B-336 TEDDY TUM TUM © Patrick Lowry/Michael Woodward Creations

SEVEN

KINDS OF

DEATH

Books by Kate Wilhelm

The Mile-Long Spaceship
More Bitter than Death
The Clone (with Theodore L. Thomas)
The Nevermore Affair
The Killer Thing
The Downstairs Room and Other Speculative Fiction
Let the Fire Fall
The Year of the Cloud (with Theodore L. Thomas)
Abyss: Two Novellas
Margaret and I
City of Cain
The Infinity Box: A Collection of Speculative Fiction
The Clewiston Test
Where Late the Sweet Birds Sang
Fault Lines
Somerset Dreams and Other Fictions
Juniper Time
Better than One (with Damon Knight)
A Sense of Shadow
Listen, Listen
Oh, Susannah!
Welcome, Chaos
Huysman's Pets
The Hamlet Trap
Crazy Time
The Dark Door
Smart House
Children of the Wind: Five Novellas
Cambio Bay
Sweet, Sweet Poison
State of Grace
Death Qualified: A Mystery of Chaos
And the Angels Sing

Kate Wilhelm

SEVEN

KINDS OF

DEATH

St. Martin's Press New York

Design by Judith A. Stagnitto

Library of Congress Cataloging-in-Publication Data

Wilhelm, Kate.
    Seven kinds of death / Kate Wilhelm.
        p.   cm.
    ISBN 0-312-08290-8
    I. Title.
    PS3573.I434S48   1992
    813'.54—dc20   92-24152
                                                         CIP

First edition: October 1992

10   9   8   7   6   5   4   3   2   1

SEVEN

KINDS OF

DEATH

One

Bob Sherwood simply kept out of the way while the two white-coated attendants got the girl in the cast aboard car seventeen. They had brought their own wheelchair, and a ramp, but, even so, all three people had worked up a good sweat before they had her settled. Her cast went up out of sight under a full skirt; she was the color of skim milk when they wheeled her past him, and by the time they were all finished, and he looked in on her, there was a green tinge under the white of her face.

"I'll come around just as soon as we're under way," he said. "Won't be long."

She nodded. They had put her on the bench that would become her bed later on; her leg in the cast was straight out in front of her. There was one big suitcase, a carry-on type of bag, a paper sack, her purse, and, leaning against the bench, a pair of crutches. The little room looked very crowded.

"You okay? You going to be okay until I get back?"

"Fine," she muttered. "Lovely."

He hesitated only a moment, then swung around to go meet the other passengers booked for car seventeen. One of the guys who had brought her aboard was waiting for him at the outside door. He thrust two twenty-dollar bills at Bob Sherwood. "Look after her," he said—something Bob Sherwood would have done in any event.

Now they were coming: a couple with too many bags; a family with two kids—whiners, shriekers, already in good voice; two women who would inspect the silverware and peer under the beds, and ask for one more pillow or blanket. . . . There was a lot of excitement—there always was for a cross-country trip—as well as a touch of boredom for a few of the passengers who had done it all before, manic behavior from some youngsters who couldn't wait to start roaming . . .

"I called you," Toni Townsend said when he got back to her. "Didn't you hear me?" She looked very near tears. "They didn't bring my bag of books!"

The green had left her skin; there was even a touch of pink in her cheeks; she looked to be twenty-five at the most, with straight, shoulder-length brown hair, no makeup, brown eyes that were quite nice. He glanced at the suitcase, the carry-on, the paper sack. "You sure? Maybe they're in one of the suitcases."

"I had a stack of books in a paper bag, and they must have left it in the station wagon. I called you," she said again, plaintively. "Four days! When's the first stop, long enough to buy something to read?"

"Well, there's Salt Lake City, around five thirty or so in the morning, and tomorrow night around eight thirty we'll be in Denver . . ."

She groaned and turned to the window, ignoring him completely as he moved her bags out of the way so she could get to the little sink and toilet across the room. He always left the curtain open long enough for the occupant to get the idea, but then he closed it out of discretion.

"Now, there's anything you want, you just pull the button, day or night. Something to drink, eat. I'll see if I can find you something to read, and I'll pick up your meal vouchers and bring your food . . ."

She kept her face averted, fighting tears, until he left again. Four days, she kept thinking, in prison, solitary confinement. She thought of the prankster god who had been playing with her and laughing at her for the past three weeks, and she cursed that god. Three weeks ago she had received the long distance call from a California firm inviting her to appear for an interview. They liked her résumé and the work she had submitted; they would pay for her trip and a hotel at that end for two days. Her roommate had shrieked with joy, and awakened the god, Toni now half believed. And that god was getting even. The interview had gone well, and then, as she had left the company grounds, her taxi and a delivery truck had collided, and she had ended up in the hospital with a broken leg. Try us again in a year or two, the company goon had said, even as he was making arrangements for her return to New York.

And the goons had kept her books. Nothing to read, nothing to see. Beyond the window heavy fog lay over the fields; the Sacramento Valley was fogged in from side to side, top to bottom.

Then she heard a knock on her door and it was pushed open; a tall slender woman stood there with a friendly grin on her face, a shopping bag in her hand. "Hi," she said. "I'm Victoria Leeds. The car attendant mentioned your problem with books and I came to the rescue." She drew near and put down the shopping bag where Toni could see; it appeared to be filled with books.

In the dining car a little later, Victoria Leeds was sitting next to an obese man, opposite his wife and her sister, who was also very fat. The wife seemed quite normal. The man was saying: "You know, I always thought I could write, if I had the time, I mean. I tell you we've had some adventures out on the farm, haven't we, honey?'' His wife smiled and nodded.

Their waiter brought soup, which Victoria began to eat with apparent concentration, but actually she was thinking: It was evident why this trio had chosen the train, not a flight; she wondered if it was even possible for them to fly. He filled three quarters of the seat they shared. And Toni Townsend obviously couldn't fly with her leg in the cast straight out like that. The families with several children would find it difficult, of course.

''Remember that poem Freddy wrote back in high school?'' the man was saying to his wife. ''Got it published in the Davis newspapers, he did.''

Across the table his wife smiled and nodded. He talked on and on. ''Always thought it was knowing the right people, being in the right place at the right time. Know what I mean?''

Victoria picked at her salad. The train was getting near Davis. As soon as it stopped, she decided, she would escape. Waiters dodged passengers who passed back and forth through the diner; a child paused at her table to eye her disconcertingly, its expression as alien as a wild animal's. She watched the woman across the table bite into her chicken sandwich, and half listened to the man next to her suggest that if Freddy just knew one editor who was interested in him, he might really make it, know what I mean? She drew out two dollar bills from her purse and put them under her plate as the train slowed for the Davis station.

''You going on in to Chicago?'' the man asked.

''Yes.''

''Well, we'll see you again in the next day or two. Nice talking to you.''

She fled. She made her way through the two cars separating her own from the diner before the train started to move again. In her tiny compartment she drew the curtain across the door, sat down, and closed her eyes. Across the hallway, down a room or two, a child was screaming lustily. She envied it.

"Why are you traveling by train?" Toni asked later that afternoon.

Victoria had been talking about her luncheon companions, the others in the diner. She shrugged. "Time out. I just wanted a little time out. Do you like that book?"

"It's okay," Toni said. "Do you get a lot of that when people find out you're an editor? Wanting you to look at Freddy's poems, their stories, stuff like that?"

Laughing, Victoria held up her hand. "First, I have a question. Are you now, or have you ever been a card-carrying aspiring writer?"

Toni laughed with her and shook her head.

"Okay. Sure we do, all of us do, I guess. And in a way that guy in the diner is right, partly it is a matter of luck, being in the right place, and so on. If they persist, I give them my card and say send your stuff in to the office."

"Do you ever accept anything that comes in like that?"

"Hardly ever," Victoria said slowly. "We deal almost exclusively through agents. As I said, he was more right than he knows."

Later, in her own compartment again, Victoria wondered at the pinched look that had crossed Toni's face. All right, she thought, Toni had a problem. Who didn't? Determinedly she watched the passing scenery; the Sierra mountains now. Then, there would be darkness, the wasteland of Nevada, the desert of Utah. . . . Soon she would think about Paul Volte, she told herself. Not this minute, but soon. For that was why she had taken the train, why she was spending four days that she could not really spare, time out, in order to think seriously of herself and Paul Volte. But not just yet.

During the next day the train wound through spectacularly beautiful river valleys and gorges, the canyons cut by the Colorado River through the Rocky Mountains. Victoria visited with Toni several times during the day; they chatted about books, movies, music, New York, but most of the time they simply gazed at the view beyond the window.

As she neared Toni's room late in the afternoon, she saw the car attendant, Bob Sherwood, blocking the doorway.

"You made this?" he said, the wonder in his voice undisguised. "I'll be damned! How'd you do that?"

More faintly Toni's voice floated out, "I don't know. I never know. My hands know what they're doing, but they don't talk to me much."

Victoria felt as if the train had lurched violently, although it had not; she felt as if she were falling, although she was unmoving. She held onto the metal of the bathroom door waiting for the vertigo to pass, and when it was over, Bob Sherwood was talking again, this time turned to include her.

"Did you know she's an artist? A real artist. Just look at this."

It was a plasticine bas-relief head, Bob Sherwood's head, rising from a smooth base no more than four inches square. Even without studying it closely, Victoria could see that Toni had caught his broad face, the widely spaced eyes, the thick nose and narrow lips. The expression was of intelligent patience, exactly right.

He held it out for her to look at, but his hand was protective, cupping the piece; he was not inviting her to touch it. When a call button sounded, he looked resigned. "She gave it to me," he said to Victoria, then turned back to the room. "I'll bring your dinner between six thirty and seven. Okay? You want anything before that?" Her response was inaudible. "Okay. You take it easy. And, Ms. Townsend, thanks. Just thank you very much."

After he had left, Victoria entered the little room, studying Toni as if for the first time. "What was that job you interviewed for? You said a computer company?"

6

Toni was on the window bench that opened to make a bed. She nodded. "In the graphics department."

"Oh," Victoria said. "Designing software packages, something like that?"

Toni lifted her chin almost defiantly. "It had something to do with art, anyway. The first job possibility that did."

"What will you do now?"

"I don't know," Toni said miserably. "Back to my job washing dishes, I guess. I'm a very artistic dishwasher."

"You have a lawyer, I hope," Victoria said. "Have you signed anything yet?"

Toni shook her head. "I was too mad."

"Good. Don't. Not until you see a lawyer." Abruptly she stood up. "I've got a bottle of wine in my room. And a book you might want to read. I'll be right back."

In her room she picked up the page proofs of Paul Volte's book, *With These Hands,* and for a moment she stood holding it tightly. She could have opened it and found a passage almost identical to Toni's words, almost as if she had been reading from the text: *I never know. My hands know what they're doing.* She retrieved the wine from her bag, and returned to Toni's room.

"Do you know his column?" she asked, handing over the book. It had an orange cover, and the stamped message, *Uncorrected Page Proofs.* It was very thick.

Toni examined it curiously, shaking her head.

"Too bad," Victoria said dryly. "His column on art and architecture appears every month in our magazine. This is his third full-length book, and it's going to be a best seller. Due out at the end of the month." She began to work with the cork in the wine. Her little corkscrew was sometimes uncooperative and crumbled the cork instead of lifting it neatly.

"How do you know it'll be a best seller?"

Victoria was turning the corkscrew slowly. "Oh, two book clubs have taken it, and advance reviews have been dynamite. And it ran as a three-parter in the magazine last winter. I was the editor for the piece," she said, even more dryly than before. She glanced at Toni in time to see a flush cover her face. The cork came out smoothly and she nodded at it in satisfaction. She poured the wine into little plastic glasses and handed one to Toni. "Cheers," she said. "Now let's talk about you and your accident and broken leg and lawyers and your future. And cabbages and kings, if they seem pertinent." Toni looked mystified and Victoria drank all her wine and poured herself a second glass.

At two in the morning Victoria finally brought her thoughts to the problem that had made her take the train. There had been far less thinking time than she had anticipated. The train was crowded and noisy. A child down the corridor from her room was unhappy and vocal about it. Intermittently the loudspeaker brayed announcements about meals, about a bingo game or something like that, about a trivia game, about movies to be shown in the lounge car, about happy-hour prices, about snacks. And, of course, there had been all that scenery.

She sat up in her bed with the curtain open to the black night with not a sign of human activity out there on the prairie, nothing to distract her. "All right," she said under her breath. "All right."

In three months she would be forty-two years old. Sometimes she looked it, most often not, but she knew. She knew. She had been married for seven years, a long time ago, so long ago she thought of that period as if it concerned someone other than her. She had a good job, with the offer of a better job waiting for her decision. And she had to face the fact that although she and Paul were a "thing," had a relationship, were ideal for each other, loved each other, nothing was going to happen between them that hadn't already happened.

"All right," she said again. "Them's the facts. Now what?"

You have to bring it out into the open, discuss it with him, her counselor had said nearly two years ago. Two years, she repeated to herself. Yes. Right. Bring it out, talk to the wind, throw the words on the waves. He wouldn't discuss it. He wouldn't go to a counselor. She had dropped counseling when the question surfaced: what are your choices then? She didn't need to pay anyone to tell her the choices. Don't rock the boat, go on with everything exactly the way it is, or get out.

Out, she thought clearly, and yanked the curtain closed. She felt as if the decision had been there for more than two years, but she had not found the words to tell herself what it was until that moment. Now it seemed so simple. One word, that was all. Out. Dawn light edged the curtain when she finally fell asleep.

"He's wonderful," Toni said the next day. "You said best seller and I kept thinking of those other books you loaned me, you know, best sellers. But this is different."

"I know."

"He understands everything," Toni went on, oblivious. "He knew how to put the questions, the answers he was after. He knew."

Victoria watched her, the sparkle that had come to her eyes, the animation in her face; she listened to the excitement in her voice as long as she could bear it, and then said, "Come to the office before the end of April and I'll introduce you to him. It has to be before the end of April. Will you be on your feet by then?"

Toni counted quickly, then nodded. "Five weeks. Oh, yes! Victoria, how can I thank you?"

"For what, for heaven's sake? It's an introduction, not a betrothal."

"It's more than an introduction," Toni said in a low

voice. "It's more than that. You know what you said about that fat man in the dining car? He was right. Being in the right place at the right time, meeting the right person, something arranges things like that. Fate. Karma. Whatever." She almost added, or a prankster god toying with you. She still felt herself to be on a string, pulled this way and that, with no choices, but now it felt wonderful, even if a little eerie. She said, "If I hadn't had the accident, I wouldn't have taken the train. If I had got the job, I'd be in San Francisco right now. But I wasn't meant to be there. We had to meet, and now I have to meet him. That's what Paul Volte understands. That's what he gets people talking about, and you feel as if, as if . . . it's as if someone managed to look into your head, into your heart, your soul even. Talking with all those other people, he could have been talking with me, making me say things I never dreamed of saying out loud. Things that are just right. I can't explain it, but he knows what it's like."

"Possession," Victoria said. "That's what he was talking about in the book all the way through. Fanaticism. Absolute egomania. An acceptance that the artist is the tool without choice." When she became aware of the anger in her voice, she stopped speaking.

Silently Toni nodded. Her face had become set in a curious expression, withdrawn, distant. For a moment her exhilaration was like an adrenaline rush of fear; for this moment she felt she could choose after all. Right now, this instant, she felt, she could still say no.

Victoria stood up, shaking her head. "You'll meet him. Give me a call at the office before the end of April." What she had not added, something Paul's book said distinctly, was that the truly gifted artist was owned by a jealous muse that would give success with one hand and snatch away happiness with the other. He had written it, she thought then, but did he believe what he had written? She did not know, and not knowing, and having no way of learning the truth made her more determined than she had been the night before. Out, she said to herself again. Out!

At lunch the next day, gazing moodily at the flooded fields of Iowa, gray and unquiet water in every hollow, every flat place as far as she could see, and if not standing water, then mud, drowned shrubs and trees, she realized that she had done what she had to do; she had made her decision. Now she could leave the train in Chicago and fly home.

She went to Toni's room to tell her goodbye, and made her a present of all the books, even Paul's. Later, in Chicago, she took a cab to O'Hare and by ten that night she was in her own apartment.

It was Friday of the last week in April when Toni walked haltingly into the anteroom of *New World Magazine* at four in the afternoon. She was approaching the reception desk, carrying a large canvas bag that she managed awkwardly; it was heavier than she had realized, the walk was longer, her leg weaker. Then she saw Victoria coming toward her.

"Hi. Good to see you on your own feet," Victoria said. She waved to the woman behind the desk, took Toni's arm, and reached for the bag. "Let me. Hey, what's in there? This way." She led Toni around the reception desk, through a doorway, into a narrow hall. Everything looked old and threadbare, as if the building had been decorated back in the thirties and not touched again since. Carpeting on the floor was worn, with holes before some of the doors; molding that was almost to Toni's shoulders was chipped here and there, with an undercoating of brown paint showing through the top layer of tan.

They passed an open door beyond which was a room that looked to Toni like chaos: long tables were piled high with papers, several people were talking in loud voices, one woman was holding up an oversized color print. Victoria continued to lead her to an elevator that creaked and groaned its way to the fourth floor; they went down another corridor as shabby as the first one, and finally into a small office, barely big enough for both women. Victoria left the door open and moved behind the desk, leaving room for Toni on the other side. In here were cartons, most of them taped closed, a few not quite filled, stacks of papers, manuscripts in piles, a wall of shelves, nearly empty, and on a narrow window sill three pots of pink geraniums.

"Home," Victoria said. She put the heavy bag on the desk on top of some papers, and surveyed Toni with a critical eye. "You look fine. How's it going?"

"Wonderfully," Toni said. "I got a lawyer, and he'll get me enough to live on for a year, he says. Maybe he will. And two different insurance companies are paying my bills, the doctors and everything. I . . . I have something for you." She opened the bag and, using both hands, carefully removed an object wrapped in a dish towel. She set it down and took the towel away. Another bas-relief, this one life-sized, of Victoria's face. It was done in a streaky blue-green soapstone.

"Good God!" Victoria breathed. "It's . . . it's very beautiful. Too beautiful." She touched the stone, then let her fingers trail over the surface, over the cheek, the forehead. The stone eyes were downcast, the expression introspective, somehow sad. Her fingers lingered over the smooth face that was pleasantly cool. "Toni, it's wonderful. Thank-you."

Toni nodded mutely. Too idealized, she knew. Too beautiful. Not quite right, but she didn't know how to make it more right. Suddenly, perversely, she wished she had not brought it, not yet, not until she was better, until she knew how to get it right. Her hands were clenched painfully; she wanted to weep because it wasn't right yet.

"Well, come on. I'll bring this. Paul's office is on this

12

floor, not far." Victoria picked up the stone carefully and they went down the corridor. She stopped before a partly open door, took a breath, then called, "I've got the artist I wanted you to meet. Are you decent?"

The door was pulled open and Paul Volte moved aside to admit them. He was tall and almost too thin, like a marathoner; his hair was gray, and his eyes a bright, sparkling blue. Although he glanced at Toni, and at the stone, Victoria was the one he looked at with a yearning so visible, so unconcealed, it was painful to witness. Victoria made the introduction.

He shook Toni's hand, and looked more carefully at the bas-relief when Victoria put it down on his desk, then nodded. "Nice," he said. "Very nice."

Toni's eyes burned more fiercely than before.

"Well, I'll leave you two to get acquainted," Victoria said. She had not looked directly at Paul, and did not now. She lifted the bas-relief and turned toward the door. "I'll give you a call in a couple of weeks," she said to Toni. "This is my last day here at the magazine, then off for a little vacation, and back to a new job. Busy time. Toni, this is one of the nicest presents I've ever had. Thank you so very much." She left the office.

Toni started to follow her. "I'm sorry," she said without any clear idea of what she meant.

Paul Volte was staring at the empty doorway. Abruptly he looked at Toni. "Can you make another one? Just like it. I'll buy it." The sparkle had left his eyes; he looked old; his voice had become harsh.

Slowly Toni nodded. She had read and reread his book many times; she had even bought a copy and read that to see if there were differences. She could quote long passages. In her head she quoted one now: *People think of it as a gift, and they're wrong. It isn't like that. A gift implies something freely given with no thought of reciprocation, nothing is asked in return.*

13

This is not a gift; it is a trade. It's as if this something promises success but at a price. With the first success, the death of a pet. Then of a parent perhaps, or a lover. On and on until you don't dare love again. You don't dare.

T w o

As soon as Toni arrived at Marion Olsen's house in the lush countryside of Montgomery County, Maryland, she knew she would not stay more than politeness demanded. Since Paul Volte had acted as if this were Mecca or something, and she felt obligated to him, she had to do this much. If he was trying to help her, and believed that Marion Olsen could help her, she would be able to say she had tried it. The problem was that Marion Olsen was about the ugliest woman she had ever seen, the coarsest, almost brutal, with a harsh, husky voice, and a peremptory manner that made Toni cringe. Toni was afraid of her.

"Is it Antoinette?" Marion demanded, surveying her as she got out of her car. She had come off a porch to meet Toni.

"Antonia," Toni said, taken aback. Marion Olsen was a large woman, looming over her like a dream menace, with ropy muscles in her arms, hands like a stevedore's; she was dressed in black sweatpants and an oversized black T-shirt that reached nearly to her knees. She wore sandals, no socks; her feet were dirty. Her hair was long, streaked with gray, tied back with a string. She glanced inside the car, at the boxes of artwork that Toni had crammed in beside her suitcases, and other boxes of her personal things. A mistake, Toni knew; she should have brought only enough for one night.

"I'd be Toni, too," Marion said. "Antonia ended up with what, nine, ten kids, living in a hole in the ground? So much for that. Come on in." They started to walk toward the house, and she asked, "What's wrong with your leg? Can you do any work?"

Toni bit her lip, then answered in a measured voice, "I am quite capable. I broke it, but it's almost healed now."

"Well, I hope it is. You'll sleep upstairs, and there's always garden stuff that needs doing. This used to be a little farmhouse," Marion said. "We've been adding to it right along." They entered by a side door that opened directly into a very large workroom with a smaller studio angled off it. Several people were in the studio working, men and women in jeans, one woman lying on the floor with her feet on a chair, hands behind her head, a man sitting cross-legged on a cushion playing a mouth organ badly. Marion did not introduce anyone, but waved and led Toni on through to a hall, past a bathroom, another room that might have been a breakfast nook but was actually an office, she said, although it looked like a dinette. Kitchen, pantry, dining room, several halls that just made it all more confusing. At the other end of the original core of the house a huge living room with a fireplace big enough to walk into had been added; a library or television or music room adjoined it. That room seemed to serve all purposes. The additions attested to various levels of skill of the builders, none of them as good as the people who had constructed the original building. The floors of the additions were wide planks; the original floors were lovely oak. The new walls were drywall with inept taping that was peeling here and there; the original walls were well plastered. It was like that throughout.

Some windows had leaded glass, others did not quite close because they did not hang perfectly straight.

But everywhere there was artwork: stone sculptures, wood pieces, bronze, iron, copper. . . . They were on every flat surface, on the floor against the walls—abstract pieces, representational pieces, some that reached the ceilings, others no bigger than her hand. Every shelf was jammed with art, every table, the top of the piano in the television room; pieces lined the staircase, mobiles hung before windows . . .

Upstairs, Marion said, were six bedrooms; Toni would share a room with Janet Cuprillo, who was out somewhere or other right now. Abruptly she left Toni and started to talk to a youngish man about a statuette he was holding. She appeared to forget Toni completely.

"Look at that line," Marion said. "Get one of the girls to model for you. You just don't contort muscles like that. You need the tension in her as a whole-body, whole-person tension, not in particular muscles. . . . What the hell? Looks like she's got grapes under her skin." They walked away, leaving Toni in the hall.

At dinner Toni did not say a word. She made no attempt to remember anyone's name, since she planned to leave again the following day. Tommy, Hal, Janet . . . it didn't matter. They were talking excitedly about a trip that most of them were taking in ten days—to Italy for six months or longer. Toni didn't try to sort that out, either.

As soon as dinner was over, Marion said, "I had Willy put your pieces in the office. Let's go have a look."

She didn't wait for Toni's response, but started out the door, and after a moment Toni followed. One of the other women in the room winked at her, but it didn't really help. She wanted to turn and run the other way; her legs felt leaden, her stomach suddenly ached, and curiously she was freezing and sweating at the same time. She should have locked the car, she thought, but rejected the notion; Marion would have got the pieces out somehow.

In the office there was a green formica-topped dinette table and several matching chairs with splits in the plastic, stuffing turned brown poking out. One wall had floor-to-ceiling unfinished wood shelves, all filled with more art objects, with boxes, glasses, a Barbie doll, a rubber frog, a wind-up bear, a mason jar filled with chopsticks. . . . Toni's few pieces were on the table: her bas-relief faces, several full-figure statuettes, some wood pieces she had done years before in art school, one studded with bits of colored glass.

Marion walked back and forth examining the pieces carefully; Toni gazed past her out the windows, which were grimy. This wasn't real country, she thought, not farming country; but countryside that had freed itself from the burden of crops, and now was reverting back to forest as quickly as possible. The country she had driven through that afternoon had appeared almost empty of people; even the developments, the projects, the subdivisions without end had seemed devoid of people and preternaturally quiet. All the people had been in cars driving on the roads. And she had lost them all, she thought then. From the interstate, to the state road, to the county road, then on to a dirt road where her car was the only thing that moved. She felt as if she had journeyed to the end of the world.

Twilight had come while they were at dinner, and the shadowless world was still, the tender May leaves that had been whipping in the wind an hour earlier were quiet, as if waiting, just as she was. Not that it mattered, she told herself fiercely.

Marion touched one of the pieces of cherry wood, carved, abstract, with such a high gloss finish it could have been metal. "How long a period from this," she asked, "to this?" Her hand went unerringly to the last piece Toni had done before Victoria's, the face of an elderly woman who lived in her apartment building in New York.

"Eight years," Toni said. Her voice came out as a whisper.

"Yes. You can stay as long as you like. You have the hands and skill. But do you have eyes? I don't know yet."

Toni swallowed painfully. "Thank you, Ms. Olsen, but I think I've already decided that this isn't my sort of thing. I don't think I would fit in."

Marion smiled. "All right. I would never try to talk anyone into going into art seriously, never. In fact, I usually advise people to keep it as a hobby, something they can enjoy doing without pain. I advise you to do that, let it be your hobby. Amuse yourself and your friends with it. You may even sell a piece, the faces especially. That saintly woman would like that on her living room wall, don't you think?"

Toni watched Marion's long hard finger trace the chin of the woman's face. The stone was a gray soapstone, very cool, very smooth. The image was exactly like her neighbor who had offered her a hundred dollars for it, a hundred dollars she certainly could not afford to part with.

"What's wrong with it?" Toni demanded.

"Nothing. Your hands did exactly what your eyes reported. It's your eyes that lied. I wonder if anyone ever suspected that she killed her first husband," Marion mused, regarding the face.

Toni gasped. "She didn't!"

"Maybe not. It was her child born without the benefit of a wedding first or a doctor, back alley stuff. She drowned it. Or maybe it was just kittens she drowned."

"What are you talking about? You don't even know her!"

Marion looked from the face to Toni and shrugged. "Neither do you. She isn't real to you. People generally aren't very real for you, are they? You invent them and your clever hands create the image you require to keep yourself safe. Stay or go, I don't care which. If you stay, you'll work very hard, and you'll learn to see. It may be that you won't like what you see and you'll wish you had left. But until you can believe that people are real, and stop inventing them, I don't know if you can create good art or not. You don't have to tell me your decision. If I keep seeing you around, I'll assume you're staying. Janet can help you stake out studio space, if you want it. And you can put these things in your room or your car, or in your space. Or just leave them where they are." She pulled at her black shirt and added, "I've got to get out of these mucky rags before Max gets home."

"Why did you say I could come?" Toni asked as Marion started to leave.

"You know as well as I do," Marion said. "Paul told me to. If he saw talent, no doubt it's there. No one has a better eye than he does." She left the room and closed the door behind her.

Toni sank down on one of the ratty chairs and stared at the gray stone face. She couldn't remember her name. Mrs. Franklin? Mrs. Frankel? She shook her head. All her life she had pretended, and at this first meeting, within seconds, she thought wildly, Marion Olsen had seen through her pretense. People weren't real. She had come to understand that very early. Her mother was a face on television telling everyone what had happened that day. Her teeth were capped, her hair tinted, her figure controlled by a careful diet and more carefully chosen clothes, and at home she did not look or sound like the television person. At home she had always been extremely busy, but that had not mattered since she had not been home very much. Unreal. Toni had not seen her for five years. Her father had managed a print shop until he left them when Toni was twelve. He had been three or four different people—a loving stranger with presents; a strange man with beer on his breath; a furious, swearing, cruel stranger; a pitiful, weepy, red-eyed stranger. She didn't believe in him, either. She hadn't seen him since she was twelve.

She remembered Victoria's words, *too beautiful,* and

Paul's, *nice, very nice.* Paul had bought the bas-relief she had made, not because the art was all that good, she understood now, but because she had created a Victoria who was lovely and not quite real, the way he wanted her to be, the way Toni had seen her. Had invented her, she corrected herself under her breath. Victoria was not real, nor was Paul. The face of the stranger from her apartment building now looked like someone she never had seen before in her life; the woman's name was gone, she was gone, hardly even a memory of her remained. An unreal woman.

She tried to conjure up Marion's face, the way she always did before starting to mold the plasticine; nothing came. She could say the words that described Marion: too large a nose, a mouth too wide, deep-set dark eyes, heavy eyebrows, long graying hair. No image came with the words. She shivered. Marion refused to be created, imagined, idealized. Marion was too real already. Whenever she thought of what Marion had said, that Paul had told her to invite Toni, she shied away from all the possible reasons she could think of for Marion's being that compliant. As far as Toni could tell Marion was not that manipulable with anyone else.

Day by day she delayed her departure. Tomorrow, she told herself. Tomorrow. She watched the others work although she did no work of her own. She listened intently when Marion critiqued a piece of work; everyone listened intently. She hung back at the group discussions. Tomorrow, she told herself again. Tomorrow.

Those heading for Italy left, and now she and Janet had private rooms; two of the men remained behind also, but still they had the group sessions, and with so few people, she felt pressured to contribute to the session both with her own work, and her critiques. The pressure did not come from Marion. She did not pressure anyone about anything. You did things or not; she never asked what you were working on, or to see what you were doing, or if you had plans for next week, next month, or next year. She was a hard critic, merciless and radiant. When she talked about a piece, Toni found herself thinking, of course, she should have seen that; it was so obvious now. Marion illuminated art in a way no one had done for Toni, and her language was earthy, never elevated, never obscure or abstract, always to the point.

Toni did only small things in clay. The others critiqued her work seriously and listened to her with concentration. But it was Marion they all wanted to hear. And Marion's face eluded her. She watched her as she spoke, the animation that changed her from second to second, from youthful, even pretty, to ancient and cruel. She memorized the coarse features, big nose, heavy eyebrows, a slight crookedness in her grin, up on the left, down on the right side . . . but as soon as she was away from Marion, the face vanished from her mind and she was left with the words instead of the image.

There was a fancy party in Washington in Spence Dwyers's gallery, to celebrate Marion's coming touring show. The young people did not attend that one, the real party would be here at the house, and to this private party she invited Paul Volte.

Now Toni started saying to herself that she would leave after the party. She wanted to see Paul again, to thank him again, but not to show him what she was doing. What she was doing was crap, she told herself, just as it always had been. She stared at her hands with hatred. All they could produce was crap.

Claud Palance from nearby Bellarmine College brought a couple of graduate students and began to teach the others how to crate artwork for a touring show. They worked in the big barn on the property across a narrow dirt road. The barn was another studio, bigger and dirtier than the one in the house. Massive pieces of granite were strewn about; what appeared to be whole trees stripped of branches and roots were behind the barn. A kiln was back there. Inside, all the work for the tour had been gathered together; only the major piece *Seven Kinds of Death* was missing. It was in the center of the living room floor, the focus for the real party, Marion said with satisfaction when the movers safely positioned it.

"You don't think it's a bit in the way?" Johnny Buell asked that afternoon, walking around it. Johnny was Marion's stepson. He was six feet tall and weighed two hundred pounds and was not fat. His dark brown hair had a nice wave; he had deep-set blue eyes, like his father's. But his eyes did not sparkle with amusement the way Max Buell's eyes did.

Marion raised her unkempt eyebrows at Johnny. "It's supposed to be in the way, damn it," she said. "That's what death's all about, for God's sake. We can't keep pussyfooting around it forever. Let it come out into the open, get in the way for a change. No one's going to trip over it, for Christ's sake!" Since the piece was five feet tall and massive at the base, with shiny metal here and there, and several kinds of wood here and there, it was unlikely that anyone would trip over it.

Toni and Janet Cuprillo had entered the house in time to hear this exchange. Janet had been Toni's roommate in the beginning. She was very pretty, with short black hair shingled in the back; her brown eyes were almond shaped and beautiful, with long, long lashes. She was extremely talented, everyone agreed, but within days Toni had come to realize that words were not the same for Janet as for other people. She liked some more than others for the way they sounded, or the way they looked, and she rarely gave a lot of thought to what they meant.

She had summed up John Buell for Toni during her first week here. Johnny took the world seriously. Living was a serious matter with him. Like a saint with arrows sticking out all over, he bled a lot. Toni had looked at her with incomprehension. "You know," Janet said, "he has a mission, and if he has to suffer for it, that's fine with him. That's what a serious person does, suffers and bleeds if he has to, but he gets his mission done."

"A mission?" Toni had echoed.

"Like missionary? A message to give. In his case buildings to build."

This was the day that Toni had come to realize that Janet took a lot of interpreting. Mission, message? Buildings as message? She wasn't sure what Janet had meant, but the gist of her comments was clear enough. Johnny was a serious young man with an important job. He took work seriously, took Marion seriously. The Max Buell Company was building a multimillion-dollar condominium complex a mile away from Marion's house, and Johnny took that most seriously of all. Then, Janet had added dreamily, if he weren't already engaged, she'd go for him. But as it was she was indivisible, and so was Toni.

Invisible, Toni decided, and that was fine with her. As far as she was concerned, Johnny's attitude was no more false and unreal than his father's: Max Buell seemed to find everything amusing, and took nothing seriously; Johnny found nothing amusing and everything was serious. He was unreal, and Janet, who was only twenty-one, was almost as unreal as Johnny.

Toni and Janet had stayed back out of the way while the movers strained getting *Seven Kinds of Death* in place; both young women were grimy with sweat and caked dust from the work in the barn, Janet nursing a splinter in her finger, and anxious to go give it a soak. After the movers left, they started up the stairs, but stepped aside once more as Max Buell came down. Unlike his son, he not only saw them but everything about them, every smudge, every scrape, every speck of dirt. He grinned as he passed them on his way to the living room.

"Message for you," he said to Marion. "Your friend Paul Volte is bringing a lady friend with him." Max was as tall as his son, and heavier, thicker in the shoulders and chest. His face was weathered dark brown, and there were crinkly lines at his eyes. He walked to the piece in the center of the room and whistled. "Hey, that looks like hot shit there! Marion, I think it's just dandy!"

"He's bringing someone," Marion said in a grating voice. "I don't suppose we know if the lady friend will want a separate bedroom, do we? My God, I'm going mad! I've rearranged sleeping accommodations a dozen times already! Why didn't he tell me weeks ago? That bastard! He didn't even tell me he was coming. What does he think, I'm running a goddam hotel or something?"

Max chuckled. "I don't think you need worry about it. It's that lady editor, and from what little I know about things like that, I think you could call them real friendly."

At the doorway Toni gasped and clutched the framework to steady herself. Not Victoria! He wouldn't! She was aware that they were all watching her as she turned and fled upstairs.

Three

Later, Charlie would be able to pinpoint the exact moment when he wandered innocently into the trap, and then the exact moment when it was sprung, but that morning in early June he had no intimation of hazardous moments ahead. Things had been peachy, he thought later, recapitulating that morning. He had done a little job for Phil Stern that had put a little money in the bank, and, more, had been entertaining in its own way, culminating in a little joust with a very good arsonist who had had very bad luck and cursed his date of birth for it. Good clean fun. The guy probably would beat the rap in court, but that wasn't Charlie's problem. And the car had not needed the overhaul he had been dreading. The sun was shining, the weather strange, but rather nice. The whole world had had strange weather that spring, but few places had it as nice as upper New York in early June.

He and Constance had corralled the cats inside and she had taken them out to the patio one by one to dose them with ear drops. Ashcan had ear mites, but you don't treat only one cat. Brutus had to be first always; he had an elephantine memory, and the sniff of medicine was enough to alert him that it was hiding time. Charlie admired Constance's ability to snag a cat, hold it in a grip that made the cat look as if rigor mortis was well advanced, and then do whatever was needed. Afterward, Brutus streaked off shaking his head, flinging medicine to the wind in both directions; he would not return until supper, and by then it would be time for another treatment. Candy complained in her scratchy voice when it was her turn, and Ashcan, who was the bearer of evil tidings this time, tried to crawl under the doormat.

Then Charlie had gone out for the mail. Constance was drying her hands when he returned and sorted it at the kitchen table. Very little, very dull looking. He was browsing through a catalogue with high-tech fishing gear that featured things like a computerized casting outfit that you attached to a box that told you what was biting, what bait to use, how to use it. Maybe if your Aunt Ethel was coming for a visit, he was thinking, grinning, when the trap opened.

"For goodness sake," Constance murmured. "Do you want to go to a send-off party for a gallery tour that Marion Olsen is having?"

"Nope," he said, and turned a page. At the time he did not hear a clash of metal, did not hear the door bang, but later he knew that was the moment. That *Nope* was the magic word. Without looking up, he asked, "Who's Marion What's-it?"

"Oh, Charlie," Constance said in that particular tone of voice that held such a mixture of exasperation and patience that it was hard to tell which was uppermost. "You remember her. We went to some of her shows. I grew up with her. We saw her all the time in New York when we were all just out of school, before she moved down near Washington. We exchange notes and Christmas cards every single year." She sounded like a saintly teacher struggling with an overgrown student who couldn't quite grasp Dick and Jane.

"Oh," he said. "You mean Tootles."

"I mean Marion Olsen," she said coldly. "She's finally surfacing again as a sculptor, after all these years. A fifteen-gallery touring show. Good for her. I'm so glad."

"She did that thing she called the *Seven Kinds of Death*, right?"

"You know very well she did."

"And she asked you if you really had married a fireman, and then she said, 'A terrible waste.' "

"Charlie, I've told you a dozen times, she didn't say that. You misheard her."

"Maybe," he admitted. "It could have been 'What terrible taste.' And everyone at that last party was a kook of one kind or another, including sister Babar."

Constance's look this time was withering. "Her sister's name is Beatrice. When she was a very small child they called her Ba Ba."

"She was never a very small child," he said. "And she's a nut. Your pal Tootles has a knack for nuts."

Constance opened another envelope, a bill, and he said, "Anyway, her husband was making passes at you right in front of me. Now is that a kook or isn't it?"

Constance ignored him. She crossed the kitchen to throw away the junk mail and envelopes.

"And you know damn well Tootles was making passes at me. You thought it was funny!" *He* had been indignant.

Constance was heading toward the hall. She paused. "Maybe she wanted to see what kind of equipment a fireman had. I did marry a fireman, you know."

"And was it a terrible waste?"

She walked from the room carrying her mail and the bill with her. Charlie was grinning again when he went back to the fishing-gear catalogue. Later, he knew if she had phrased the question differently, he would have said sure, let's do it. The way you ask a question is important, he would have said. There was no doubt that he didn't want to go, and that was the question she had asked, after all. A yes or no answer was required, and a yes would have been a lie. If she had said she wanted to go, he would have agreed without question, maybe with a few jabs at Tootles, but without real argument. If she had brought it up again in any way, he would have said he had intended to go with her all along, just teasing a little that morning. If she had left the invitation lying about, he would have picked it up and said something like *Why not?* None of those things happened, and neither of them mentioned Tootles or Babar again until two weeks later when he found Constance poring over a road map.

"What's up?" he asked. He had mowed the lawn and carried the fragrance of newly cut grass with him into the house, which already was perfumed with roses in just about every room. Mowing his own lawn always made him feel virtuous; shoveling snow did also, although he complained about both chores.

"I thought I might drive down," Constance said. "The flights are awful, with changes at La Guardia or Philadelphia or somewhere. Or else the shuttle and then rent a car. And the train's even worse. Three hours in Penn Station."

"Down where? Are we going on a trip?"

"I am. Marion's party. I'll leave on Thursday, get there that night and start home on Sunday. If I'm too tired, I might stop at a motel Sunday night. Depends on what time I get away."

"You'll drive more than three hundred miles for a party?" He heard the incredulity in his own voice.

She looked up at him and said yes. Her pale blue eyes were glinty.

It was that damn Viking blood surfacing, he thought then, a streak of stubbornness, a fierce loyalty that verged on insanity, a perverse determination. . . . If she thought he would yield just like that, he also thought, she was wrong. Why didn't she come right out and ask him nicely to drive down with her? Make a little vacation out of the affair.

It wasn't that they never did things apart. He did little investigative jobs for Phil Stern's insurance company from time to time. They both did other investigative jobs now and then that took him to one place, her to another. She had presented a paper at a psychology conference just a few months before and had been gone almost a week. He went fishing now and then, and had done some workshops in the past year on techniques of arson investigations. It wasn't that they would be separated for a few days, it was the glint in her eyes, the too-cool, too-aloof expression on her face that made this different.

"Watch out for the husband," he said coldly.

"I think I'm a little old for such a warning, but thank you. You needn't worry, that one's been gone a long time. Actually, she's married again, to a millionaire, a fact I've mentioned more than once—when it happened, and again this past Christmas, as I recall. I sometimes worry about your memory, or is it that you didn't want to hear anything about Marion? Anyway, she probably will keep her eye on the current husband."

The fact that Tootles could snag four or five husbands, and her looking like a horse, meant to him that Constance could have had a dozen, if she had chosen that route.

To *his* eyes Constance was the best-looking woman he had ever seen; she had been the most beautiful girl he had ever seen back when they were both students in Columbia, and the years had been loving and kind to her. Her platinum hair had never darkened, and now that it was starting to turn gray, it looked no different from all the years he had known her. She moved with the grace of a dancer, and her slender body had not changed that much. The little bit of weight she had picked up over the years was a plus, he thought. Back when Tootles either had said what a waste, or hadn't—he really wasn't all that certain—he had been cut sharply, because he had believed it. Constance was wasted on anyone but a god, he had thought then. He knew the theory that the passion of youth matured and became companionship, if the couple was lucky, and he knew that if he were a religious man he would thank God that the theory was baloney. They had the companionship and the mutual respect their maturity demanded, and they still had the passion. But also they were individuals, not a matched set, and by God, he thought then, she was the one who had to give a little; just a fraction of an inch would have been sufficient, but it had to come from her.

If he had said any of those things at that moment, if he had simply kissed her, he thought later, they probably would have gone to the party together. But he said, ''Send me a postcard,'' and stalked from the room.

Constance knew almost precisely what had gone on in Charlie's head during those few moments, not the word-by-word struggle, but the essence. She knew far better than he did if he gained or lost a pound; she knew to the day when the first gray hair had appeared in his crinkly black curls. She knew the way the light came into his eyes and then left them flat and hard black, the way his face softened or turned to stone, the way the muscles on his jaws worked, and each nuance spoke multiple meanings for her. The words had formed in her mouth, ''Oh, Charlie,'' meaning, this time, we're having such a silly quarrel. Her hand had nearly spasmed when she restrained its motion toward him. The moment passed that could have ended all this.

The day the invitation came, she had been dismayed by his instant reaction, his instant refusal to go to the party, but after no more than a second or two, she had decided he was right and probably he should not go. Actually, she did not want him to go with her. When Charlie first met Tootles— she bit her lip in exasperation with herself, but that had been her name from the time they both wore diapers and it was hard to remember it was no longer appropriate. When Charlie first met Tootles, she started again, he had been deeply offended. Charlie, so faithful and steadfast, so young, had not approved of promiscuity, and Tootles was promiscuous. Honest and truthful, he had not approved of lying, and Tootles sometimes seemed to make little or no distinction. He suspected that people who talked of their work as Art, always with a capital A, had to be phonies of some sort, and Tootles had talked of her WORK as ART, and of little else in those days. Charlie, unstinting in his own generosity, was suspicious of people who were born to be takers, and Tootles, he had said, was a saltwater sponge.

Those first impressions had endured for more than twenty-five years and nothing else about Tootles had stayed with him, although they had been with her subsequently half a dozen times at least. He had failed to see the three or four other artists Tootles always maintained because they were even hungrier than she was. He found no virtue in her real appreciation of the work of others. He never had seen her working with a child, a teenager, any talented novice.

Constance began to fold the map. She had not shown the invitation to Charlie, had not left it lying on the table for him to see because Tootles had written a message on the bottom in her scrawly script. *Please, Constance, please come. I am in desperate trouble. I have to talk to someone I can trust. Please.*

The message would have confirmed his worst feelings about Tootles and the little spat would have been blown out of proportion because he would have tried to prevent Constance's going. He believed Tootles was never happier than when she had created a maelstrom, when she had her stick in the waters muddying them more and more, involving everyone possible.

Aware of all this, Constance had phoned Tootles, whose voice had been husky with desperation. "I have to talk to someone," Tootles had whispered. "I have to! I'm in so much trouble. You know me, Constance. You know the good and the bad, all of it. You can tell me what to do if anyone can. And if there's no way out, I'll just kill myself!"

F o u r

By Friday afternoon Constance was wishing she had stayed home with Charlie. At first she thought she could never admit that to him, but then she knew she would. *You were right, darling,* she would say as airily as she could manage. *Tootles is a basket case, and Ba Ba is a kook.* Babar was wrong, though. She was more like a great sleek seal, with dark, almost black hair beautifully styled; she was expensively gowned, manicured, painted and powdered, bedecked with jewelry, but still a nut.

"It *is* you!" she had exclaimed, when Constance arrived. "I always said there was something fey about you. You have the gift and you tried to tame it by studying science, but the gift is there, I can see it in your eyes." She said over her shoulder to the room in general, "She's clairvoyant, you know. You can see the aura, feel the power of her gift coiled, ready to spring. You don't change, that's the other side of the gift, you know," Ba Ba was going on, and would continue to run on as long as anyone was in range, Constance had remembered belatedly. She had passed her to find the living room filled with people.

She had kissed Tootles and met Max Buell and his son

Johnny, and the two young women students, and two male students who were taken away by a man called Claud Palance, an art teacher, she gathered, but it was difficult to be certain because too many people were talking at once, and most of them were Ba Ba.

Claud Palance was on his way out with the young men. "We'll come back Monday to finish up the crating. Have a good party." They left.

"Well," Tootles said, "that does relieve the bedroom pressure, I guess. Men hate parties," she added to no one in particular. She was in black sweatpants and black T-shirt, and sandals that revealed dirty feet. "God, I need a drink or three. Constance, have you had any dinner? I can get you a sandwich or something."

And from that moment until after lunch the next day Constance had not had a second alone with Tootles, who, in fact, was apparently avoiding her. On the very few occasions that they might have talked for just a moment, Tootles remembered something that had to be done instantly and dashed off. Ba Ba, on the other hand, was everywhere all the time. Constance had escaped her by taking walks; Ba Ba did not walk much, she had said positively. It was easier to imagine her sliding through water with hardly a motion of her hands or feet than to see her in walking shoes making her way through woods. Constance roamed through the back of the property where an unkempt garden seemed extraordinarily productive, through a grove of massive oak trees, down to a tiny brook. Across the dirt road in front of the house, she wandered into the barn where the show pieces were being crated. There were still a few things to be boxed up, but many crates were already secured with screws. The big barn doors had been closed, making it dark and airless inside. In the gloom she could see that people had been working in here with very big pieces of stone and wood. She already had gone through the studio in the house; it did not surprise her to find another bigger one here.

She left the barn by a small door, walked around it, and found a path through the woods. She had been here years before and was pleased to find that she remembered the property rather better than she had realized. The woods had grown up thicker than she recalled, but that was the only difference as far as she could tell. Up half a mile or so, she knew she would come across a small stone building, a one-room house from some distant past, Tootles's retreat. She smiled, remembering the story Tootles had told about it: a Civil War romance, Northern woman, Southern man, trysting place, death from a broken heart.

But eventually she always had to return to the main house, where chaos was developing rapidly. Caterers were unloading equipment and food; kitchen help had appeared; someone was going upstairs with an armload of fresh towels, and Tootles was running around barefoot, giving orders, getting in the way. Constance retreated to the living room where she regarded the work called *Seven Kinds of Death*, and she was struck by a very vivid memory of the evening when she and Charlie had seen it together, when it was first installed in the National Gallery seventeen years ago. They had overheard a group of people walking around it, pointing. "I can see at least five kinds of death in it," a narrow-faced young man had been saying. "There's death of a forest, obviously, and death of innocence, and death by war, and death by starvation, and this could be death . . ."

At that moment Charlie had whispered in her ear, "Death by boredom."

She was still there when Johnny Buell arrived and asked Ba Ba, "Has he come yet? Paul Volte?"

They entered the living room together, Ba Ba talking about Paul Volte; Tootles, close behind them, said to Constance, "He and Max made me invite him. Paul, I mean. You remember Paul, don't you? That's all Johnny is thinking about. Paul Volte. Maybe he'll do an article about the condos. Not bloody likely. They made me ask him."

The two girls followed her into the room. Constance thought of them as Toni-sad-eyes, and Janet-the-manic, who bounced a lot. They reminded her of her own daughter, and that made her think again of Charlie and how much she would rather be home with him than here with these people.

Moments later Paul Volte and Victoria Leeds arrived. Each carried a small overnight bag; she had a book and a sweater, and her purse. They put everything down in the foyer and entered the living room to be introduced. Johnny Buell turned shy and left, muttering he'd meet them later. And Paul made it clear almost instantly that not only were he and Victoria not sleeping together, they were hardly even speaking. He called her Ms. Leeds, and did not look directly at her, but thanked Tootles for permitting him to bring a friend. Victoria Leeds did not look at him, and also thanked Tootles. But the most interesting thing, Constance thought, watching, was how the expression on Toni's face changed. From a deep-seated sadness, or even fear, or a clinical depressive withdrawal, she became almost as manic as Janet. She hugged and kissed Victoria and Paul both, and smiled broadly even as Tootles groaned and cursed.

"What the hell am I supposed to do about beds? I thought it was all fixed!"

Victoria said she would go to a motel in the village, and Paul said they would both go to a motel, and Toni said Victoria could have her bed and she would sleep in the studio in her sleeping bag, and Janet said no, she would do that. Since Victoria was Toni's friend they should share the room . . .

Ba Ba said maybe one of the twin beds from her room could be moved somewhere. Then Tootles was shaking Paul's arm and saying he did this on purpose, and he was a son of a bitch for not calling to explain the situation. By now Victoria had drawn apart and was merely watching with a trace of a smile on her lips. Constance moved forward and took Tootles's hand.

"Calm down," she said. "Janet can have the second bed in my room. Toni and Victoria can share a room, and Paul can have the room you meant him to have."

"Victoria, do you mind?" Toni asked anxiously. "I can sleep in the studio if you want a private room."

"I think it's all been arranged very nicely," Victoria said. She smiled at Constance.

"Well, I'll just move some things off the other bed," Constance said to Janet who was watching it all, very bright-eyed, apparently breathless. "And you can move in whenever you like."

Toni led the way upstairs to show them the rooms, and Constance followed. At the top of the steps when she turned one way, and Paul, Victoria and Toni went the other, she heard Victoria murmur, "You didn't warn me that it was a madhouse, Paul." Constance laughed softly to herself.

Charlie always said people were either coaster-carrying types, or wet-glass-and-hardly-a-second-look types. He put his wet glass down where it was convenient, sometimes remembering a napkin or even a coaster under it, but not usually. From what little she had seen of Victoria, Constance decided, she was another wet-glass type, while Paul without a doubt was a coaster carrier. She imagined that his house, apartment, wherever he lived, would be like a museum. First impressions, she knew, could be misleading, but there they were. Victoria found the world interesting, the people in it more interesting; her bright eyes and little smile of acceptance said as much. And Paul was a sufferer who suffered most especially at Victoria's hands. Why? Constance wondered. And why did it amuse Victoria, as she felt certain it did, to see him in pain? She shrugged and began to move her things in the bedroom to make space for Janet.

A little later Constance was saying to Max, "I saw your fence when I drove in. An impressive fence."

He laughed delightedly. "Isn't it, though? And tomorrow you get a tour behind the fence—the first building is ready for a grand unveiling." He raised his voice a bit. "Paul, Victoria, you want to see inside the condo tomorrow? A grand tour."

Paul and Victoria had been trailing after Janet who was putting names to the various pieces of art in the living room. It appeared that most students who ever had passed through here had left pieces behind. When Constance glanced in their direction she saw that Johnny Buell was at the doorway and had come to a complete stop with the question.

"I'd love to see inside the fence," Victoria said, and Paul shrugged.

Johnny Buell entered the room and joined Victoria and Paul; Janet introduced him, and soon they were all laughing as they drifted into the hall, out of sight. It was not yet four thirty; Toni and Ba Ba had taken Tootles upstairs to get ready for the party. Toni was good with hair, Tootles had said vaguely. Victoria had not changed yet from her jeans, nor had Paul, and Johnny was in tan slacks and a matching shirt, his working clothes. Constance assumed they would all drift apart now and adorn themselves properly. The cocktail party was scheduled from five to seven, and then, Tootles had said emphatically, she intended to vanish until eight, or else the guests would never leave, and they had to eat a real dinner, didn't they?

Constance had decided to go up to change when Max said, "I suppose you shouldn't ask an art critic to write up something, should you? Her show, I mean. Or the condos either, far as that goes."

"Let me tell you about a client who consulted with me once," Constance said. "He was a poet, and quite good, according to his reviews. The problem was his lover. This was what brought him to me for advice. He said that every time he became really involved with a woman, it ended when he asked for an honest opinion about his work. He was afraid to ask the current lover, and he couldn't stand not knowing exactly what she thought. He respected her opinion, of course."

Max laughed. "Old rock and hard place choice. What did you tell him to do?"

Constance said gravely, "I told him that when the current affair ended, to find himself a woman who was illiterate in English." She left Max chuckling.

Cocktail parties, Charlie always grumbled, meant funny food that you never would make for yourself or order in a restaurant, and standing up too much being polite to people you didn't know or give a damn about. If numbers meant anything this was a smashing success of a party. There was a crush of people in every room. Now and then Constance glimpsed Janet bopping around explaining the art pieces; apparently that was her role. And Toni appeared looking anxious, casting an eye at the tables, the drinks left on tables, just checking on things; her role was to be responsible.

Constance found herself standing next to Max once. He was beaming, to all appearances having a remarkably good time. He looked past her and his face changed subtly; the pleasure was still there, but he looked softer, and very proud. Constance glanced in the direction he was looking to see Tootles arm in arm with two men, holding a drink in one hand, laughing. Apparently she was teaching them a dance step. Toni had done her hair in a chignon that was very flattering; she was wearing a long green skirt and a gold top tied at the shoulders, leaving her arms bare. Although she was more muscular than most women, she looked very handsome that night.

"Isn't she wonderful," Max Buell said in a soft voice.

"Yes," Constance said. "She really is."

He smiled at her then. "I'm glad you came. Have you met Spence Dwyers?"

A man had joined them. "Hello, Spence," Constance said.

"My God! It is you! I thought I recognized you. Constance Leidl, isn't it?"

A long time ago, when Tootles's first husband died suddenly in a car wreck, Spence had rallied about, as he put it. He had married her and they had stayed together for several years before the slow drift apart started, or fast split, or whatever it had been. Constance never had been told, but whatever had happened, it had not changed one important aspect of their relationship. Spence Dwyers owned the gallery where Tootles had shown her work then, and he had arranged the tour they were celebrating now. Throughout the years he had been her most steadfast patron.

He looked like a boxer, which he had been in his youth, with a thick chest and heavily muscled arms. His nose had been broken and retained a crook, and he wore heavy, thick glasses, almost bottle-glass lenses. When he smiled it was like looking into a gold mine.

Max left them chatting about the old days; the party shifted this way and that; groups formed, broke up, reformed. Constance looked at her watch often, counting the minutes until seven. Once she saw Toni whispering urgently to Max, and they left together heading toward the porch. Champagne running short, Constance assumed, and smiled at a woman whose name she had not learned. She met Johnny's fiancée, Debra Saltzman, and was not surprised that she turned out to be a most expensively casual young woman, a bit bland and pretty with long, blond, permed hair that looked windblown, and would always look windblown. She said, wasn't it *exciting* that Marion's work was going on tour; it was so *exciting* to know a famous artist.

Constance drifted over to Paul Volte and congratulated him on the success of his latest book. He nodded in an abstracted way, and she realized that he was searching the room. He held a highball glass that was nearly full, twisted it around and around as he studied the shifting patterns the guests made.

"Have you seen Victoria?" he asked, refocusing his eyes on her. It was obvious that he had heard nothing of what she had been saying.

She thought a moment and realized that she had not seen Victoria a single time that evening. She had meant to speak with her, in fact, because she had been so attracted to her. She told him no and abruptly he walked away. It was five minutes before seven.

Then it was over. Tootles was gone, and Johnny and Debra were telling Max goodbye, Johnny speaking in a voice loud enough to carry. They left with another young couple. Right on cue, Constance thought with amusement.

"Constance," Ba Ba said at her elbow, wheezing slightly, "have you heard yet? No one can find Victoria Leeds. She isn't in the house and she never changed her clothes or anything."

Constance and Toni looked through the upstairs bedrooms and closets, the three bathrooms. When they returned to the first floor, Paul was entering from the back of the house. Toni's fingers dug into Constance's arm. The young woman was staring at Paul, her expression a mixture of anguish and fear; she was ashen. She turned and ran.

"Would she have walked to town, to take a taxi back to Washington, perhaps?" Constance asked Paul.

He shook his head. "I called the two taxi companies and asked. I called the train station and the bus depot. No sign of her." He glanced beyond Constance; a few guests were still partying, no more than five or six. "We need to organize a real search," he said. "Why don't they clear out?"

Spence joined them. "She's not on this side of the property, I'd swear to it. Did she even know there was the rest of it across the road?" His voice was gravelly; a frown etched deeply into his forehead.

"She never came out here before, but someone could have told her. Let's start over there." Paul Volte was nearly as pale as Toni.

Constance saw again the look of terror that had come to Toni's face, and although she had no idea of why these people were all assuming the worst, their fear became her fear. She said slowly, "Paul, perhaps we should call the sheriff's office. Two or three people can't really search the woods thoroughly." It was fifteen minutes before eight.

Later, when Charlie asked Constance exactly how she got rid of the lingering guests, she said simply, "I told them to go away." It wasn't quite that abrupt, but very nearly. Max called the sheriff, and Spence and Paul left to search the woods across the road.

Ba Ba came up to Constance to complain about the summary dismissal of guests and Constance didn't really tell her to shut up, just something like that, and then Tootles appeared again, coming from across the road. She had found time to change into her black pants and shirt.

"What's happening?" she demanded. "I met Paul and Spence and they practically ordered me to get my butt over here."

"And she's ordering everyone in sight," Ba Ba said aggrievedly, glowering at Constance. "All I said was that I was still having a conversation with Susan Walters, and here she comes and—"

"Ba Ba, shut up," Tootles said and asked Max, "What's wrong?"

"It seems that Victoria Leeds is missing," he said with a shrug. "Personally, I think she must have decided to take a powder and just forgot to mention it to anyone. I called the sheriff."

Tootles's eyes widened, then narrowed to slits. "Good Christ! Not Paul!"

The sheriff's deputy arrived a minute or two after that,

and he called back to his office for help for a real search of the woods before it got too dark. It was nearly eight thirty.

Dinner was a buffet; since the cook had no clear idea of how many people she would be feeding that night, it had seemed the simplest way to go, Ba Ba explained, and then started to explain again. This time Max told her to shut up. They picked at food that was very good. Paul and Spence had returned, and Paul didn't even attempt to eat. He sat in the living room with his eyes closed and started at every sound from outside the house.

The deputy returned at nine thirty. It was still day-bright outside; he was sweating heavily. He was a florid-faced man in his twenties, blond, blue-eyed; his shape was somehow not right, too narrow in the shoulders and chest, too wide in the hips. "What's in the big boxes in the barn, Mr. Buell?" the deputy asked, standing in the doorway to the living room.

"Artwork, pieces going on tour," Max said.

Everyone had stood up, and as if managed by a choreographer, they all began to move toward the door. The deputy looked surprised, but did not object, and the group went outside, across the porch, through the front yard that was several hundred feet deep, across the dirt road, and finally into the barn. The big double doors had been opened, and interior lights had been turned on. The crates were in the center of the building; leading to one of them were red spots.

Janet screamed shrilly and Toni grabbed her; they stood with their arms around each other.

"Hey, take it easy," the deputy said. "It's just paint. But it looks to me like someone's opened a couple of the boxes, and didn't take the time to close them again, not like the others, anyway."

Constance moved closer and saw what he meant. Some of the screws had been removed evidently and replaced, but were no longer in all the way.

"Open it," Tootles said in a croaking voice. "For God's sake, just open it!" She flew at the crate and tried to rip the front off. Max drew her back and nodded to the deputy, who began to take out the screws. Max held Tootles against him until the box was opened.

Constance was aware that Janet screamed again, and Tootles made deep, hurt-animal sounds against Max's chest. There were other sounds of incredulity, of fury, anguish. . . . Inside the crate was a wooden sculpture about three feet high, two feet in diameter, securely fastened to the crate with straps, and covered with red paint. The paint had splashed against the wood of the box, turning the interior into a grotesque red stage.

Wordlessly Spence went to a worktable and came back with another screwdriver. He opened another crate. More paint. A piece of wood had been broken off the sculpture and was lying on the bottom of the box.

Janet was keening, her voice rising and falling. Constance moved to Toni, who was holding the younger woman. "Take her back to the house, will you? And stay with her. And Max, you should take Tootles back." Ba Ba, stunned into silence, left with Max and Tootles. Toni pulled Janet out the door. The deputy and Spence opened more crates. Paul had found another screwdriver and was opening crates also.

Out of fourteen sculptures that were already crated up, eleven were paint-daubed, or broken. There were five pieces yet to be boxed; none of them had been damaged.

When they finished, the three men gazed at the spoiled pieces, and finally Spence said, "Why in God's name did she do it?"

"Who?" the deputy asked.

"The missing woman, Victoria Leeds, obviously. She must have come over here, and destroyed a lifetime of work. For God's sake, why? Is she crazy?"

For a second or two Constance thought Paul was going to

hit Spence Dwyers. Paul's muscles tensed; his face became set in a grimace of hatred, but then he relaxed. And she could think of the expression that replaced the hatred only as one of hope. She thought then that nothing she had seen or heard since all this started made a bit of sense, including Tootles's original note to her and the mysterious words she had uttered over the phone.

F i v e

When Constance returned to the house, Ba Ba was talking shrilly: "Well, he shouldn't have brought her out just to fight with her! They could fight back in New York."

Tootles and Max were on one of the sofas, his arm around her shoulders; she looked dazed. Ba Ba was sitting near them, leaning forward speaking into Tootles's face. Janet was huddled on another sofa looking terrified, and Toni, only slightly less frightened, was sitting close to her. Ignoring Ba Ba, who had glanced up without interrupting her stream of words, Constance went over to the young women.

"Why don't you rearrange things one more time," Constance said to them. "Both of you take my room, and I'll move into Toni's room for the night."

"Would you?" Janet asked. Her voice was tremulous.

"No problem," Constance said, but she wished she knew the girl better, knew how close to the edge she really was. Too close, she thought. "Let's go up and do it." They had to walk around *Seven Kinds of Death* in order to leave the room. At least, Constance thought, the best of the lot had been safe, under the eyes of sixty or more guests all evening.

"Why she had to carry the fight beyond Paul is more than

I can see . . ." Ba Ba's voice floated out with them. In the room Constance had used, Toni said they'd do it themselves, if that was all right, and Constance left them moving bedding and clothes.

The search was called off when it became dark enough to justify abandoning the effort to find a woman who apparently was missing only because she chose to absent herself. The deputy clearly was no longer interested in searching for Victoria. Paul looked murderous, and he paced the entire downstairs jerkily. He would be exhausted, Constance knew; his muscles were so tight, and all that walking with so much anger or worry would exact a high cost physically. Spence slouched in a deep chair and scowled at the floor.

Two women from the village who had cooked and served and cleaned up were gone, and the house felt eerily quiet after so much commotion. Ba Ba was talking steadily; she seemed quite unaware that no one listened, no one responded. She was talking about her premonition about the weekend.

"No show," Tootles said to Spence during that evening.

"We'll assess the damage tomorrow," he said. "I think everything can be put together again, cleaned up. We'll see tomorrow."

She shook her head; she appeared to have aged ten years or more since the party. "No show," she said again, and put her head on Max's chest. He stroked her hair.

"I knew something evil would happen, you see, just not what it was. That's how it works for me so much of the time . . ." Ba Ba talked on and the others drifted away to go to bed.

The next morning Constance talked to Janet and to Toni, and she talked to Paul, and to Spence, and began to think she was learning much more about all these people than she needed to know, or even wanted to know. But she did not talk with Tootles, who had a headache and was staying in her room. And she talked as little as possible with Ba Ba. Actually she talked not at all to Ba Ba, and she tried to avoid listening.

Victoria had not returned to her New York address; she had not shown up anywhere.

"Well, I don't think it's fair for her to spoil the weekend for all of us," Ba Ba said at lunch. It was not at all clear to whom she was addressing her complaints. "I mean we have only until Monday, and today we're supposed to get a peek at the condo that will be home for Max and Marion any day now." So she wasn't talking to Tootles, Constance thought. The air? Was that her audience, just that simple: the air? ". . . and tomorrow we're having brunch in that nice old inn, aren't we? They used to have Bay clams, remember? They did them in a champagne sauce. I wonder if they still do that. That means out until late in the afternoon . . ."

Wearily Tootles said, "Ba Ba, for God's sake, stop. We'll go look at the condo. Let's walk over. I feel as if I'm going stir crazy!"

"I'll meet you," Ba Ba said hastily. "I'll drive."

"Good, you drive. I'll walk. Paul, Spence, Constance, who else wants a walk through the woods?"

So even this walk would be semipublic, Constance realized, and she also heard herself making plans to start for home as soon as they got back from inspecting the condo. Say she left at two, she was calculating, she could make it home before midnight without pushing too hard. And before she left, she had already decided, she would give Tootles what-ho for alarming her with talk of desperation and suicide.

Max drove over with Ba Ba; Toni and Janet, who had already seen the condos, chose to stay behind, still huddling together, still wary around Paul. Whatever had been bothering Toni seemed to have infected Janet, who now regarded Paul with fear also. He ignored them both. Constance doubted that he had even noticed their fear. He was very pale, and his hands trembled; a tic jerked in his cheek over and over. He seemed unaware of it. Constance walked next to Spence, with Tootles and Paul leading the way, talking in low voices. Tootles strode along briskly; he walked with a hunched shuffle like that of an old man. The day was heating up; it would be very hot before evening; already the woods felt close and too still, with no air in motion.

"Have you had a chance to assess the damage yet?" Constance asked Spence.

"Yeah. Son of a bitch, what a mess. It can be cleaned up, most of it, but it's going to take patience, and she doesn't have the heart for it right now."

The stretch of woods covered uneven ground that rose and fell, rose again. The path was the only sign of any usage here; on both sides the undergrowth was dense and wild. There were many brambles with blackberries starting to turn color, the brilliant red giving way to black.

Then they reached the tiny stone structure, a one-room house built of gray fieldstones; Tootles led the way around it, to the right and downhill twenty or thirty feet. Across a train track, and the state road that ran parallel to it, they could see the high construction fence and the tops of several condos. Only one of them was finished, Constance understood, but there were six in all being built more or less at the same time. It looked like an alien city rising from behind the wide-board fence.

Max had already arrived with Ba Ba; they had driven over in Tootles's ancient station wagon and were standing by it; Johnny had borrowed Max's Continental, Constance remembered, and Ba Ba was not a likely candidate to ride in a Corvette. In the compound, enough landscaping had been done to be impressively pretty, if artificial looking—too institutional.

Ba Ba appeared to be the only one in the group who had any interest in the condo. Spence and Paul were both impatient, and Constance, thinking now of driving home, was eager to be on her way. The building they entered had a wall of handsome, dark, carved doors, each with a smoked glass oval insert, most of them numbered: 6, 5, 4. . . . The numbers were eight or ten inches high, in brass, very rococo. Max inserted a computer card at 6. The oval window lighted up, and the door opened. It was more like a small foyer than an elevator; there was a mirror on one wall, and a shelf nearly overwhelmed with a large arrangement of roses. Their perfume was cloying in the small space. A small helium balloon floated over them with *Congratulations* printed on it.

"Hey!" Max exclaimed. He peered at the card and then turned to Tootles. "You did this?" His voice was husky.

Tootles looked embarrassed; she shrugged, but when Max took her hand and held it, she did not try to pull away.

There was no sense of motion whatever after the door closed, and then a moment later a door opposite the entrance swung open. Dedicated elevators, Constance realized, and this really was a foyer, of a piece with the bigger foyer that they now entered. A blast of frigid air hit them; the air conditioner apparently was super efficient, and set far too low.

Straight ahead was a wide hall, bright with sunlight. A door to the left was partly open to the kitchen area. Max was smiling broadly, and Ba Ba was praising everything, even the sunlight. They paused while she exclaimed over a curved hallway, broad enough to permit bookcases on one whole wall. Then they took the few remaining steps toward the living room. Spence and Max were in front now, Ba Ba close behind them, Constance, Paul and Tootles trailing. And Ba Ba screamed.

Constance darted away from Paul and Tootles, passed Ba Ba, and caught Spence's arm just as he reached out toward Victoria Leeds, who was on the floor. She was lying on her stomach, with half her face visible; both arms were outstretched, one hand clutching a tarpaulin partially dragged off a table. Around her throat was a piece of rope buried in the swollen flesh; only the ends could be seen. Her face was grotesquely swollen and discolored, her eye wide open and blind.

"Don't touch that," Constance said in a low voice to Spence, who was reaching for a slip of paper. He was as white as the newly painted walls, his eyes seemed not to be focusing properly. Constance looked back at the group still in the doorway, and realized that Ba Ba was still screaming, over and over. She said sharply to Max, "Get them out of here and call the police." He nodded and just then Paul Volte started to move toward Constance and toward Victoria. He walked like a man in a trance. Constance caught Spence's arm, pulled him back a step from the body, and said in a very brusque voice, "Get Paul out of here. Take care of him."

Spence looked at the body, at Constance, and ran his hands down his face; then he seemed to focus his eyes again, and he moved toward Paul and took him by the arms. Max had already herded the others out the doorway. "Come on, old buddy," Spence said. "Can't do anything for her now. Come on. Let's go." Slowly he got Paul turned around, moving in the opposite direction. Constance doubted that Paul would remember any of this. Without touching the body on the floor or anything else, she also moved to the door, where she stood studying the room.

A conference table and chairs were in the center, covered with tarpaulins. Opposite the door was floor-to-ceiling glass, with a balcony beyond it. No drapes or curtains were at the windows. She could see into another room with another long table with blueprints and a typewriter on it. A temporary office apparently. It looked as though more tarps were on the floor in that room, and now she could smell the paint, and she could smell death. She turned and followed the others into the foyer, back into the elevator, and down to the lobby to wait for the police.

This time the sheriff came with the deputies. Bill Gruenwald, he said, examining them all very carefully and quickly. He looked like a man who took good care of himself; he was muscular and trim, in his early forties, with a brush mustache and short brown hair neatly cut.

Ba Ba had stopped screaming to take up moaning. Gruenwald turned his gaze to her, and she said, "I knew it would happen. I knew it would. I had a premonition of evil. I usually listen, but my own sister called me to come, and I did. But—"

"Ba Ba, shut up," Tootles snapped. "Sheriff, can we please go back to the house?"

He sent a deputy to follow them, and they all rode in the station wagon.

"I have to tell Toni," Tootles said when they entered the house. "My God, just my God!" She started to walk toward the studio; the deputy made a motion as if to stop her, and she looked at him in a way that made him flinch and move aside. She went on, and in less than a minute Janet screamed, and she and Toni ran from the studio, up the stairs, and banged a door closed.

Johnny Buell arrived only seconds after that; he shook his head in disbelief when Max told him Victoria was dead.

"Murdered? Why? How did anyone get in the building? That unit? I was over there at seven, I took Debra and Phil and Sunny, and got my briefcase. A little after seven. And I locked up, but anyway Pierce was working by then. We saw him. How did she get in?"

He stopped abruptly. He had looked stunned, disbelieving, but now a different expression crossed his face. He suddenly looked sick. "I have to call people," he said dully. "How long will it be before we can get into Six, clean it up, make it accessible again?"

Max glared at him, and Paul left the living room abruptly. After a moment, Johnny walked out.

When the sheriff finally came to the house, he was met by his deputy, who talked to him in a low voice on the porch.

Sheriff Gruenwald looked particularly grim when he entered the living room, grim and angry.

"John Buell?" He looked at Johnny who had come from the studio area when the car drove up. Johnny nodded. "You went to the condo last night with some other people?"

"That's right. We left here right after seven and drove over there. We went up to Six and I got my briefcase, and we went down again. The watchman came over and we talked a minute or two. I remember that it was ten after seven when I went up to check out the other units, to make sure the painters hadn't left anything. That couldn't have taken more than a minute or two, and then we drove into Washington."

"We who?"

Johnny gave him Debra Saltzman's name and address, and the names of her friends whose addresses he did not know. Gruenwald looked very unhappy. "Our report from yesterday says no one saw Ms. Leeds after about four forty." He looked them all over again, as carefully as he had done before; Toni and Janet had come down, and his gaze rested on them.

"Ms. Cuprillo?"

Janet nodded.

"Right. You were still talking to Ms. Leeds, I understand, after the others left to change their clothes. Is that right?"

She nodded again. Her eyes were very large.

"Fine. Did she say anything about meeting anyone? Did she mention an appointment or anything of that sort?"

"No," Janet whispered.

Toni looked from her to Paul. "She got a letter, remember?" she asked Paul. She said to the sheriff, "I showed them their rooms and there was a letter for her, in Paul's room."

Patiently Sheriff Gruenwald asked Toni to elaborate. When she led them into Paul's room, there had been a letter propped up on one of the pillows, addressed to V. Leeds, typed. She and Victoria had not gone into the room with Paul. He found the note and brought it to the door and handed it over. Toni didn't remember what he had done then, only that Victoria had opened it, glanced at it, crumpled it, and put it in her pocket as they walked towards the room she was to have used.

"Okay, Ms. Townsend. Did you get a glimpse of it? Hand written, typed? Half a page of type, full page, a few lines? What did you see?"

She hesitated, thinking. "Not much. A few lines, typed, I guess."

"Good. Was there a signature? Ink? Blue? Black? Felt tip? What did you see? Could there have been a map of the area?"

Constance watched this with admiration. He was very good, but Toni could add no more to what she had already told him. If there had been a signature, she had not seen it. If there had been a map, she had not seen that, either. She had gone up with Tootles and Ba Ba before four thirty to do Tootles's hair, and she had not seen Victoria again.

"When did you miss her?"

Toni looked at her hands, tightly squeezed together in her lap. Her voice was nearly inaudible. "Not until after six. I was so busy. And I didn't look in the bedroom and see that she hadn't even unpacked until after that, six thirty maybe, when Paul told me he couldn't find her."

"I see. Thank you."

He took them back over their movements of yesterday. Constance had gone up while the group was still talking and laughing, about four thirty, she said. Johnny had left right after he saw Constance go upstairs; he had gone back to the condos to send home a few guys who were still painting in the sub-basement and to shower and change his clothes. Then at five, he had gone to meet Debra's train and they had come to the party.

"Did you set the air conditioner at the minimum setting?" Constance asked. "It was freezing in the apartment," she added to the sheriff.

Johnny shook his head. "We keep it around eighty," he said, shrugging. "I didn't touch it."

Sheriff Gruenwald had looked surprised at her question, but he nodded very slightly, as if to say message received. Fingerprints, she wanted to suggest, might be on the controls. He turned to Paul Volte.

Paul said he had gone up soon after Johnny left, leaving Janet and Victoria.

"She said she wanted to step outside for a cigarette," Janet said. "I didn't see her again. I had my other clothes in the studio and I went in there to change."

Paul said, "She quit smoking three years ago."

"You're sure that's what she said?" Sheriff Gruenwald asked Janet. She nodded. "Okay. We didn't find any cigarettes in her purse, you see," he said almost apologetically.

"Oh!" Janet said then. "Something else. She said he," she nodded at Paul, "was being worn down by his ironic pose. She seemed worried because he was tired and sick."

The sheriff narrowed his eyes at her. "I don't get it," he said. "She said what?"

Janet repeated her words and then shook her head. "I didn't understand either," she said. "But I felt funny asking her what she meant. I pretended it made sense."

Sheriff Gruenwald studied her for another moment, then turned back to Paul. "Does that mean anything to you?"

Paul shook his head.

"You handed her the letter you found on the bed. Did you see the contents? Could there have been a map of the property, do you suppose?"

Paul shook his head. "She didn't open it in the room. I didn't see it."

Sheriff Gruenwald said then, "How it looks at the moment, is that the lady went out to meet someone, and on her way she could have stopped in the barn and made the mess you folks found last night. That could account for the missing time. We know she was still alive at ten past seven when John Buell and his friends were in the building. What I'll need now is to find out where everyone was, starting at seven ten and for the next few hours last night."

"We were all right here, saying good-bye to the party guests!" Ba Ba cried. "We had a party, you know, dozens and dozens of people were leaving from seven on and we were talking and saying good-bye. And then we were all out looking for her."

He waited for her to wind down, and then asked softly, "All of you were here? All the time?"

"Yes! Yes, of course," Ba Ba said shrilly. "You have to tell your party guests good-bye. Haven't you ever given a cocktail party to celebrate something? Haven't you ever gone to one? Doesn't someone tell you good-bye and I'm happy that you came and—"

"Ba Ba, shut up," Tootles said. "I wasn't here," she said to the sheriff. "I went to the little stone house at the end of the property and stayed there until nearly eight."

He let out a long breath and nodded.

S i x

The sheriff asked questions, he talked to Paul alone, and then Tootles alone. Although this all took several hours, Constance knew it was not yet a serious interrogation. They didn't have the time of death yet, the exact cause of death. . . . All the routine things would take a few days, and then they would come back and start the serious interrogation.

"I know some of you are from out of town," Sheriff Gruenwald said to the group that afternoon. "I'll want statements from each of you before you leave again. We can do it in the morning, nine o'clock. If that isn't possible, tell me."

No one moved or spoke. They were all in the living room, where *Seven Kinds of Death* now looked obscene. He nodded at them generally, and told them he would return in the morning, and then he left.

No one moved except for Johnny, who was chewing on a fingernail and looking at his watch. He jumped up suddenly and said, "I've got calls to make." He ran from the room.

Paul said to Marion, "The sheriff thinks you invited her out. I told him she didn't know you."

Tootles shook her head. "I know. He was asking me the

same thing: did I ask her, why? Paul, just when the hell did she decide to come along? How the fuck did she know about the party if you didn't tell her?"

"I don't know," Paul said miserably. "Last week she called me, the first time we've talked in several months." He looked at Toni. "Since the day I met you, in fact." He rubbed his hand over his face, over his eyes, and stood up. "She knew about the party, and said she'd like to come along with me. I didn't ask how she knew. I thought . . . I thought we might be getting back together again, that maybe this was her way to come back." He laughed with great bitterness. "We said hello in the taxi, and sat together on the airplane. I asked her how she was doing, and she asked me the same, and that's all we had to say to each other. I thought during the weekend there would be a chance. I didn't press it." He looked at Spence. "I'm going to walk to the village. You want a beer?" Spence nodded and the two men left together, one looking like a tired pugilist, the other like a half-starved art critic.

Janet had watched and listened, as motionless as a carving; when she moved she was as jerky as a badly managed puppet. And Toni was only slightly less rigid; whenever Paul was within sight, she did not shift her gaze from him.

Once more Ba Ba started to describe exactly how Victoria had looked. With a cry Janet leaped up and ran from the room, tore up the stairs; Toni was close behind her.

"For God's sake," Tootles exclaimed, "Ba Ba, can't you stop just for a while?"

"I can't get over how her face was so swollen—"

"If you don't cork it," Tootles snapped, "I'm going to hit you in the head with something hard and maybe lethal."

"Well, if that's how you feel," Ba Ba cried, "I'll just go home, now. This minute!"

"You can't leave until tomorrow," Max said quietly. "And you do have to stop babbling."

Ba Ba drew in a sharp breath, and walked from the room with her chin quivering.

"Tootles," Constance said, "I want to talk to you before I leave tomorrow."

"Yes, of course," Tootles said. "I mean, you came all the way from wherever you live now and we haven't had a second together."

Then Janet came back, red-eyed, jumpy, and nearly in tears. "Johnny's still talking," she wailed. "I have to make a call. I have to call my mother."

Max strode from the room; in a minute he returned and nodded to Janet. Johnny was at his heels. "But make it quick," Johnny snapped. Then he softened his voice, and looked contrite, even ashamed. "Sorry." Janet was already out of the room, running toward the office.

"I'll go to town and finish," Johnny said abruptly. "I'll come back when I'm done. God, I haven't been able to reach Stein yet. I'll be back." He hurried out, and soon they heard his car throwing gravel.

In another minute or two, Janet said from the doorway, "I called my mom. And I have a reservation for tomorrow at twelve." She drew in a quick breath and added in a rush, "I have to get out of here. I have to get out! I have to!"

Tootles had been on the sofa; she got up and went to Janet. "Come along upstairs," she said quietly. "We can talk, and I'll help you pack. Of course, you have to go home for a while. Come along." She put her arm around Janet's shoulders and walked out with her.

After they were gone Max said reflectively to Constance, "You called her Tootles. I like that. From her childhood?"

She nodded.

"Right after we acquired the land for the condos," he said, walking to a sideboard where there was a bar setup, "I took a stroll over this way to meet the artist and her crew. I'd been warned that it was an unconventional bunch over here. They were all out in the front wrestling a tall wooden figure, eight feet, nine feet, into a truck. It wasn't even her work, but Marion was right there with the kids, all of them filthy, sweaty. I pitched in and helped, too." He poured a glass of mineral water and sipped it. "Next thing I knew she was asking me if I'd had dinner yet, and we all came in to eat chili and homemade bread. Marion's bread; one of the kids made the chili. I don't think they had a cent between them, her or the kids. It was the best food I'd had in years." He drank the water and said, "I wish I'd known her when she was Tootles."

Constance wanted to tell him that would have been a mistake. Before Ed Holbein, or after? Before Spence Dwyers, or after? Before Walter Buckman, or after? None of that really mattered, she understood, not to Tootles, possibly not to Max.

"You're going to live in the condo?" she asked.

"Yes. I'm out here about half the time, in downtown Washington the other half, and this is better. I'm ready to slow down a little, and, of course, she wants to be close to the work, to the kids."

"I'm just surprised you got her to agree to go even that far," Constance said. Then she added, "Max, I think you should talk to a lawyer, you and Tootles, maybe before the sheriff asks any more questions."

His face became very still, the smile frozen in place. "You think it's going to come to needing an attorney?"

She nodded. "It could. Maybe I can get to the telephone now." She went into the dinette-turned-into-office and dialed, only to get the answering machine at the other end. She frowned and said that she would be delayed, please call her, and gave the number. Then she cursed under her breath.

That afternoon Constance mounted outside stairs that led up to a sun deck that ran the length of the house, facing south. Her bedroom, which Toni and Janet now shared, opened to it, as did a number of other rooms. Up here there were lounges, chairs, pillows, tables; Toni and Janet were sun-bathing on mats.

"Hi," Constance said as she approached them. "Toni, I wonder if I might borrow Paul's book. I noticed it in your room earlier, but it isn't there now."

"Oh," Toni said. "Marion has a copy."

"She doesn't know where," Constance said.

"I'll look for mine," Toni said after a moment. "I'm not sure where I put it."

"It's on the table by your bed, the bottom shelf," Janet said. "I remember seeing it there."

Toni stood up finally; she was in a bikini that revealed a beautiful body evenly tanned all over. She pulled on a terry shirt that reached to her knees, and went to the bedroom window, where a screen had been removed and propped against the house. She stepped over the sill to enter the room. Constance sat in a chair near Janet.

"Yesterday, when Victoria and Paul came downstairs, you introduced them to Johnny Buell, and then you were all laughing. Remember that? It seemed such a lively and pleasant little group, telling jokes so soon, having a good time."

Janet raised her head from the mat in order to look at Constance. "I know. And then . . ." She buried her face in the mat again.

"What was the joke?" Constance asked, ignoring the young woman's distress.

"I don't know," Janet said, her voice muffled. "Something about opposites attracting."

"Ah," Constance said thoughtfully. "Like Max and Marion. Or Spence and Marion in the distant past."

"Yeah, just like that. I was thinking of Spence and Marion, in fact. You know, how crazy he is about her and all. Victoria said jocks often were attracted to artists, like that. And, how often real ladies seem to love prizefighters.

Spence used to be a fighter. Victoria said she got a proposal from a jock recently. That's why she came out here, to get away from him or something." She had raised her head to speak, and now lowered it again. "It doesn't sound a bit funny now, but it did then." Her voice became muffled again.

"Then Johnny left," Constance said. "Did she say anything then? Maybe something to you and Paul?"

Janet shook her head. "Next thing she said was when Paul left, how his ironic pose was wearing him down." Janet scowled at Constance. "It sounds so dumb, but I can't help it. She said it, I didn't. Then she said she was going to check out a smoke. And she went out to have a cigarette. That's all she said."

"Check out a smoke?" Constance repeated. "Were those her words?"

"I don't know," Janet cried. "It's how I remember them. I don't know!"

And apparently her memory was all they had to go on, since Paul would have missed whatever Victoria had said about smoke, and whatever she said about his ironic pose. Constance studied the young woman in silence for a time, until Toni stepped through the open window again carrying Paul's book. "I couldn't find my copy," she said. "But I remembered where I saw Marion's down in the music room. This is hers." Her face was sweat-shiny and her breaths were coming hard and fast. She had been running.

Constance stood up to take the book, and then started back toward the stairs. "Thanks," she said. "See you later." Toni lay down again, her head turned so that she could watch Constance.

The deck had been added by inept carpenters; the floor was not level, and the slope was toward the house, not away from it. At the far end where the steps had been built, there was a walkway that led toward the rear of the house. Constance followed it to an outside door that opened to a very narrow hall, then to the central hall of the upper floor, and on to her own room that overlooked the back of the property, the kitchen garden area, the ancient oak trees in the distance, shrubs that needed pruning. It was very quiet out there today. She sat at a window in her room with the book in her lap, wondering why Toni did not want to lend her copy. She must have written in it, Constance decided, underlined passages, highlighted it, annotated it in some way. And by now probably no one would be able to find it without a prolonged search. She opened the copy she held and began to read.

Alice Weber, the woman from town who had made lunch, returned to cook dinner. Ba Ba joined her in the kitchen and their voices rose and fell, rose and fell. Spence and Paul returned from the village; Paul looked as if he had been sleep-deprived for a week; his eyes were red-rimmed, bloodshot, and sunken deep in the sockets. Spence went straight to the little bar. Johnny came back and talked in a low voice with Max for a few minutes, exactly like a child checking in, making a report. Afterward, he said to Tootles, "I had to leave this number for calls to be returned. You can't find anyone on a Saturday afternoon." It sounded almost like an apology, but not quite; it was too sullen for that. He glanced at his father as if to say, okay, I did it. Max's expression was unreadable. Tootles shrugged.

Dinner dragged interminably. No one except Ba Ba had anything to say, and no one paid any attention to her flow of words. As soon as possible Constance went up to her room to finish Paul's book, only to find that after she was done with it, she was too restless to settle down. What did he believe? She saw again his haggard face, his trembling hands, and realized that she did not have even a clue about the man behind the appearance. She knew his column, read it with some regularity, in fact. He was witty writing about art, with a dry humor that was lacking in personal exchanges, as far as she could tell, and that wasn't a fair judgment, she knew, not under the circumstances. And, of course, he was so knowledgeable, recognized as a world authority. But what did he believe? Possession? A jealous muse? A price that must be paid for every success? What did he believe? And more important at the moment, what had happened between him and Victoria Leeds? Tomorrow, she thought, she would find an opportunity to have a little conversation with Paul Volte, not more than that. Just a little talk to satisfy her own curiosity before she started for home. She finally went to bed and was lulled to sleep by the music of crickets, tree toads, a frog chorus.

When she woke up, it was fifteen minutes past eight. She started to roll over, to pull the sheet over her head, to go back to sleep, but she remembered that today she was going home, that she had packing to do, and she forced herself out of the bed, to her feet.

Spence was in the kitchen drinking coffee, reading the *Washington Post*. He had already been down to the village. He grinned his crooked grin at her silently and she was just as silent. What a homely man, she was thinking, and such a charming man. Years ago she had not seen the charm, or had it developed with maturity? He seemed to have traded in a certain belligerence for a great dollop of charm. A fair exchange, she thought, a fine trade. She poured coffee, sat opposite him, and started to read another section of the paper. Yesterday Toni and Janet had made breakfast; Alice Weber had come in to fix lunch, and again later to make dinner. Whatever the arrangements were between the young people and Tootles, teacher and students, hostess and not-quite-guests, boss and slaves, chief and Indians, it seemed to include a bit of work on their part, and they seemed to find that perfectly acceptable. Constance found it perfectly acceptable also.

The others were drifting down, helping themselves to

coffee, no one talking much that morning. Spence got up to make another pot of coffee. "Don't touch that paper," he said over his shoulder from the sink. He had left it open to the editorials. Max was homing in on the newspaper. He looked sheepish and drew back.

Toni appeared, looking for coffee for herself and for Janet, who was packing. Ba Ba came in and said she would make breakfast if people would just get out of the way, and she began to talk about the stacks of pancakes and fried eggs they used to have when she was a girl. . . . The sheriff walked in then, along with one of his deputies and a woman he introduced as a stenographer, and by now the kitchen was quite full, with several people talking at once.

Then another voice cut through it all: "Of course, I'm coming in. I'm looking for my wife."

Constance had never been so glad to hear that voice in her life.

S e v e n

When Charlie heard the message from Constance on the answering machine he had tried to call back; the line had been busy. When he heard on the evening news that Victoria Leeds had been murdered while attending Marion Olsen's house party, he had tried to call repeatedly. The line had stayed busy. Finally he had called the airport instead, and at five that morning he had flown into La Guardia; at seven he had boarded the shuttle, and by nine he was at Tootles's house, where, it seemed to him, they were having a party.

At that moment Mrs. Weber arrived carrying a large bag of pastries. She looked at everyone with astonishment, and without argument they all left the kitchen to her. Charlie held Constance's hand and permitted himself to be led to the living room, where dominating everything was the monstrosity that Tootles had named *Seven Kinds of Death*. Charlie had hated it when it was first unveiled; he saw no reason today to change his opinion about it.

"I'd like a room where we can take statements," the sheriff said to Max Buell. Max nodded and they walked out together. At the same time, others came downstairs and introductions were made all around. Everyone was up, in the living room, waiting for the sheriff, waiting for breakfast, just waiting. Ba Ba was talking about how many calories were in doughnuts compared to whole wheat toast. Doughnuts won. Charlie and Constance crossed the room to the far side; his gaze remained on the work, *Seven Kinds of Death,* as Constance filled him in rapidly and concisely in a very low voice. When she paused, he shook his head.

"What?" she asked.

"Craziness," he murmured. "If Tootles found Victoria Leeds destroying her art, why go all the way over to the condo to do her in? The Tootles I used to know would have picked up the nearest blunt instrument and finished her off on the spot, yelling bloody murder all the while."

They stopped talking when Sheriff Gruenwald and Max returned.

"Sheriff," Johnny Buell asked then, "when will your men be done with the condo? Can the guys get in tomorrow to finish up?"

"Yes, I think so. We'll probably clear out by evening."

"And can I go home?" Ba Ba asked shrilly. "I want to leave here now. Today. I knew I should have stayed home. Larry said I should stay home and he was right. He's my husband and for once he was right. He wouldn't come, and he said I shouldn't either."

Sheriff Gruenwald waited patiently until she paused. "We have no intention of holding anyone here longer than absolutely necessary."

"And Victoria? Her body? When will you release her?" Paul asked. He had trouble with the words; his voice broke and he had to swallow before he could finish the question. "Have you been in touch with her folks?"

"Yes. We'll ship her remains to her family in Michigan just as soon as the autopsy is completed." He went to the door. "I'm expecting the state investigators to arrive any minute now. Meanwhile we'll begin. Ms. Cuprillo, this way please."

"Well," Charlie said. "Is there coffee left in that pot?" He went to the sideboard where sweet rolls and coffee had been arranged, and poured himself a cup, then one for Constance.

"I'll stay if you want me to," Ba Ba said to Tootles. "I didn't mean to run out on you if you need me. You know I wouldn't do that. Larry didn't mean you were the reason he didn't want to come. It was business really, but if you want me to, I'll call him . . ."

Tootles didn't even glance at her. She was looking straight ahead with a distant expression. "He thinks I did it," she said in a low, very hoarse voice. "My God, that man thinks I did it! Did you see how he looked at me?"

Max made a comforting sound and put his hand on Tootles's shoulder. She shrugged it off and jumped up and swung around to glare at Constance. "You told Max I should get a lawyer before I answer any more questions. You think I did it, too! Don't you? Don't you?" Her voice rose until she was shouting.

"No," Constance said without hesitation. "That isn't what I think."

Tootles jammed her hands down in her pockets and began to stride back and forth through the room.

In a few minutes the sheriff returned and nodded to Constance. "Ms. Leidl, please. I'd like to ask you a few questions."

Charlie stood up. For a moment he and the sheriff regarded one another without expression. The sheriff shrugged slightly, turned, and walked out; Constance and Charlie followed him. The sheriff motioned the stenographer away in the hall. She nodded and went out to the porch.

"You're private investigators," the sheriff said in the little breakfast room that he had turned into an office. He stood at the table; Constance sat in one of the old wrecked chairs and Charlie wandered around the room looking at the various objects. His gaze lingered on the Barbie doll. "I just got some stuff on you, Meiklejohn, and I remembered your name. Are you working on this case? Have you been hired?"

Charlie raise his eyebrow in surprise. "Nope. I just got here, remember."

"She's been here several days."

Charlie shrugged.

"I've known Marion Olsen all my life," Constance said. "We grew up together."

Gruenwald sat down heavily and regarded her for a few moments.

Charlie picked up the windup bear and turned the key a few times. The bear danced. "You have a time of death yet on Leeds?" he asked, his back to the table and the sheriff.

"Why, if you're not working?"

"Curious," Charlie said.

After another moment of silence Gruenwald said, "As soon after seven as we can put her in the apartment. It's going to be tough to pin down. The air conditioner was set nearly to freezing."

"Ah," Charlie said. "I see. Quarter after seven? I suppose Tootles is in pretty good shape, isn't she? She could have sprinted over there in a few minutes, waited for the Buell crew to depart, waited for the watchman to hie himself off on the rounds, got herself up to Six, and accomplished the foul deed. Then, of course, she had to reverse every action, dash back down, out, through the woods, and so on. Doesn't leave her much time to discover the damaged art, though, does it? And without that knowledge, it's hard to imagine a motive for her. Of course, she could have stumbled across Leeds in the process of closing crates up again, and chased her through the woods, into the condo complex, and so on. But who unlocked doors, if that's the case?

Leeds? Not bloody likely, is it? And why would Leeds take it on herself to be the ultimate critic? Good luck, Gruenwald. You're going to need it."

Gruenwald nodded. "I know. Yesterday, I would have bet you anything we could put a tramp in that room, something like that. Nothing pretty, but neat. No way. Watchman was on duty from six on; the building was locked when he got to work. John Buell locked it up at five fifteen, and unlocked it when he took in his group at a couple minutes past seven."

Charlie shrugged. "Hard to fit a tramp in, all right. Same old story. Spot a likely suspect and the hunt ends. Bingo. She won't be convicted, you know."

"Maybe, maybe not. But it won't be in my hands." His voice changed subtly. Now he sounded as if he were talking to the chamber of commerce about a highway project that didn't interest him very much. "The state is taking over the investigation almost immediately."

Charlie knew about things like that, too. A small-town killing, domestic murder, break-in and death at a convenience store, all that the sheriff would be expected to handle. But this had turned into a big-town killing; big time builder involved, with his backers; New York editor as victim; some of the party guests, no doubt, wanted this all taken care of pronto. He knew about things like that very well.

Gruenwald said, "The state investigator is named Belmont; he'll want it closed as soon as possible. And he doesn't know Marion Olsen."

Charlie studied him thoughtfully for a moment, then asked softly, "And you do know her?"

"Yes. But even if I didn't, I'm not in the habit of railroading anyone. I just wanted you to know."

"Why?" Charlie asked in honest curiosity.

Sheriff Gruenwald flushed a shade or two, and muttered,

"I've studied some of your cases, the arson cases in particular. They're good."

For a second or two Charlie was speechless. Then he said kindly, "Sit down, Sheriff. Let's talk." He pulled a chair around to sit down also. "First, the note you found is probably a fake." The sheriff started to say something, refrained. "She told me," Charlie said, nodding at Constance. "She saw it. The note Leeds got when she arrived was in an envelope; she took it out, crumpled it and stuck it in her pocket. The note in the condo was smooth, not wrinkled. Right?" He didn't wait for an answer. "So you have a fake note that you will claim puts Tootles at the scene. Maybe it does and maybe not. How did Victoria Leeds get into the condo? She couldn't have gone in on her own, could she? I suspect most of the building is under a security system that needs special keys, computer cards, something of the sort." The sheriff hesitated a moment, then nodded. "Yes. So someone had to be there to let the victim enter, or she had to enter with her killer. Since the watchman was around at seven fifteen, after the Buell gang took off, we have to have our pair wait behind a tree or something while the watchman closed and locked the fence gate, right? It starts to get a little weird, doesn't it? Or else the killer and victim were both already in the building, maybe in the apartment before Buell and gang arrived, but that means someone other than Tootles. She couldn't have got there before seven ten even in a car. At seven she went up and changed her clothes, a matter of several minutes at least, and then she took off into the woods on foot. Guests were leaving; she couldn't have driven off without being seen, and anyway I bet her car was in the garage, hemmed in by a dozen others. We could make her run a mile and time her, I guess, to prove it one way or the other. She must have collected Leeds somewhere along the way." He shook his head. "Weird. Where was Leeds from before five until then? Smashing and splashing paint on art?" He frowned at the formica tabletop, and began to run his finger in a circle, around and around. "It just refuses to make much sense, doesn't it?"

He stood up. "Well, I doubt you'll be able to get enough on Tootles to make it stick. With what you have right now, I know I couldn't."

"But it's early," Gruenwald said. "Lots of time to dig around and see what turns up."

They all turned toward the front of the house. Cars were throwing gravel; brakes screeched. The state investigators had arrived, Charlie decided. The sheriff went to the door with them and pulled it open. "Don't wander away," he said. "They'll want to talk to you."

Charlie nodded; he knew the game rules very well. "I suppose we can get some air," he said. The sheriff shrugged and started to walk toward the front door. Charlie took Constance by the arm. "Let's take a walk." They went out the back door.

E i g h t

As soon as they were away from the house Charlie stopped walking to take Constance into his arms and kiss her in a way he had not been willing to do in front of others. "There, now," he said when he drew back finally. "That's better."

"I'll say," she murmured. "And it was only three days."

He grinned and took her hand. "We don't count by days," he said. "Onward. Let's mosey down to the little creek. I remember when Ed Holbein called it his private trout stream."

"Poor Ed. Remember how happy he and Tootles were? I wonder if she's been that happy with anyone else since?"

"How about Max?"

"He's fine. I like him a lot, but it's different. He adores her apparently. And from what little I've seen, she appears content. I never thought that was a word that could be applied to Tootles."

He nodded. Tootles content was an oxymoron as far as he was concerned.

"You think she's really in for it, don't you?" Constance said a moment later. They were walking under the giant oak trees; they could hear the soft rush of water over stones.

"She's in for it," he said. "Trouble is they just don't have anyone else. Could anyone else have left the party, stayed out at least half an hour, starting at seven?"

She shook her head. "Not the overnight guests. I've tried and tried to make any of them work, but they won't. People were either paired up looking for her, or in plain sight telling other guests good-bye. It could be," she added, "that it really was an outsider we know nothing about. Or someone she knew in the area and was in touch with. We just don't know enough."

He spread his hands. Neither of them believed an outsider had entered the house before Victoria's arrival in order to leave a note for her on Paul's bed. They had reached the little brook that was only six or eight feet across and inches deep. It had a pleasant singing voice, he thought in approval. Unpretentious, nice. And if trout ever had been present in those waters, it was back in prehistoric times. It was at least ten degrees cooler here by the running water in the deep shade.

He looked around for rocks or logs to sit on, and had to give that up and lean against a tree instead; grasses and weeds grew right down to the edge of the water. "You don't think Tootles did it," he murmured. "Why? Just because you've known her all your life?"

"I don't think it's that." She considered it with her head cocked, accepting that bias could be a factor, accepting that if it was, she could do nothing about it. "But you said it before. If she had found anyone messing up her work, she would have thrown a fit on the spot. She isn't devious, not that way. Action/reaction are never very far apart with her. Deviousness and a cold-bloodedness just aren't her style." She drew in a deep breath and went on to tell him about Tootles's note, and the phone call.

Charlie scowled at her. "Good God, that's all the cops need," he said. "She says she's in desperate trouble and someone gets killed! Think she'll blab about it?"

"Of course not." And it went without saying, they both knew, that neither would Constance. "But I can't believe it had anything to do with Victoria Leeds. I'd bet a lot that they didn't know each other before Victoria showed up here. Paul said that, and so did Tootles, and I believe it; I was watching when Paul introduced them."

Charlie knew that if Constance was willing to put up money, it meant she was certain, not that anything was at risk. He grunted as he pushed off from the tree; there simply wasn't anyone else, he told himself again. It was Tootles or a stranger. And he didn't believe in strangers wandering in through locked doors to commit murder that apparently had nothing to do with robbery or rape.

"The sheriff's pretty good," Constance said a moment later, but without much conviction. "The old Sherlock truism comes in just about here, doesn't it? If you rule out all that just won't work, you're forced to take whatever is left. I'm so afraid that's how his mind will work, and apparently he's very much afraid the state investigators will take Tootles with even less struggle than he's having."

She watched a monarch butterfly pose against an umbel of Queen Anne's lace, and then rise without effort to catch a ray of slanting light that made it glow like a magical creature. It drifted away, and if she blinked, or if it did a vanishing act so fast she could not follow, she could not have said; the butterfly was there, then gone.

"Charlie," she said, "you keep calling Tootles a nut, and Ba Ba, of course. But why? I mean, Ba Ba talks incessantly, but does that really make her a nut? And what is it about Tootles?"

She kept her gaze on the spot where the butterfly had vanished; it must have fallen through a hole in space, she thought distantly.

The silence that followed her question had become too long, too intense, so that no matter now how it was broken, there would be that interval when her question hung between them. Charlie squatted and picked up a handful of stones that he began to toss into the fast little stream.

"It was a long time ago," he said at last.

"I know. We were all little more than children."

Not Tootles, he thought; she had never been a child. The funny thing, he also thought, was that he had been invited in, but had not entered, and yet the guilt he had felt then had made it seem that he might as well have yielded. Now he could admit that the cloud of pheromones that Tootles had moved in was almost more than a fellow could resist, but in those days he had been terrified. He and Constance had only recently married, and he could not have been less interested in another woman; and that state had endured. But there were all those pheromones calling, beckoning. The spell had been there; he had been targeted more than once, and he knew that others, including Babar, probably believed he had taken that next step. Over the years he had met other women like Tootles, and men also, who exuded sex appeal the way the Greeks in the deli he had grown up near had exuded the aroma of garlic and olive oil. But sex appeal alone did not qualify anyone for nuthood, he also knew.

Slowly he said, "When we were all still living in New York, Babar and Tootles had that rattrap apartment down on Twenty-second. Remember? Just before they moved down here, the last place they had in the city, I guess." He remembered clearly a series of ratty apartments that he associated with Tootles and Babar, all firetraps, walk-ups, infested with vermin, and all vibrating with a feeling of excitement nearly uncontainable.

That last day, he had gone to their apartment late in the afternoon, planning to meet Constance there after she finished a class she was teaching; then half a dozen or more of them were going to go eat Chinese food—cheap, abundant, good. None of them had money for restaurants; he had started his career as a fireman by then, but Constance was still in school, working on her doctorate, teaching. A long time ago, he thought again.

"Anyway, there I was, dead tired from coming off the four-day stint. Remember, four days on, four off?" She nodded. "I conked out on the floor, out like a light, and when I came awake enough to hear anything, they were having a go with that damn Ouija board they used to play around with. But this time it was different. I think Babar was in a deep trance, or something, and she scared the shit out of me. And Tootles, too, I'm sure."

Constance turned to look at him with an expression of bewilderment. "You were afraid? They used to do that back when we were just kids. What was frightening?"

He shook his head. "I was half asleep, just waking up, and Babar was going on about a spirit she had summoned, and damned if I didn't see something like a cloud form behind Tootles, and then settle over her, and disappear. Okay," he said hurriedly, lifting his hand palms out, "I admit I was groggy from missing sleep. But that wasn't even the scary part. It was what Babar was saying, and how she was saying it, and how Tootles was reacting. I think they both believed every word. And that was scary, their belief, their acceptance. Talking to the air as if it held a genie with wishes to hand out, payments to exact, you know, cutting a deal. I was wide awake by then and made noises and broke it up. They were both really sore, especially Babar. Apparently this was the most successful trance she had achieved, the best spirit she had called up, or some damn thing. Anyway, they were furious with me, and kicked me out, just like that. Both of them were like . . ." He shrugged then. "Nuts," he said. "Two nut cases if I ever saw any."

"Oh, Charlie," she said in a soft voice. "You never even mentioned any of that. I thought . . . I don't know what I thought. That Tootles had really tried to seduce you, I guess."

"You were willing to pal around with her thinking that?"

"It didn't matter," Constance said. "I knew you wouldn't, and she didn't mean anything by it. She was never out to hurt anyone, just to give everything a try. She gave spiritualism a try, and Catholicism, and Zen, and TM. Heaven alone knows what all she's tried over the years."

"Especially men," he said darkly.

Constance nodded. "I know. Especially men. And as for the fortune telling, they used the I Ching, various kinds of cards, including the Tarot, the Ouija board, maybe even entrails. I bet right now Ba Ba has a drawer full of crystals, talismans, fetishes of all sorts. . . . She's intrigued by the occult and always was, and yes, maybe a bit of a nut where the supernatural is concerned. I just never realized that you had seen them going at it. I wish you had mentioned it years ago."

Even thinking about mentioning it at a time when it would have been meaningful brought back the memory of near terror he had felt that day. He had been incapable of talking about it then; he couldn't have explained the fear he had felt, couldn't have justified his aversion to both women after that day and for years to come. Over the next ten years they had attended a Marion Olsen opening or two, they had gone to a show or two, had come out to the farm twice, neither time staying more than a few hours, and in his mind Tootles and Babar were still the nuts he had come across nearly thirty years ago. That had not changed a bit with time.

Constance was frowning thoughtfully at the stream; she nodded, as if reaching a decision. "Tootles has left all that far behind, I'm certain," she said. "Ba Ba is still interested in the occult. Not that it matters; it doesn't have a thing to do with what's going on now. Information, data. Just sorting out things."

"Let's walk," he said, and for the next few minutes neither of them spoke. They had nearly reached the house when Charlie stopped and put his hand on her arm.

"Honey, you know, don't you, that they won't just let us walk away from this one? I think there are times when I can look into the future without a crystal ball or the Tarot cards, or any other damn gimmick. One of them will ask us to take this on, prove Tootles didn't do it, find out who did. Bet?"

She shook her head emphatically. "You know I don't. Ever."

He laughed. "Okay. Want to make book on who will ask? Max?"

"Maybe," she said cautiously. "Or maybe Paul Volte." He looked surprised, and they continued to walk toward the back door of the house. "But, Charlie," she added, "we can say no. You can say no. You don't have to hang around and ask questions, or do anything else about this mess."

That should have been an option, he knew, but it wasn't, not really. They would manage to hang this one on Tootles if someone didn't do something to prevent that, and no one else could be expected to have this deep belief in her innocence—as far as this murder was concerned, he had to add to himself. No, if he believed in fate, karma, any of that stuff, he would have to accept that this was the trap that had opened weeks earlier; finally it was shutting all the way.

"Check," he said. "One thing, though. I don't want to stay in the house even if we hang out for a day or two. Agreed?"

She nodded. He would have to throttle Ba Ba, and that could be serious. Or she might decide to throttle the woman. "We probably can get a motel room, or a hotel in the village, or something."

He snapped his fingers in irritation then. "Damn," he muttered. "Forgot about that car." He glowered toward the driveway where a rental car was parked next to their Volvo. "How much would you say it's worth not to have to drive in to National?"

"That bad, hm?"

"Tourist season," he said. "You wouldn't believe down-town Washington in the summer."

She eyed him curiously. "Why were you downtown?"

"Never mind," he said. "Just a little wrong turn, that sort of thing that can happen to anyone at all."

"Fifty dollars? Forty? Whatever the kid you ask says he'll charge," she said.

He knew she was right. Some things he refused to bargain over. They both stopped again when Janet appeared with a deputy and got into a taxi. The driver put her suitcase in, and drove off. Janet had looked infinitely relieved; standing in the drive watching the taxi vanish down the road, Toni looked forlorn and miserable. She ducked her head and slouched back into the house.

Two hours later the state investigator, Lieutenant Belmont, told Constance she was free to go.

Constance found Charlie on the back porch. "Done," she said wearily. "Statement accepted, signed, tucked away where maybe no human eye will ever spot it again."

"Rubber hoses and all?"

"On both sides, and bright lights, the works."

"Let's scram. Onward to the village green. You hungry or anything?"

He drove down the gravel road, crossed the railroad tracks, and came to the state road where he turned left. He was watching the odometer closely. It was nine-tenths of a mile to the gate of the construction fence at the condominium complex. He slowed there and pulled to the side of the road, surveying the fence, the railroad tracks a few hundred feet away, parallel to the road, and beyond the tracks the stand of trees that was Tootles's property.

"Problems," he said then. "This is pretty exposed, wouldn't you say?" From here he could see that there was the big gate, double doors that could admit trucks, cranes, whatever equipment the job required. Next to it was a door no more than three feet wide. Both were closed now. The gate was at the corner of the fence, a car length off the road; to one side the undergrowth was cleared away, no place to hide there. On the other side of the gate a parking lot had been bulldozed and covered with gravel. The fence on that side appeared to go back to the river bank. "No lurking space at all," he said morosely. "You'd have to stay all the way over there in the woods."

"And then cross the tracks and hope no car came while you were in the open," Constance added. "It doesn't work very well, does it?"

He made a grunting noise and started the car again, put it in reverse and backed into the parking lot, where he surveyed the length of the fence. There was no other gate in it, just the two entrances at this corner. He drove out of the lot and very slowly along the frontage of the condominium property. The fence was unbroken after they left that first corner.

"Okay," he said then and pressed the accelerator.

The village of Maryville had a population of twelve thousand two hundred residents; there were three motels within a few minutes of downtown, and a hotel in the center of town, but there was no vacancy in any of them.

"Tourists," Charlie said with resignation, joining Constance at the car. She had gone in with him the first two times, before accepting defeat.

When they got back to Tootles's place, all the police cars were gone. Paul Volte was standing on the back porch, his arms crossed over his chest, a deep frown on his face.

He watched Constance and Charlie without speaking until they were within touching distance, and then he said in a low voice, "I think that idiotic lieutenant plans to arrest Marion!"

"What's been happening?" Charlie asked.

"The questions he asked me all kept leading back to

Marion. How did Victoria know about the party? Was she interested in Marion for literary reasons? Planning a book or something about her. Like that."

Charlie nodded in sympathy. "Way it works," he said. "You find a good likely suspect and work and work with it, just to see how long it takes to shake it apart. If it doesn't come apart, you begin to think you've got the answer. So far, everyone keeps coming apart, except for Tootles. They'll keep at her until they make a case, or she falls apart before their eyes like everyone else is doing."

"Christ!" Paul said. "It's the most ridiculous thing I can imagine!"

"Paul, exactly when did Victoria tell you she wanted to come to the party?" Constance asked. "Could there have been a news item about it?"

He shook his head. "What for? Marion's not really a hot news item, you know. Victoria called me on the fifteenth, one week before we actually came. She said she understood there would be a party for Marion, and that I was invited, and would I mind if she tagged along. Would I give Marion a call and make sure it was all right? I said why didn't she call for herself, and she said she didn't even know Marion Olsen, who might not accept a call from a stranger, and a party crasher. So I made the call, and a week later we got together and came by plane and rented a car at the airport to drive the rest of the way." He had said all this so often it now was singsong. He ran his hand over his face and closed his eyes wearily.

"Would you have considered an article about Marion's touring show?" Constance asked.

He looked at her in surprise and shook his head. "No. *Seven Kinds of Death* is the best thing she's ever done, and it's eighteen or nineteen years old. I wouldn't have written about her, and she didn't think for a second I would. I wouldn't have written about the condominiums, either," he added. "The International Style passed through the corridors of the Chicago School, interpreted by Le Corbusier, diluted by Howe and then translated into binary by a hacker, who invariably selected the worst features he could find to produce a CAD program. For fifty dollars extra you can get variations."

His contempt was so blatant that for a time no one spoke. Constance gazed at a willow tree fluttering gently, and finally Charlie said, "We have no authority to ask questions, no reason to expect anyone to answer them, but for what it's worth, I don't believe Tootles killed Victoria Leeds. I've known her for more than twenty-five years, and I just can't see her doing it. For what it's worth. And I could be wrong, natch."

"What do you want to know?" Paul Volte asked. The animation that his scorn had enlivened vanished and weariness settled over him again like a miasma.

Constance had already told Charlie about Paul's relationship with Victoria, and with Toni; there seemed little point in rehashing any of it now. "You asked Tootles to invite Victoria Leeds?" Charlie asked, and Paul said not exactly. When he called, Max had answered, not Tootles. Charlie sat down on the top step of the porch; Paul left the rail he was leaning against to sit down also. Constance pulled a lounge chair closer and stretched out on it.

"This is all meaningless," Paul said. He sounded dispirited and despairing; his voice was monotone. "I called here and got Max," he said in a flat voice. "I said I'd like to bring a friend, Victoria Leeds, and would that be convenient. And he said he would be delighted to meet Ms. Leeds. That was all."

He said he had not paid much attention the day he and Victoria arrived and Johnny Buell joined them for a few minutes. Janet and Victoria had been laughing at something, but he didn't know what; he had not heard the joke. He had, he admitted, taken a dislike to Johnny Buell when he realized that he was the one who had been responsible for his, Paul's, invitation. Just two weeks before the party, he had received the invitation, and he would not have come if Victoria had not called him. Inviting him was obviously an afterthought, he said bitterly. Johnny had read his book, had been flattering about it, but it was obvious that he was looking for a free lunch.

"Did you notice what time it was when you realized you hadn't seen Victoria at the party?" Charlie asked.

"I came back down a little after five thirty, and I sort of looked around for her, but there was a crush already. It must have been close to six thirty before I started to worry about it." He described the half-hearted search at first and then the real search, and finally calling the police. A little after seven when the party was officially over, they finally had crossed the road to search the barn. He had not paid any attention to the crates. "It probably wouldn't have meant anything to me even if I had seen the loosened screws. I hadn't seen them before and hadn't worked on crating up, so I doubt I would have noticed anything out of ordinary there. We were looking for a woman, remember."

"That was near seven?" Charlie asked.

"A little after. Johnny and his friends had left already; most of the guests had left, I think. Seven fifteen, something like that."

"And as far as you can say, the crates had been opened by then?"

"I don't know," he said. "I just don't know."

Charlie glanced at him unhappily. "Can you think of anyone who might have wanted to kill Victoria Leeds? Or a reason?"

Paul shook his head. "There isn't anyone, and there isn't a reason in the world. I've tried and tried to come up with anything, and there's nothing." He caught his breath in sharply, closed his eyes, and then added, "She was one of the kindest, gentlest, most understanding people I've ever known. No one could have had a reason." His eyes gleamed with unshed tears.

There was a silence following this. Paul gazed blindly past Charlie, who felt almost embarrassed. Constance broke the silence.

"I understand that you recommended Toni to Tootles," she said. "Is that something you do often? Recommend young artists to study here?"

He shrugged. "This was the first time. Victoria asked me to do something for her, and when I saw the relief Toni did of Victoria, I agreed that she would benefit."

"Is she exceptionally talented?" Constance asked.

He shrugged, but now he looked more alive than he had only a moment earlier. "She's good. There's talent. We'll have to wait and see."

Charlie stood up and stretched. "You leaving today?" he asked.

"I don't know, but in any case not until I've had a chance to talk to Max and Marion. I can't believe that policeman intends to saddle Marion with this. It's the craziest thing I've ever heard of!" His respite from grief, guilt, whatever it was, had been short-lived; he looked miserable again. He had got to his feet as he spoke, and now he started to walk toward the door of the house. He hesitated before opening it. "What about you? Are you leaving?"

"Haven't decided," Charlie said.

"Hang around if you can," Paul said suddenly. "Are you free to take on an investigation now? Would you be interested? I have to talk to Max and Marion first, but if they agree, would you be interested?"

"Mr. Volte," Charlie said softly, "do you know anything about me, about us?"

Paul nodded. "I called my lawyer yesterday and briefed him about what was going on here. Your name came up because of her." He nodded toward Constance. "I believe my lawyer would approve if we hired you. And if that lieutenant really tries to hang this on Marion, we'll want to hire you, I'm certain."

He reached for the handle of the screen door but stopped again when Constance asked, "Paul, why do Toni and Janet think you had something to do with Victoria's death?"

He hunched his shoulders for a second as if to ward off a blow, then he said, "Because I'm responsible. Not for the act itself. I didn't do it, or hire anyone to do it. But I'm responsible. If it weren't for me, she'd be alive now." Abruptly he yanked the door open and hurried inside.

Nine

Whatever Charlie had intended to say next, he forgot because Spence Dwyers came shambling around the corner of the house. He spotted Charlie and Constance on the back porch and headed toward them, straightening his back, raising his head, as if his awareness that he was being watched had pushed a button. Charlie had sparred with Spence once many years ago, and had been trounced, but not hurt. He remembered how careful Spence had been not to hurt him.

"Charlie!" Spence said as he drew near them. "Thank God you're here! Has Paul spoken to you? Or Max? We want to hire you to get to the bottom of this mess. My God, I can't stand seeing Marion like this!"

"What happened?" Charlie demanded. "Is Belmont giving her a hard time? Doesn't she know she doesn't have to say a word without a lawyer at her elbow?"

"No. No. It isn't anything like that. They haven't come down hard yet. But she's . . . I think she's shrinking right in front of our eyes! It's awful, the way she looks."

"Are they through with you?"

"Yes, they told me I could leave. But who could leave now? With her like that? We have to talk, make plans."

"Sit down," Charlie said, indicating the top step. He waited until Spence sat down, and then sat beside him. "Did you know Victoria Leeds before she showed up here?"

Spence shook his head. "I never even met her. I got here after the party started, and she never put in an appearance. I don't think any of us knew her, except for Paul and Toni. You know about that? How they met and all?"

"Yes, we know," Charlie said morosely. "Spence," he went on, gazing out through the trees, "if we take this on, we're going to need all the help we can get. You understand? I mean no holding out, no half truths. It's not going to be a snap, and we may not be able to take the heat off Tootles, but I'll try."

Spence nodded. "Yeah, Charlie, goes without saying."

Charlie became aware that Constance wanted to ask something. There was nothing he could have pointed to; he was certain she had not cleared her throat, or shifted her position, or touched him. But he knew just as surely as if she had run her hand down his back.

And she knew he was pausing to allow her question. She asked, "Why did you arrange a touring show for Tootles at this late date in her career?"

Charlie continued to look out over the trees, but he was fully aware of the rigidity that had come over Spence Dwyers; the man hardly seemed to breathe for what seemed much too long a time. Charlie waited, mulling over the question.

"It's never too late," Spence said finally. "She has some very good pieces, after all. A lot of them I've had in my gallery over the years. Nice work. She can use a little appreciation, we all can, no matter what stage we're at."

Constance said, "Hm," and Charlie said, "Knock it off. Whose idea was the traveling circus? Yours or hers?"

Again the silence stretched too long. Pay dirt, Charlie thought then, and he hadn't even known what they were scratching for this time. He got up and brushed off his trousers. Very slowly Spence stood up; he didn't look at Charlie or Constance. "Damn it," he said finally, "her work, the show, it's got nothing to do with the Leeds woman. She was just someone Paul knew. Let's let it go at that."

"Can't," Charlie said with regret. "We'll come back to it."

For a second or two Spence hesitated with a curious look on his face, partly embarrassment, partly surprise. "Jesus," he said in a low voice, "the way we're talking about her, Victoria Leeds, as if she didn't matter. Me, I mean. The way I was talking about her. Jesus. It's just that I didn't know her, and I do know Tootles."

"Paul's certainly taking it hard," Constance murmured.

"Yeah. I know he is."

"Too hard?" Constance asked in a low voice. "I understand Victoria Leeds wanted to marry and he wouldn't do it. She left him months ago apparently."

Spence nodded. "That's what I heard, too. So now he's having all the guilt in the world settle down around his shoulders. Way it goes. Anyway, I don't know anything about their private lives, you understand. I only met him a few times over the years, not like a bosom buddy, you know."

Constance nodded and said *of course,* and now Charlie asked, "You know of a place where we can get a room, an apartment, anything for a day or two?"

"Out here, or in town?"

"Here."

"Not offhand. Let me give it a little thought. I'll ask Max. There's got to be something."

Constance now asked, "Spence, is Toni any good? Is she going to make it?"

He looked surprised, then shrugged. "Who knows? She's clever, smart, good with her hands. More than that? Not yet. But she's pretty young. Give her a few years, see what develops." He grinned lopsidedly, "Tootles wouldn't have invited her to stay if she hadn't thought the kid will make it eventually." Shaking his head, he repeated, "Tootles. I haven't called her that in thirty years. Tootles. Still fits, doesn't it?" He sobered again quickly. He glanced at his watch, then started to move toward the door. "I'll make some calls, see if I can find you a place to stay. And, Charlie, later, this evening, let's get together again with that other question. Okay? Just need a little time first, that's all."

"Sure," Charlie said. "Sure, Spence."

One by one the others drifted out to wander around in confusion; no one seemed in a hurry to leave now, not even Ba Ba. She appeared, hesitated, turned and reentered the house. Spence came back and handed Charlie a piece of paper with the name of a motel and directions—ten minutes away, he said, no more than that. Then Toni appeared and said there was a phone call for Charlie. "I think it's the sheriff," she said, leading them to the telephone in the office. She watched Charlie as he lifted the receiver. He returned her gaze pointedly and did not speak until she flushed crimson, turned, and walked away with her head very high, her back very stiff. She pulled the door closed behind her unnecessarily hard.

"Meiklejohn," he said then, grinning at Constance.

"Mr. Buell said they might hire you," Gruenwald said. "You working now?"

"Not yet."

"Want to go with me to talk to the guy who was crating up the artwork? He's due back around nine. Thought we might like a word with him."

"I'd like that," Charlie said. "We'll be staying at . . ." He glanced at the paper Spence had given him, "Lakeside Inn."

"Know where it is," Gruenwald said. "Pick you up around eight forty-five. Okay?"

Charlie said okay and added, "You understand that I might be working by then," he said.

"I know. See you later."

Constance was watching him with a slight frown as he told her about the invitation. "But if the state police are handling the investigation, why is he doing this? And why ask us to go with him?"

"Good questions," Charlie said. "Let's ask him."

He looked past her at the hall door, and then went to open it to listen to voices raised somewhere around the front of the house. He motioned, and they walked quietly down the hallway toward the foyer.

"I don't give a shit!" Tootles was yelling. "That pip-squeak can't come and go like that, give orders to stay put like that. Who does he think he is?"

"He's the law," Spence said.

Paul's voice was lower. "Marion, just don't let him get to you. Talk to your lawyer first thing in the morning."

Max said, "He isn't after you, Marion. I'm sure he isn't."

"And you're wrong," Ba Ba cried. "Of course, he's after her. I knew it would happen! I read the cards and they were full of death omens, catastrophes . . ."

A strange voice said, "Mrs. Buell, you want lunch in the dining room? I can put out sandwich stuff, and salad. I wasn't sure what to do, what with all those men hanging around . . ."

Max said, "The dining room's fine. Fine. We need coffee, and something to eat. Sandwiches are fine, aren't they, Marion?"

"You're hungry? How can you be?" Tootles cried. "I can't stand this! Food. Coffee. Let's all pretend nothing's happened, nothing's going to happen. That man plans to arrest me, for chrissake!"

Charlie took the next step or two into the foyer and Tootles ran to him, caught his arm. "You will help, won't you?

You can find out who killed Victoria Leeds. Charlie, some-one has to help me!"

He looked at her in wonder. She could still do it, he realized. The hormones, the appeal was still there in this coarse, not at all handsome woman with unkempt graying hair, unkempt, not-very-clean clothes, dirty feet . . . He pried her fingers loose from his arm, and took her by the shoulders, moved her back a foot or two. "Let's make one thing clear," he said. "If I take this on, you don't lie to me. Is that a deal?"

She looked bewildered. "Of course. Why would I lie to you?"

He sighed and looked past her to where Constance was standing, watching all this with a very bright look. Probably no one else would recognize it as amusement, but he knew that expression. He scowled at her.

"I thought he was a fireman," Ba Ba said.

"And you'll all cooperate," Charlie said to them all generally.

"What difference does it make, if he's a fireman?" Ba Ba asked. "We haven't had any fire, thank heavens. At least, we've been spared—"

"Babar, shut up," Charlie said. Count the small blessings, he thought with relief; when you told her to shut up, she did. For a few minutes. And she didn't seem to hold a grudge. She assumed a pout now and pointedly looked out the window as if she had suddenly gone deaf. "I'll want to ask you as a group about the night of the party. I'll want to ask some of you questions not in a group. And I'll want to have a look at that condo. Can we get in yet?" he asked Max.

Max glanced at Johnny who shrugged and said, "The lieutenant said they'd clear out by four at the latest."

Charlie nodded. "Four it is. And right now, I want a sandwich." They all followed him meekly enough into the dining room. It was nearly three already.

Asking questions of the group was a bust, he decided later. Nothing turned up that he had not already heard. Constance went upstairs to gather the few things she had unpacked, and now it was going on four, and they were ready to leave.

Johnny Buell met them at the door. Although he looked serious, there was also an underlying eagerness in his expression, his attitude, like a Boy Scout after another merit badge. "Now what?"

"Exactly the same as it was the other night. You said good-bye to everyone, and your group went outside. Where were you parked?"

"Across the road," Johnny said. "I knew we'd want to leave promptly at seven and I didn't want to get blocked. I had moved the car over there already. Dad's car," he added. "Mine's a Corvette, a two-seater."

"Good," Charlie said. He looked at his watch. "Let's pretend it's about three minutes after seven. We've said good-bye, and it's time to leave. Let's go."

Johnny would have hurried them through the yard, but Constance did not permit it. "I noticed Debra's shoes," she explained. "High heels, sandals. And this is rough ground."

They reached Max's Continental, and got in. Johnny drove fast, but not dangerously so, and probably at his usual speed, to the condominium fence. No one spoke until he stopped. "I had to get out and open the gate," he said, opening his door. He unlocked the gate and swung it back, returned to the car and drove on through, to the first of the buildings. An iron-grille gate closed the driveway outside the building itself. He touched a signal button on a box on the dashboard and the gate swung up; he drove in and down a long ramp. "Basement," he said. "This will all be parking space for the occupants." They drove past some elevators and stairs. The parking spaces were marked by pale green lines painted on the floor. He drove slowly to the far end of the basement and made a partial turn, touched the signal button again, and the second grillwork gate opened.

"We got out here," he said.

"You opened the gate there before you left the car and went upstairs?"

Johnny nodded with a crestfallen look. "I don't know why, no reason. I just did. I know. Someone could have entered the building while we were upstairs."

Charlie nodded and opened the car door. The wall to his right housed many elevators, a staircase, and two or three unmarked doors that he assumed were maintenance closets. All the doors were the same dark green as the walls. Stenciled on panels on the elevator doors were oversized numbers on one side and the letter A on the other in the same pale green as the floor stripes. The numbers and the stripes seemed to glow against the dark green; easy to spot late at night, after a hard day, Charlie thought. Johnny went to Six A and pushed the button. He had to use a computer lock card to open the elevator door; they entered the small foyer that looked almost exactly as it had when Constance had ridden it up before. Now the roses on the shelf were dying and their fragrance had turned to a musty odor.

No one spoke until they reached the sixth-floor apartment and entered. Charlie said, "Seven ten. Was the timing about the same as the other night?"

Johnny moistened his lips and nodded. His subdued eagerness had vanished; he looked apprehensive and seemed reluctant to leave the foyer and advance into the apartment until Charlie realized the cause of his nervousness. "She's gone," he said kindly. "Believe me, it's all right."

They walked through the hall into the spacious living room where even the chalked outline of Victoria Leeds had been cleaned up. The tarps were back on the furniture.

"Now what?" Charlie asked.

"I went on through to the dining room. I had left my briefcase in there. The others didn't move from the doorway. No one wanted to get paint on their clothes. It smelled pretty strong, you know, wet paint. The walls, the door facings . . .'' He hurried across the room to the dining room, went in, came back out and rejoined Charlie and Constance at the door. ''Then we went down.''

They reentered the foyer/elevator and rode to the basement, where they got back in the car, and Johnny drove out of the building and touched the button to close the gate after him. ''I stopped here,'' he said, pulling on the hand brake. The iron gate had already closed. ''I began to wonder if there were tarps, the heavy odor of paint in the other units, and I knew I wouldn't rest unless I checked them out. This was a big weekend,'' he added. ''You know about the two tours through the buildings we had planned?''

Charlie nodded. ''Let's go in and go through the exact same movements you made before. Honey, you want to chat with the watchman?'' Johnny looked around in bewilderment; there was no watchman in sight.

''Oh,'' he said, and then led the way back into the building; they were now on the first floor; here the elevators had the big brass numbers that Constance had seen on her tour. ''I went up to Five A,'' he said, and held up a wallet with computer lock cards. He used one to open the elevator to Five A and they entered it. ''I used the stairs to go to the other floors. Each elevator is dedicated to its own unit at this end of the building.'' He glanced at Charlie who nodded in understanding. They arrived at the foyer on five, and glanced inside the unit without entering, went to the end of the hall and down the stairs to four, and repeated the inspection, then to three, two, and finally they were back on the first floor. It had taken no more than five minutes in all. The apartments all appeared to be identical. Only Six A still showed the evidence of recent painting activity. Six A and Five A had both been outfitted with a conference table and chairs in the large living room. In Five A coffee service had been added. Probably they would have had doughnuts,

Charlie thought, for the money men. This side of the building had the biggest apartments, the most expensive, the only ones with their own elevators.

"The watchman was here when I came out," Johnny said on the first floor, walking toward Constance and the car. "I didn't talk more than a few seconds with him. Then we left. Pierce, the watchman, followed us to the construction gate and closed it after us."

He started to open the car door, and Charlie said, "Hold it just a second. What about the briefcase??

Johnny looked blankly at his hands, as if trying to remember. Then he said, "Yeah, I tossed it inside the trunk." He went back around the car and opened the trunk and made the motion of throwing in the briefcase, and then they all got inside the Continental again, and he drove to the gate.

Charlie looked at his watch, more unhappily than before. Fifteen minutes, at the very least, and eighteen was more likely.

"Okay," Charlie said. "Back to the house. Thanks. You were over here earlier, weren't you?"

"I'm over here every day," Johnny said. "It's our job, I'm riding herd on it."

"I see. But you came over Friday and sent some workers home, and told them to come back Saturday and finish up? Is that right?"

"Yes. I came back to change clothes, and they were doing the stripes on the floor or something. I told them it could wait until the next morning, and I locked up when I left to pick up Debra and her friends at the train station in Maryville. I don't know what time that was. I had to wait a few minutes at the station, not long. The train comes in at five thirty."

"Um," Charlie said. "What I really wanted to know is did the men return Saturday morning and finish? Would they have been likely to go up to Six A to clean up their stuff?"

"No," Johnny said. "I told them I'd pull the tarps off and put them in one of the closets sometime Saturday afternoon. All they had to do was finish up in the basement and clear out the brushes and cans and stuff. They did that. At least the stuff is all gone now. This is the first time I've been back over," he added, disgruntled. "They wouldn't let me back into Six A at all to get those tarps out and look around."

"Then you and your friends drove into Washington and you didn't come back here until afternoon on Saturday. Is that right?"

Johnny's voice was hard and tight when he said, "I drove to the city and we had dinner, and I was with Debra Saltzman until after two thirty in the morning. I slept until noon on Saturday, and after I showered and ate, I came out here, and have stayed on since then. Is there anything else?"

Charlie looked at him in surprise. "Okay," he said. "Take it easy. Were you able to reach everyone about canceling the tour?"

"Finally," Johnny said. "Sorry I jumped on you like that. This is my first . . . investigation of this sort. Edgy."

They had reached the house again; this time he pulled into the driveway and drove through until they were even with the back door. "I'll go park," he said. "You can get out here if you want."

They got out and he continued to drive toward the garage. "Did you find anything new?" Constance asked as soon as the car left them.

"Hm, not sure. Look," he said, and pointed. At the far side of the yard Paul Volte and Toni were walking together, her hand on his arm, his head bowed as if listening to her.

"Looks like she's over her fear of him," Charlie said. He continued to face their direction, but he was no longer seeing them. Something, he thought, something about the crates. "You saw those boxes before and after they were opened," he said slowly. "Was there anything on them to identify them, stenciled addresses, names, contents listed, anything?"

She had to concentrate on visualizing how the crates had looked. No marks. No names. No contents. Nothing to identify the contents to anyone who hadn't already known. She described them and said, "Oh." But someone could have told Victoria about them, she thought swiftly then. From inside the house Ba Ba's voice screeched suddenly, and Tootles yelled something at her, and then they were both yelling.

Charlie took Constance by the arm and turned her toward their car. "You know what would be nice along about now?"

"Tell me."

"A nice quiet room, eventually a nice tall drink, and no Babar, no Tootles, no Johnny."

"You say eventually?"

"Well, I always say first things first. Let's wrap it up here and scram, kiddo. Show you some interesting etchings, or something."

He loved the way she laughed then, and later in their room he knew he would love the way she would agree that first things should be first.

Ten

Claud Palance lived in an apartment near Bellarmine College; about ten miles from Maryville. That's how this part of the world was, Charlie brooded. You think you're out in the country, and then there's another bedroom community, another town, another complex of apartments, schools, shopping centers. He thought gloomily of a megalopolis stretching from above New York City down to the Keys, one bedroom community, one city center, one parking lot after another all the way. He shuddered. To get to country, real country, you would have to turn inland and even then it wouldn't start for another fifty miles, a hundred miles. At *their* place in upper New York state real country began at their door.

Sheriff Bill Gruenwald drove five miles over the speed limit in his unmarked green Ford. He appeared to be in deep thought and was silent for the fifteen-minute drive. He had called ahead; Palance was watching for them and met them at the door of his apartment before they had time to ring. His rooms were at ground level, spartan, obsessively neat, the sort of place where you asked permission to move a paper or chair, maybe to breathe. He led the sheriff, Charlie and

Constance out the back door to a shared courtyard with several grills, comfortable chairs, and a small swimming pool. The young men he had banished to camping in the wilderness were now taking turns tending sausages at the grill, plunging into the pool, returning to stand dripping once again at the grill.

Claud Palance was in his early forties, with thinning light-colored hair, smooth-faced, with watery pale blue eyes. They had camped near the Appalachian Trail at a lake, hiked in seven miles to it. They had heard no news, he added. He mentioned the name of the lake they had camped by and Sheriff Gruenwald nodded. No news out that way, he agreed, and proceeded to give a concise rundown of the events of the weekend. Palance was stunned and speechless over it. It seemed difficult for him to make sense of the questions the sheriff asked; he had to go inside and get a Diet Coke first, and then he did a few breathing exercises before he began to describe the boxes of artwork for Tootles's show.

"Do you know without a doubt that the crates had not been tampered with Thursday night?" Gruenwald asked.

"Yes, at least up to the time we left. We worked until dinnertime on the project. Six maybe. After we ate I reminded Marion that I planned to take the boys away for the weekend. We left then, but they were okay at that time."

"Do all of them stay over at Marion Olsen's?" Gruenwald asked, indicating the boys, who were splashing each other vigorously; they looked like high-school kids.

"Two of them do," Palance said. He pointed them out. The other three were his students, or had been, and all of them had worked on crating up the pieces at one time or another.

"Why?" Charlie asked then. "Why you and your students? Did she hire you to do it?"

Claud Palance looked startled at the question. "No, of course not," he said. "When it came up, I just said we'd do it. She didn't know how and neither did the kids at her place. I did. It's that simple."

Charlie was studying him curiously. "But that doesn't really get to the question of why, does it? Volunteer work? I take it that it was dirty, time-consuming, exacting. You were over there a couple of weeks already?"

"Yes. Each piece requires its own unique box, its own straps or braces, supports, whatever. You don't just pack up art with newspapers and hope for the best. You need to crate each piece in such a way that the gallery people, or museum people who are going to show it can uncrate it and then box it again when the show comes down. They aren't expected to reinvent the wheel, but simply follow instructions, and that means the instructions must be exact. Crating up a show that size might take weeks if you're using novice labor, as I was, teaching them as I went."

Sheriff Gruenwald was following this with narrowed eyes. "How long would it have taken to open twelve of them, slap paint on them, break a piece here and there, and then close up the boxes again?"

Claud Palance hesitated. "It really would depend on how careful the person was, how hard he was trying to hide what he had done. Couple of hours probably. Maybe more. Did he open one and destroy that one and close it up again and then go on to the next, or open them all at once and then have to find the screws again to close them? If you want fast and malicious damage, why bother to close them up again afterward?"

And that, thought Charlie, was one of the best questions yet. Another good question, he realized, was why not mess up all the pieces? Why leave two untouched? It sounded to him as if the guy had run out of time.

"Did Marion Olsen help with the crating?" the sheriff asked.

"Once or twice." He grinned, and something about his musculature made his ears stand out, almost pop out.

Charlie tried not to stare. "It went much, much faster when she didn't help," Palance said, the grin fading away.

Across the apartment complex a young woman appeared with two small children in tow. They all hesitated at the sight of the college boys playing in the pool. Claud Palance called, "Hey, Ron, settle down, okay?" One of the boys looked at him, glanced at the woman and children, and nodded. All the boys climbed out and sat on the grass.

"You know Marion Olsen at all?" Claud Palance asked the sheriff then; he glanced at Charlie and Constance as if inviting them to answer or not.

"Some," the sheriff said cautiously.

"Well, let me tell you something you'll run into. People either love her and will do anything on earth for her, or else they want her driven out of the state. I don't want her driven out of the state."

"That's a school over there?" Charlie asked. "She's running an art school?"

"A one-woman art academy," Palance said. "No credentials, no diploma, no grades, nothing to show for it except some of the best instruction you can find in sculpting. That's what she does, and as far as I know she's never charged a cent. Some of them pay, if they can, whatever they can, but they don't have to. And I don't know anyone in the business who wouldn't trade years at any accredited school for a year under her tutelage. I would be her student like a shot if I could be."

"Why aren't you?" Charlie asked.

"Because I'm not good enough. She knows it and so do I."

The sheriff drove them back to their motel. He had to pass through Maryville, out the other side, and on for another few miles. They were all silent during the drive. It was deep twilight now, the countryside very still.

"There's a coffee shop, isn't there? At the motel. Or a bar or something?" Gruenwald asked.

"Yep. Nice little lounge. You knew pretty much what Palance was going to say, didn't you?" Charlie commented; it wasn't really a question.

"Yeah. Some of it." He slowed down as he neared a congested area, and then turned off the highway and stopped at their motel. Lights from the building turned his face pink and green. He glanced at Charlie. "You working yet?"

"I'm working," Charlie said.

"Come on. I could use a beer or something."

The lounge was almost deserted; a man and woman were having a quiet talk at one side, and at the other the bartender watched a television screen with the sound turned way down. They took a booth; the bartender came quickly and they ordered, beers and wine.

"Charlie," Gruenwald said then, "let me tell you about the first time I saw Marion Olsen." He sprawled back in the seat on his side of the booth, his arm across the top of the backrest, gazing away from Charlie and Constance. "About seven years ago," he said, then shook his head. "Exactly seven years ago in May. There's a children's hospital not far from Bellarmine College. For what they call special children, exceptional children in some places." He stopped when the bartender came with a tray, and then he took a long drink from his glass of beer before he continued. "Okay, special children. I had reason to be in the hospital seven years ago, and I saw this woman come in and head straight to one of the activity rooms. That's what they call them, activity rooms. She had a big box of stuff that she lugged in. I was curious and followed. The room she went in already had about eight or ten kids in it. Not doing much of anything, hanging out. Little kids, five years old, six. So Marion Olsen goes to a long table in there and begins to unload her box. It's full of partly-made clay things, some you could tell what was intended, but mostly not. One little statuette could have been a horse, I guess. Hard to tell. Without a word she starts to mold that clay they use, plasticine. And pretty soon one of the little kids comes over and picks up one of the other pieces, whatever it was, and begins to squeeze it, change it. It was hers, apparently. And it was like that. Marion never said a word, and neither did the kids, but before long nearly all of them were working on something or other, purposefully working." He drank again and put down his glass hard. "For some of those kids this might have been the first time they did anything with any purpose. I asked about Marion. She showed up one day with her box and said if she could have space, maybe some of the kids would play with her. Just like that. At first they said no way. Only trained personnel allowed. She threw a fit, and they gave her space just to shut her up and prove you can't reach those kids with anything not analyzed and planned and presented by a shrink of some kind. That was seven years ago that I saw her, and she'd been doing her thing for three or four years by then, and she still does it once a week."

They were all silent for several seconds until Constance asked gently, "Is your child any better now?"

He nodded. "Not much, a little. A girl, Nancy. She's thirteen."

Charlie signaled the bartender, who came over with two more beers, another glass of wine. No one spoke until he was gone again.

Then Gruenwald said, "That place of hers, what Palance calls a one-woman art academy? She doesn't dare call it a school or the county would close her down. Fire trap, they call it. A few people complained; they go around and inspect it regularly, but what the hell, it's a private residence. She doesn't do anything by the books, get the right credentials, stuff like that. She'll take in anyone she damn well pleases, and if there's any formal education or training, it's kept a secret. She's turned down some people who've made a royal stink about her and her place that she won't call a school. And she's taken in some that have made people hereabouts want to scream. Blacks, gays, weirdos of every make you can imagine. But no one can prevent anyone having guests. As long as they don't pay her, she doesn't call it a school, she can do what she damn well pleases. She does and it drives a lot of folks nuts."

"You love her or want to run her out of the state," Charlie said.

"I don't want to run her out of the state," Gruenwald said deliberately. "I don't want anyone to hang a murder charge on her, either."

Charlie nodded. "They hired me today. I've known some of them for more than twenty years. It's possible one or another of them might tell us something they wouldn't tell you. Just possible. So far no one has told us diddly. What was in the note you found by Leeds?"

"I think it's a fake, like you suggested, but still there it is. It was typed on the machine in the condo apartment, in the dining room. It said *Meet me at the condo, Six A, at seven thirty.* Signed M. Typed M, no handwriting anywhere. No prints recoverable. Paper and envelope from the house. There's a drawer with stationery in the office. The state lab has all that stuff now, but I don't think they'll come up with more than that."

"No map or directions?"

"No. Just that."

"Too pat," Charlie said after a second. "And it would make her out to be too dumb, to leave it in plain sight like that. But those who want to run her out of the state will buy it. A jury could be talked into buying it."

"I know," Gruenwald said. He lifted his glass and drained it. "I'll be around tomorrow. You going to stay here at the motel for a while?"

"Couple of days. Then New York City. Why did Victoria

Leeds invite herself to the party, that's the question, isn't it? Without an answer to that, we're stuck exactly where we are right now.''

Gruenwald nodded. ''You might want to do it again, but I checked out the group that went over to the condo Friday night. Debra Saltzman, Phil Michelson, Sandra Door. They call her Sunny. Good upstanding types, with fathers in Congress or counting their millions, that sort of thing. They confirm John Buell's story. No body was in that apartment at ten past seven.''

''Right,'' Charlie said gloomily. ''The way it stands now, the artwork was okay Thursday evening. Friday night it was a mess. Victoria Leeds vanished a little before five Friday, and is unaccounted for for the next two hours. Where the hell was she? Smashing art? Why? Everyone who was an overnight guest or regular in that house, except Tootles, is covered by nearly everyone else from seven onwards. Have you talked with the watchman yet?''

''Pierce? Sure. He got there at six Friday; gate was closed, locked. He made the rounds, everything locked up tight. Nothing out of ordinary. They are being careful because there were a couple of accidents earlier on, one was fatal. So they're being very careful.''

''Accidents?'' Charlie asked, perking up.

Gruenwald shook his head. ''Nothing for us. Some kids got in the grounds when they were still digging holes, and one of them had a fall, broke his ankle. That was over a year ago. This spring a guy fell from the roof of one of the buildings. Died instantly. Insurance company got antsy, I think, and now they're super cautious. Both good and bad for us. But Pierce says the gate was closed and locked when he got there at six. Then Buell and his crowd came in a few minutes after seven, left ten minutes later, and he locked up again. No one came in after that. The buildings that have doors were all locked, and he checked the others. Nothing.

He's a pretty good guy. He's sure. And like I said, they're being careful."

"Someone else got in," Charlie said darkly. "The delivery man with the flowers?"

Gruenwald shook his head again. "Nope. Pierce met him when he arrived for work and carried the flowers inside himself; that's when he checked out the building."

"And those young people, they really went in far enough to be certain no one was there?"

Constance made a slight noise, then said. "You couldn't have missed seeing her. Even if they had stayed in the foyer, Johnny had to pass within two feet of where her body was."

"They all say they went through the hallway to the living room doorway," the sheriff said with finality. "They would have seen her. When Buell went back to check the other units, it took five minutes probably. They agree on that. Pierce had joined them by then and confirms that Johnny was gone just about long enough to glance into the rooms, but not a minute longer."

Charlie's gloom deepened as he considered this. It could be a conspiracy, he thought, and mocked himself for the thought. Pierce, the son and daughters of public figures, Johnny Buell, all in a conspiracy to hide the fact that Victoria and her killer had to have entered those grounds, that building, that particular room at the same time that they were all coming and going without seeing a thing.

Slowly he said, "Suppose Johnny goes to the dining room and sees Victoria Leeds hiding, or even just there. He says, stay put and I'll be right back. He gets rid of the other young people, returns with the rope and kills her."

Sheriff Gruenwald waited him out patiently. "How did she get in? Where did the rope come from? Was he expecting her? What would his motive have been? Why was she hiding? Why didn't she just say *hi* to the gang?" He looked apologetically at Constance and added, "Besides, it wasn't really a clean kill. She was trying to crawl away apparently, grabbing at the tarps; the killer held her with his knee in her back, used some weight to hold her, bruised her pretty bad, and it took a few minutes. I'm not saying your scenario is totally impossible, only that I don't believe a word of it. I doubt that anyone who isn't a real psycho could have killed her and then appeared normal immediately. Psycho, hired hit man, there's some that could, but we don't have them around here, far's I know. Just don't believe it."

Nor did he, Charlie had to admit to himself. "That still leaves the time that Buell took his friends up to Six A and left the gate open. She and her killer could have got in then. At least that gets them inside, instead of lurking behind a tree somewhere."

Gruenwald nodded. "That might be the only scenario that will work, and it brings in an outsider." He looked very unhappy about it. "Belmont doesn't like outsiders wandering into locked buildings with so many people milling about. Can't say I blame him." He took a deep breath, shook his head, and went on. "We're checking the guests who drove past the condo that evening. It will take time. That's a long guest list. But maybe someone saw something." He did not sound hopeful. "Well, I better be on my way."

Charlie motioned the bartender over, signed the tab and showed their room key, and, when the bartender left again, Gruenwald stood up. "I've got to get home and get some sleep." He glanced at Constance, then at Charlie. "You know that I'm off the case officially? I mean, anything I do now is just because I'm interested. A responsible citizen, that's me."

Constance nodded and Charlie walked part way out with him. She watched the two men go through the ritual of shaking hands; she listened to the words, *keep in touch, take care, I'll let you know,* but she was brooding over the many men who felt the great urge, the need even, to help and protect Tootles. Charlie returned.

"You want anything else?"

She shook her head.

Slowly, hand in hand they left the lounge and walked through the lobby to the elevator to ride up to the seventh floor where they had a minisuite. They had spent some time in the room earlier; she had remade the bed more or less, and she had unpacked for both of them while Charlie showered. Now he moved back and forth from bedroom to bathroom, yawning widely often. But she was not at all sleepy yet; she picked up Paul Volte's book. There were a few things she wanted to reread before going to bed.

It was hard to remember, she thought much later, that a writer like Paul Volte was a true artist, as much as any poet, or playwright, or novelist. His craft was as demanding, and his knowledge of people possibly even more so; he could not make it up, only report and interpret what was. His prose was lucid and beautifully rhythmic, very precise. A true artist, she repeated to herself, deserving of the various awards he had gathered over the years. Coming from a background of art history, art appreciation, criticism, he had developed a superb talent for spotting what was wrong with a piece of art, or, more important, possibly, what was right about it. His word was the word of God in that world, enough to make or break, to send the artist to the heights, or bring him or her down to the gutter. Yet, talking to him, observing him, thin, hungry-looking, abstracted, it was hard to discern any self-awareness in him of the power he wielded. Until you looked closer, she added, remembering the small glint of satisfaction he had revealed when she asked about Toni's talent.

Was Tootles as unconcerned about his opinion as she appeared? What had the students thought of him? Filled with fear and awe? Toni had shown both, and then, curiously, had dropped both attitudes to show something else, a demanding persistence about something that overrode her earlier fear of him. And Johnny Buell? Had he really thought Paul would write about the condos? What a coup for him that would have been. Worth conniving to get Paul to appear and take the tour. There was little doubt that a good word in Paul's column, or a paragraph in his next book would send Johnny's stock off the chart. The people Paul had chosen to write about were all doing extremely well, she had read. The kiss of an angel, his words had been called.

But the wild current that ran all through his book was the common acceptance of possession that surfaced again and again in artist after artist. The artist as one possessed, helplessly yielding to the power possessing him or her, or giving up art, that was the subtext that had turned the book into a best-seller, she was certain. That mysterious power to possess, to demand, to exact a terrible price for success, that was what people had wanted to read about; that was what people wanted to believe, did believe, and he had handled it with such conviction, such delicacy and even humor that to the believers, it must be like an *ex cathedra* pronouncement from the Pope himself, while to the nonbelievers, it was just another one of those superstitions that artists professed to believe in, no more powerful than the old wives' admonitions: no hat on the bed, salt over the shoulder, no open umbrella in the house . . . all very *in* right now, very much New Age. But she heard her own voice arguing: Just because something had become acceptable that had been scorned by so many for so long, didn't mean it couldn't be true. Popularity didn't automatically make it false.

She yawned and stood up then, stretched, and got ready for bed, disturbed by something she could not quite define about Paul and his book. She got into bed beside Charlie, and he turned in his sleep, his hand seeking her the way it did if he was asleep or awake. She settled in close to him, their bodies touching here and there, their breath mingling, and she began the long slide into sleep.

He believed it, she felt almost certain, Paul believed all that he had written; of course, a good writer must believe, but when had he started to believe it? Before or after writing the book? Could he have written that particular book without first knowing what he had to ask, what he was looking for? She could not think now why the question was important, why this entire line of thought was important. The slide was moving her faster and faster downward, her thoughts becoming more and more jumbled, surreal even. She imagined, then saw, Paul Volte digging a hole that looked very much like a grave. A line of people stretched out of sight over the horizon, each person carrying something—a basket with a kitten, a St. Bernard dog, a tin of muffins, an old woman in a pail, a case of leather-bound books. . . . When they reached the hole that Paul was digging furiously they tossed in whatever the burden was, and then trudged away with bowed heads, downcast eyes. The line did not diminish.

E l e v e n

"All right," Charlie said, after finishing his second cup of coffee the next morning. Breakfast had been decent—not good, not bad—decent, and filling. He did not expect much more than that from motel restaurants; decent was a plus, in fact.

"So, all right," Constance said, watching him. She liked Charlie in the morning. He always woke up so chipper, ready for anything, eager. Youthful, she thought with surprise. Charlie in the morning was very much like the youthful Charlie she had married; as the hours passed, he grew up and matured all over again, day after day. She knew he had seen too much, had been through too much with a big city fire department, then the arson squad, then as a city detective in homicide. Just too bloody much. You can take the boy out of the city, she went on, but you can't take away the synapse tracks, the traces, the imprinting, the knowledge, the memories of what he had done, and what he had not done, what others had done. . . .

"What I'd like," Charlie said, gazing past her innocently, "is to tackle Tootles, but she would close like a clam if I attempted it, so that's your department. I'll put in some time at the condo, and inspect that fence and do other pretty important things like that.''

"Charlie," she asked in wonder, ''how can you take on a job to save the life of a woman you can't even bear to spend five minutes with?''

"But I thought I explained," he said, and began to search for the bill.

"You already signed, remember?"

"Oh, yeah, I forgot. Anyway, it's not Tootles so much as Babar. My God, she's worse than ever.''

They walked from the restaurant. "I thought she'd be gone by now," Constance said, heading for the Volvo. "Oh, dear, we have to do something about that rental car today.''

"Babar won't leave until the excitement is over," Charlie said, "and God knows how long it's going to take to reach that point. Poor old Larry will just have to rough it alone. I hope he's eating all right with her gone.''

Constance frowned at him. "All right, darling," she said coldly. "I'll talk to Tootles. You've made the point, don't try to stretch it too far.''

He looked at her with renewed innocence.

"Tootles, this is ridiculous, and you know it!" Constance was saying a bit later. They were in the office in the main house; sounds of hammering, pounding, banging echoed from within the nearby studio.

"I don't have an idea in the world what you're talking about," Tootles said, but with an absent look, as if she were paying little attention to her own or Constance's words.

"For heaven's sake, what are they doing in there?" Constance asked then, as the hammering noise increased.

"Roger, one of the boys who stays here, is making a birdhouse, a memorial. His way of reaffirming life, I guess.''

Constance bit back a retort, and drew in a deep breath. "Let's go someplace quieter. I have to ask you some questions, and you have to answer them. Do you grasp the danger you're in?''

''Don't be silly,'' Tootles said with a quick laugh. ''But it's quieter in the other side of the house. Let's go to the music room.''

It would be the music room for her, Constance realized; Tootles played the piano with gusto and not a trace of talent. Today she was wearing faded blue jeans, and a handsome silk-screened T-shirt with a panorama of butterflies and flowers front and back. Dressed up for the reporters, she had said grimly; they had been snooping all morning, and they would be back. Tomorrow she would wear her T-shirt with dragons.

Constance followed her to the living room, on through to the adjacent room where Ba Ba was watching television with headphones on. Constance glowered at Tootles, who, she was certain, had known they would find Ba Ba in here. She took Tootles by the arm and turned her, marched her out of the room again. ''Out to the porch,'' she said with grim determination.

The front porch had a pair of wooden benches and several bentwood chairs. Constance did not release Tootles until they reached the furniture, where she almost shoved the other woman into a chair and then dragged a second one closer.

''Now, you just listen to me,'' she said crisply, her anger as evident in the coldness of her voice as in the stiffness of her posture. She made no effort to conceal it; she wanted Tootles to see how furious she was. ''You're the only one from this house who could have found time to get over to the condo and kill Victoria Leeds. That's for openers. Someone, possibly Victoria Leeds, made a mess of your art, providing you a very fine motive for getting even. How much more does it take to convince you that this is serious trouble?''

''But what makes you think I doubt it's serious? I didn't

do anything, that's all there is to that. And what good would it do for me to scream and cry and wring my hands and come on like some poor damn bedeviled ingenue? I don't even know the fucking words! I sure as hell couldn't improvise that role with any conviction."

"Why did you ask me to come here? What's the crisis you claimed threatened you? Why that note on my invitation?"

"Constance! What a dumb-ass question! To share my success, to celebrate with us. To have someone from home witness this crowning achievement. All the above. Emergency? Of course, my very first touring show! Ruined. Maybe I had a premonition. Maybe it rubbed off from Ba Ba."

"Stop it, Tootles! I mean it, stop or I'll just walk out and take Charlie with me!"

Tootles shrugged eloquently. "I threw myself on his mercy, and he agreed to help. I think he's more a gentleman than you give him credit for."

Now Constance laughed, without guile, a pure laugh of real amusement. "Do you really think he'd stay if I said I wanted to leave?"

For a long time Tootles examined her with narrowed eyes, the way she might have looked at a piece of work one of her students had presented for judgment. She shook her head and leaned back in her chair. "I asked you because I was afraid the weekend would be too much for me. I wanted to lash out and hit Johnny for topping my party with his own viewing of the condo, even trying to get a write-up about it, and then assuming I would play hostess for him without so much as 'if you please, Ma'am.' He ordered flowers in my name and told me I was supposed to pour the coffee for the financiers! He suggested I might even wear a nice dress, or at least a nice pantsuit! And have my hair done. The little shit! As if I give a goddam about the fucking condos or his long-range goals! My instinct was to wear the crummiest sweats I have, and show up barefoot! And I couldn't. I didn't know what it would do to Max if I lashed out at Johnny. Or poured scalding coffee down the crotches of a bunch of fat bankers. Johnny wants the company to become another Bechtel, you know. He has plans, five-year plans, ten-year plans. Christ, he has plans for the next century! All this mess probably set his plans back five years. I hope to hell it does."

And she was lying in her teeth, Constance thought distantly. Everything she said could be true, it sounded plausible if a bit weak, and it didn't really sound like a lie, but it had nothing to do with why Tootles had begged her to come. This was how Tootles had been as a child, a teenager: once she started on a plausible story she could keep spinning it out interminably, until her questioners forgot the original question and simply gave up in fatigue. Constance had watched this kind of performance many times. The beauty of Tootles's stories was that they were always based on a foundation of truth that appeared strong enough to support whatever she constructed on it. No doubt she really had resented Johnny's topping her party with his own. No doubt she had hated being dragged in in any capacity. Tootles playing hostess to businessmen who were not *her* business men was a ludicrous idea.

Constance finally put her hand on Tootles's arm to stop her.

"Do you have the computer card key for Six A?"

Tootles had to blink several times to return to the real world.

"Sure. It's going to be our new home."

"Where is it?"

Tootles shrugged and looked blank. "I don't know. Usually it's in my purse. In my wallet. It's sort of flimsy, like a cheapo credit card. They're made that way because, according to Johnny, they're supposed to be changed every month or so. You know how that works? They key in an order for a random number or something and that's your lock number and the printer issues a card that gets laminated and if you lose it, presto changeo, a new random number."

"You weren't carrying a purse or a wallet Friday night when you returned," Constance said, interrupting her. "Were you?"

Tootles shook her head, then suddenly brightened and sat up straighter. "That's right! I knew you could do it, you and that gorgeous man of yours. I just knew it! Maybe this is why I asked you, and I just couldn't explain it ahead of time. Ba Ba's right, after all! We're in touch with more than we can explain, more than we know. Constance, that's so smart!"

Constance watched her silently. A datum, she thought; that was all that was, another datum, not a reprieve.

"Tootles, knock it off," she said after another moment. "Why does Paul Volte accept any responsibility for Victoria's death? Does he believe that superstition? That each success must be paid for?"

Tootles became very quiet, as if she had fallen into a deep sleep with her eyes open. She seemed not to breathe, even.

"It's all through his book," Constance said impatiently. "He can't deny the book. But how strongly does he believe in what he wrote? Does Toni believe it? Do you?"

With a jerky motion Tootles jumped up and went to the porch rail and stood holding it with both hands. Constance followed her to lean against the rail at her side. "Tell me about it," she said in a low voice. She glanced at Tootles, then turned her gaze away, toward the trees, the sky, anywhere but the woman holding the porch together, possibly holding her own world together with white-knuckled fingers.

"You remember how it was in the sixties?" Tootles said in a rush. "How poor we all were? At the beginning, how poor we were. But did you know that a few of my things had already been well received, well reviewed? It wasn't much, no money involved, there seldom is in art. At least, I never expected money from it. That didn't matter, I was on my way." Her voice had dropped lower and lower, and had become hoarse, almost a whisper. "I had the gift," she said. "Ba Ba knows; she was there when it happened. I had it, and I was on my way. I didn't know what the price would be. Ed and I got married and came down here. Remember? My God, Ed was the only man I've ever loved like that, with innocence and passion in equal amounts, and enough awareness to know what you're doing! My first real love. You can't have it twice, can you? He was a beautiful man, beautiful." She stopped speaking, gazing straight ahead, her hands white on the rail, the muscles in her forearms like knotted ropes.

"Then Ed died. My first show was up in Spence's gallery. My first real success, something else you can have only once." She laughed harshly. "That's when I learned the price. Ed got killed in a stupid wreck. Later that year I married Spence. Remember? Everyone was so shocked that my grief didn't last longer. It was a marriage of convenience, as the saying goes. I would be safe with a man I didn't love. Or more to the point *he* would be safe. He was great in bed, maybe the best fuck I've had—something to be said about doing it without love, I mean if there's a real interest there. Anyway, I could go on making things, doing good work, and we'd both be safe; no one would be at risk. What a deal!

"Spence was good for me," she said after a moment, much quieter. "He was a good guide, a good critic for me. But he began to notice that he was the one doing all the loving." She shrugged again and turned to look at Constance. At that moment she looked to be a hundred years old.

"I began to see other men," she said deliberately. "And along in there I met Paul and a friend of his, Gray Axton. They came down together the first time. Gray Axton," she repeated. Tiredly she thrust her hands in her pockets and walked back to the chairs and sat down, her legs sprawled out, her chin sunken against her collarbone, scowling into the distance. Constance trailed after her and resumed her seat. "Gray was the second Ed for me, the second chance at love, all that mushy stuff," Tootles said; her voice had gone very flat. "It wasn't the same, not the thing I'd had with Ed, nothing could have matched that, but I fell hard, and so did he. He was a painter, and damn good. Spence was excited about his work. And Spence never made a fuss about him and me, or anything else. He just moved out, back to his Washington place. After a few months with Gray I finished *Seven Kinds of Death,* and he went to Vietnam. Back in 1972, winter. My piece made the National Gallery, and Gray was killed."

She ended it in such an uninflected tone that it was another few seconds before Constance realized that without prodding Tootles would stop there. Constance leaned forward. "You believe, that's what the point of the story is, I take it." She kept all compassion out of her voice, all warmth, allowed only an intellectual curiosity to come through.

Tootles looked at her with dull anger now. "Yes, damn it! I believe! You stick your damn hand in the fire once and you learn something about pain; do it again and learn something about idiocy. Ed was the first one that I knew about, knew I was responsible for. Poor Mitch Phillips was the first, before Ed even. But I thought he just died; people did now and then. We were eighteen, and he died the same week I was accepted as a student by the New School of Fine Art in New York. I didn't make the connection, not until years later. I made it right away with Ed, and with Gray. Yes, damn you, I believe! So does Paul. As for Toni, ask her!"

"Hm, I don't understand," Constance said after a moment. "If you had it at eighteen, why didn't Ba Ba know it and make it clear then? Why didn't you understand for years?''

Tootles sighed theatrically. "She developed her gift later. I mean, for God's sake, when I was eighteen, she was just fifteen! She got in touch with . . . with whatever it is after she came to live with me in New York. She was eighteen by then. And Mitch had been dead for years. It just didn't come up. I mean, there were other men, but . . . you know what was going on in the early sixties. It didn't mean much.''

"Hm," Constance hmmed again. "So after Gray, there was Walter. Is that right? Where's Walter now?"

"God knows. But let's get this straight. After Gray there were a lot of guys. A whole lot. And none of them meant shit to me. Now, we can move on to Walter. It was fun with him. You know he dug for gold back by the brook? And he built onto the house as if he thought he was Noah, and this was the Ark, and the water was rising. We learned to hang glide together. Fun. That was Walt. Just plain old fun. He sort of drifted away after a while. No surprise; we both knew he would one day.''

"And now there's Max," Constance said quietly. "He really cares for you.''

"I know," Tootles said, and then she threw her head back and laughed as raucously as a teenage boy. "You know what he said to me? Bastard. He said it turned him on to see a woman my age with dirty feet. The first time we met, I guess I had dirty feet. I don't remember." Her voice was affectionate, and her face had become soft; almost instantly she had shed the years that pain had put on her face just moments earlier. "He said he never had met anyone like me before. I bet the bastard didn't.''

Constance nodded. "Did you ever even consider that the deaths might all have been simple coincidence?''

Tootles sounded mocking now when she said, "Isn't that the first explanation a sane person would consider? Sure I did. And Paul has done the same thing. Everyone does.''

"Why are you afraid for Max?" Constance asked, still quietly, still being a professional, not the life-long personal friend who might have yielded to sympathy or impatience by now. "In spite of yourself, did you come to care for him?"

Tootles was startled by the question apparently. She snapped her head around to glare at Constance. "Don't be stupid," she snapped. "You don't know what you're talking about."

"I know. That's why I asked. If you really believe in the curse, or gift, whatever you call it, you must be afraid to love him. Afraid you'll lose him maybe. You begged me to come here for something; is that it? To get you out from under this curse? Are you afraid for Max?"

"I'm not afraid of anything. Period." She stood up.

"Just one more thing," Constance said, standing up also. She was taller than Tootles. As a professional psychologist she rarely would have put herself in a position where she would actually look down on a client or a patient; a few minutes earlier she had leaned against the rail in order to maintain equal eye height, but now she drew herself very straight and tall quite deliberately, forcing Tootles to look up. "When you left the party, what did you do? Minute by minute."

Tootles made an impatient gesture, as if she would sweep the question aside if she could. "I've told it over and over. I went up and changed my clothes and went out on the upper deck, down the outside stairs, up the driveway to the road, across the road to the path and on to the little house where I sat down for a few minutes, and then walked home again."

Constance was following this with her head tilted, frowning slightly. "I just don't see why," she murmured, as if to herself. "You wanted to be alone, that I can understand, but why so far? Altogether that's a two-mile walk? Why? You could have gone down to the brook. Or you could have just stayed on the sun roof. Or in your room."

"Aren't you leaving out one of the other things I could have done?" Tootles snapped. "I could have hurried over to the condo to kill Victoria Leeds."

Constance shook her head. "No. I don't think so. I mean, I don't know who killed her, but I don't think you could have got over there that quickly and then back again by eight. Do you have a dirt bike, something like that that you could ride through the woods?"

"Jesus! No!"

"Where did you go?" Constance asked, just as if they had agreed that Tootles would now answer. "Not the retreat a mile away. Where?"

"I told you," Tootles said harshly, breathing too fast, too shallowly. "I told everyone. I have things to see to. So long, Constance." She wheeled and reentered the house, nearly running.

Constance watched her go; she hoped Charlie was having more success at the condo than she was having.

Twice, at least, Charlie had hoped the same thing about her, that she was getting something worthwhile from Tootles, because he wasn't getting a thing.

In a few minutes he had an appointment with the construction superintendent, Thomas Ditmar, who was in a trailer office near Building C. Someone could have climbed over the fence, Charlie was thinking moodily. No marks, no grappling lines, no indentations of ladder feet, nothing to show that they did, but it was still possible. Someone could have come up from the river, he went on, scowling now. No mud, no messed-up banks, no trace of mud found in the building, but it was possible. Someone could have been dropped in by an eagle, he thought then. Right.

He had talked to the painters, who confirmed Johnny's story; he had sent them home a little after four thirty. They had come back to finish up on Saturday. They had put the panels on the elevator doors, finished the stripes on the floor for parking spaces. They had not gone up to Six A; what for? They had washed up their brushes, gathered the buckets and stuff and put everything away in the sub-basement, and they were done.

Charlie looked at the sub-basement, full of heating equipment and plumbing, and individual storage compartments for the tenants. The brushes were there, dry and clean: rollers, small finish brushes, large ones. The paint was there, and tarps. Stencils for the door numbers and for the numbers on the storage compartments that were as big as commercial ministorage units. Like them, these compartments were metal, rows of them, with four-foot aisles between them, all neatly numbered.

He inspected the scene of the death again. She had entered the living room, he decided, had gone in several feet and had been attacked from behind. The killer had been there already, he thought, waiting for her. You need a little bit of distance to reach out and put a rope around someone's neck; if they had come in together, it would have been hard, unless the killer had hung back, let her get to the right distance. Someone could have said, go have a look out the windows. Great view. Then the rope over her head, jerked tight, no time for her to try to run or even to try to turn around. He remembered what Bill Gruenwald had said: she had tried to crawl away.

He walked through the apartment, dissatisfied. The police had taken the typewriter, but some tarps were still on the long table, still in the dining room, on the floor and on the table there. The police had taken the one she had grabbed and pulled partway off the table. He went to the window and looked out over the river and the woods. It seemed a wilderness out there. Finally, still dissatisfied, he left the apartment.

* * *

"Thomas Ditmar," the man said, in the doorway of the trailer. He was built like an elephant, thick in every dimension, very powerful looking. His hair was sandy colored and fine, his eyes clear, pale brown, his skin weathered to a deep brown.

They shook hands and he stepped aside for Charlie to enter the room he was using as an office.

"Max says you're hired on to clear up this goddam mess," Thomas Ditmar said. "I hope to God you do, and do it quick. We had goddam reporters messing around this morning. Reporters!"

The trailer was small for a mobile home, but large enough for a comfortable office. A coffeemaker on a counter was nearly full; half a dozen mugs were upside down on paper towels near it. A gray corduroy sofa, two small matching chairs, a table, and a desk with a computer were the furnishings. The table was covered with blueprints and pencils, pens in a mug, note pads, drafting paper. . . . The tiny kitchen was super efficient, it seemed, with everything built in and nothing used, from all appearances, except the sink where more mugs were draining.

Ditmar poured coffee for them both and sat down on the sofa, cradling his mug in both hands. "Max says you'll ask questions. I'll answer. Your turn."

Charlie laughed and took one of the small chairs; to his surprise it was very comfortable. "That makes it sound pretty neat," he said. "Like erecting a building. Get the plans, the site, the materials, and up it goes. No problems."

Ditmar grunted and shook his head. "Always problems. That's what life's all about, solving them. But my problems usually have solutions. Think this one does?"

Charlie shrugged. "Always a solution, sometimes you just don't find it. History corrects the mistake you made, sometimes. Been with Max long?"

"Ever since he went into this business, twenty-eight years."

"So you're the last one to ask what's wrong with him," Charlie murmured.

"Nothing is," Ditmar said matter-of-factly.

"What I mean," Charlie said. "Know his wife?"

"Yep. Best thing ever happened to Max."

"Knew his previous wife, too?"

"Yep. A very good lady, very, very good lady. Gone to her just rewards in heaven, at God's right elbow, no doubt." Nothing at all changed in his voice; his eyes did not sparkle with amusement, no laugh lines deepened, but it was there.

"Making sure he stays on the straight and narrow?" Charlie asked lazily. Ditmar nodded, and finally a gleam of amusement lighted his eyes. "What about Johnny Buell?" Charlie asked.

"Learning the business the way he should. Not half the man his father is, but Max wasn't half the man at that age, either. He'll be all right."

"Will you keep on with the company if Max retires, turns it over to Johnny?"

"Nope."

"Look, Mr. Ditmar," Charlie said then, "I don't know what the hell I'm after. Just talk, okay? I mean, I could ask you simple questions all afternoon and get nowhere, because I don't know where I want to go yet. For instance, what's with you and Johnny?"

Thomas Ditmar regarded him for several seconds in silence. At last he said, "You retired, from the New York police department, something like that? Isn't that right?"

"Yep."

Ditmar grinned and nodded. "Okay, then you know. You do things one way all your life, a pretty good way it looks to be, and then someone comes along and says that's hokey, from now on we do it this way. No harm intended, you understand, just different ways. You must have seen it in your field. I know damn well doctors know what I mean. When Max wraps it up, so will I. Tired, ready to retire, hit the road off-season, leave winter behind a couple of years, head for mountains when it gets hot, do things like that, things I never could do before. Not ready to learn my trade all over again. There's plenty others ready and able to step in and run with it."

"How bad is it with Johnny?" Charlie asked. He understood exactly what Ditmar was talking about.

"Not bad at all. Max is still in charge. It's a good company, one of the best, some of the best construction anywhere around, never lost a penny of anyone's money, good times or bad, but things change. That's all. Things change. You ever try to draw building plans on a computer?" Charlie shook his head; Ditmar did, too. "And I don't aim to learn now. Max never wanted a company so big he couldn't oversee everything personally; Johnny's already planning to expand, get managers, go public maybe. Max never would have thought of trying to get a big write-up, not without paying for it. You know, advertising. Different philosophies, that's all. Max leaves, so do I."

"Is Max planning to leave?"

For a second or two Ditmar regarded him without expression. Then he shrugged. "Eventually. Won't we all?"

"This is his last job maybe?" Charlie had no idea about this; a random shot, he thought, no more than that.

"If you already know that, there's not much more I can add," Ditmar said. "It'll take close to a year to finish up here, and then . . . let Johnny diaper the baby, I guess." He shrugged. "This is his solo flight, with the instructor in the next seat, but next time out, no copilot, just him, if he's ready." He examined Charlie closely. "Let me ask something, Mr. Meiklejohn. This have anything to do with the killing?"

Charlie had to admit probably not. "What I really need is a way to get someone in that building and out again past your watchman, Pierce. And so far, no dice."

"What times you looking for?"

"Between seven ten and about seven thirty."

Ditmar shook his head. "Johnny and his gang, then Pierce was on this side, closing the gate, things like that. I left the party with my wife and a friend of ours at ten after seven. Johnny pulled out of the complex in front of us, and I turned in at the parking lot over there and we had a little discussion about looking around. Decided not to, not until another building is finished, but we were there until twenty after seven probably, maybe a little longer if you count the time we had to wait for traffic to clear so's I could enter the road again. Lots of folks were leaving the party along about then, you know. Fifteen, twenty cars must have gone by while we sat there."

Charlie stared at him, aghast. "Jesus Christ! Have you told the sheriff?"

"Nope. Haven't been asked."

Charlie thought of the two scenarios he had come up with so far: one in which Victoria and her killer entered the building while Johnny and his group were all up on six. That one didn't explain how they had got into the apartment on six, but at least they were in the building. And the other was the little scenario in which Johnny left his friends for five minutes in order to return to Six A to kill Victoria Leeds (who had obligingly set herself up for him without a sound), and then drove his girlfriend and her pals back to Washington to have dinner, and do a little screwing, he added darkly.

At this moment one or the other seemed to be the only one that would work at all.

T w e l v e

Charlie had walked to the condos from Tootles's house, and now as he left the trailer/office to start the trek back, he saw Johnny Buell coming forward to meet him. Johnny was wearing good-looking tan work pants, a matching shirt, and a hardhat. He could have been dressed for an ad for an expensive liquor, or a sports car. He looked a lot like the boss's son.

"How's it going?" he asked, falling into step with Charlie.

"About what you expect this early. How many people have keys to the gate?"

Johnny looked startled, then thoughtful. Finally he said, "Damned if I know. Various foremen, Ditmar, of course. Dad. I do. Maybe Marion, but I sort of doubt that. Why would she? Pierce. Half a dozen, a dozen at the most."

"How about the computer card keys?"

"Maybe the same list, with a few additions. I know Marion has one to the sixth-floor unit. She's been in and out, picking out colors, drapes, that sort of thing. Ditmar has them all, and I do. I guess Dad does, too. A few others."

In other words, a bust, Charlie thought regretfully. Too

many people with access. They had come to Building A. One of the workmen had already explained the building designation: A is for Applegate, first in the row. B is for Birmingham, upscale, don't you know? C is for Carlton, Rich, rich, rich, rich; D is for Davenport, a son of a bitch. E is for Ethridge, first among peers. F is for Farmington, or maybe for fears. Charlie thought the workers did not take the project quite as seriously as Johnny did.

He paused at the grillwork gate to the below-ground parking section. The gate was open now. "When you drove out on Friday, did you close both gates?"

"Sure. The system's electronic. Going in, the thing closed after me, and coming out I just touched the button and it slid down when I drove up to the street level. I went back inside on the first floor."

Charlie walked into the lobby at street level; the dedicated elevators with brass numbers lined the wall to his left, flanked by the door to the stairwell, broom closets, whatever. . . . He walked to the center of the building and gazed down the long corridor, with another bank of regular elevators at the far end, and apartment doors in between. "Are the rooms all kept locked?" he asked Johnny, who had remained at the entrance.

Johnny said they were, and Charlie sighed and shrugged. So it would take more computer card keys to enter them. He walked back to the front of the building. "Okay. See you later. Thanks." He continued to walk toward the gate. It was open during working hours; trucks came and went, workmen came and left, there was a steady flow of traffic in and out. It had been open on Friday until Johnny closed it when he left to pick up Debra Saltzman and her friends, five thirty or thereabouts. The train had arrived at five forty and Johnny was waiting for it. So, he followed the thought, Victoria Leeds could have entered the grounds before five thirty without being seen. All right, he mocked himself.

Now tell us why, Mr. Bones. Step one, and then step two, he told himself firmly.

He went through the gate and came to a stop at the edge of the road; a movement across the train tracks near the woods caught his eye. When he looked more carefully, the scowl on his forehead vanished and he smiled broadly. It was purely reflexive. Constance had stepped from behind the trees, and was walking toward him. Seeing her unexpectedly usually gave him a jolt of pleasure like this. He quickened his steps to meet her on the other side of the train tracks.

She held out both hands to him, and he kissed her lightly before they turned toward the woods. "Anything?" he asked.

She shrugged. "I was trying to put myself in Tootles's place," she said. They had reached the trees, where she stopped to look back at the road. "It's Friday evening, and I am tired of the party, and want people to go home. I go upstairs and change my clothes, go out by way of the sun deck, dodging anyone who might be outside smoking or something. Across the road, and then through the woods to the little retreat. So far, okay. It's fifteen, twenty minutes after seven. I can get this far, but then I'm stumped, why didn't someone see me?" She eyed the train tracks, the road, the condos across the road. "There's just no cover at all. And people certainly were driving by at that time."

They stood together looking at the clearing maintained by the railway, twenty feet on both sides of the tracks at least, then the state road with the cleared shoulders, and then the condo complex. No cover. He told her about Ditmar. "He sat there waiting to enter the road until twenty-five after seven probably. They were still coming out of the dirt road when he finally took off. I'm just glad that's not our chore—to interview all the guests and find out if anyone saw anything." He sounded glum and not at all hopeful.

They started to walk through the woods now, holding

hands. It was very warm, no wind stirred, and the humidity was climbing. Summer had arrived without fanfare, simply heating everything, sweating everything. The woods seemed unnaturally quiet.

"I think it's time to look beyond our little circle of old buddies," Charlie said.

"New York," she said unhappily. "Charlie, I don't have a thing to wear for New York. And from the glimpse I got of your suitcase, neither do you."

He laughed. "When we lived in the city, you would go out dressed exactly like you are now and think nothing of it. I think you look great." She was wearing tan slacks and a pale blue shirt, a red belt, red sandals. She looked wonderful to him. No matter what came up, what they did, she was always dressed exactly right for it.

"That's different," she said patiently. "If you live there you can dress casually, do whatever you want, but if you go there from outside you have to dress differently."

"Why?"

"Because."

"Okay," Charlie said later; after half a dozen phone calls he was now driving the rental car in to Washington. "I'll go to the precinct house and go through the stuff they hauled in from the publishing office. Since the BB's have the case, no problem there." The BB's were Bergdorf and Beckman; Charlie had known them for many years. "And while I'm doing that, you can talk to the people at Magnum Publishing. How's that sound?" She hated the precinct stations. "Then we meet at Phil's, do something about dinner, and crash. And tomorrow go together to see her apartment."

"Not okay. Not quite. First I go shopping. A power suit, maybe," she said with a thoughtful expression. "And a shirt for you. Anything else?"

"You might pick up a toothbrush for me," he said, paying

close attention to a semi that wanted to pass, but not enough to go ahead and do it.

"You forgot your toothbrush?" There was a note of disbelief in her voice.

"It's okay," he said quickly. The truck driver had given up and was back doing a sedate seventy-five. "I've been using yours."

"Charlie! You haven't!"

He looked at her, startled. "All right. I haven't."

"But you have, haven't you?"

"Which do you want, yes or no?"

She turned to look at the passing scenery. If she had turned any further, he thought, she would have broken her neck.

At four that afternoon Constance walked into the office of Lewis Goldstein at Magnum Publishers. "It was good of you to see me on such short notice," she said, shaking his hand. "I appreciate it."

"Not at all. Not at all. Please, sit down. Poor Victoria. Such a shock. I just can't quite believe it, you know?"

He was a handsome man in his fifties, well tanned, with beautiful silver hair that was thick and lush looking, gleaming. His office was small, much like other editors' offices that she had seen, with stacks of manuscripts, baskets of unanswered correspondence, boxes of manila envelopes, few of them opened. A wall calendar displayed an icky May—illustrated by a big-eyed child sniffing a buttercup.

"Had you known her very long?" Constance asked.

"Years and years. We offered her a job here over a year ago, my suggestion. She was a superb editor. Just super."

"She was the magazine editor of Paul Volte's book, I understand. Were you the book editor?"

He nodded, beaming. "A delightful book, purely delightful, wasn't it? She did a wonderful job helping him develop the material, guiding it all along the way. That's what she was so good at. What a tragic loss."

"Did you work together?"

"No, not really. She came here in the middle of May, along about then, and I was gone for nearly ten days in late May. Of course, Paul's book was through production many months before that, while she was still at the magazine. But people acknowledged her role in the tremendous success of the project. A few proposals followed her here from the magazine, things of that sort. People had been stirred by the articles, her work. We expected very good things from her. Such a tragic loss!"

"Were the things that came after her the result of Paul's articles? How could you tell?"

"Well," he said, his broad smile returning, "at least one of them made it abundantly clear. It was addressed to the magazine, to the attention of the editor of Paul Volte's articles. Right there on the envelope."

She smiled ruefully. "That would seem to be clear enough. If it was addressed to the magazine, why did it come here?"

"You know, everyone believes editors pounce on the mail carrier, can't wait to get their hot hands on the treasures they know will be delivered. It isn't like that. Probably when that manuscript turned up it got handed around like a hot potato for a while before Sammy got the bright idea of forwarding it to Victoria. It must have been delivered to the magazine while she was on vacation, before she started working here, or she would have returned it herself then."

"Sammy?"

"Sam Stover. He's at *New World*. He might know something about that manuscript, if you think it's important. I can't imagine why it would be, though. One of thirty thousand that pour in year after year."

She didn't point out that she had not led him to this digression about the manuscript; she had followed, and it now occurred to her to wonder why it had stuck in his mind if it was one of such a great number. "What was unusual about the manuscript?" she asked, taking it for granted something had been, inviting him to take that for granted also.

"Not the manuscript. At least, as far as I know. I never saw it. See, we put it on her desk here as sort of a joke, that and a pile of other stuff, all to be taken care of instantly. A joke. Make her feel as if she was already one of the gang here. But for some reason she singled out that one to respond to. I never saw the proposal, and maybe it was great, but it surprised me that she read it and wrote the guy a note or something. A hell of an editor," he said, and for the first time Constance had the feeling that he meant it.

He said he didn't know why she had gone to the party. He had never even heard of Marion Olsen. He had suspected that Victoria was getting together again with Paul, and he had hoped that was the case, but she had not mentioned any of that to him. In fact, they had said hello in the corridors that last week or so, and that was the only contact they had with each other.

Matter of factly, she asked him where he had been the weekend of the party, and after a pause that held a mixture of disbelief and outrage, he answered. Sailing with two authors and their wives, over to Connecticut. She thanked him nicely and he was excessively polite when he stood up to see her out.

At the door she paused to ask, "Did Victoria have a secretary here, or an assistant? I'd like to ask that person a question or two."

That person turned out to be Beverly Swandon, a plump young woman with dimples in both cheeks and very curly hair of an improbable chestnut color.

"I remember that manuscript, you better believe. Some joke, loading up her desk like that! As if it wouldn't happen in the normal course of events, you know? But that manuscript that came from Sam Stover, from some nerd out in the boonies. I remember because this guy sends in the manuscript and a week after that he moves, and begins to make phone calls to get his right address on the return envelope. I mean, come on, you don't know you're going to move a week in advance? Yeah. You never heard that the post office will forward mail? Right. But Victoria Leeds took it like a lady and she even wrote him a little note when she sent it back."

"He called here? When? What name did he give?"

"Not here. He called Sam Stover. Anyway, Stover called Ms. Leeds and told her the right address. I never heard a name."

"And she rejected the manuscript?"

Beverly Swandon shook her head. "She put a note on it, something like if he fixed it up, wanted to talk about it in the future, to let her see it again. Anyway, the note was on her memo, you know? 'From-the-desk-of' kind of thing. She didn't put his name on it, just wrote out the couple of lines and clipped it to the manuscript. That's why I never saw a name, I guess. I had to make out a label with the new address. I remember that part. A Washington, D.C. box number. I stuck it over his old address."

"You must have seen his name on the envelope?"

Beverly shook her head; she had reached the limits of her memory, the name eluded her.

It was getting close to five, Constance realized, and she asked Beverly about the rest of the time Victoria had worked here. There was very little beyond the fact that Beverly had liked her a lot, a whole lot, she repeated. She didn't know anything about the party, why Victoria had gone, who Marion Olsen was, or even when Victoria decided to go. She had simply said she wouldn't be in on Friday, and then they found out that she had gone off and got herself killed.

* * *

135

No one should have to be in New York at five in the afternoon, Constance thought a few minutes later, standing outside the building that housed Magnum Publishers. She was on East Tenth; Phil Stern lived on West Fourteenth. As far as she could see there were people, walking, rollerblading, on bikes, in trucks, in buses, in taxis, even in private cars that were virtually gridlocked. People running for the next bus, for the subway entrance, pushing, and creating a strange constant noise that was partly roar, partly high-pitched voices, brakes squealing, horns blaring, voices shouting, cursing, singing, even a cornet from somewhere seemed to belong to the overall sound. She started to walk. An image presented itself to her mind. She had seen a cloud of smelts moving up a river once, heading they did not know where, for a reason they could not explain, but determined. Yes, determined. She walked briskly.

One of Phil Stern's little jokes was that he and Charlie had gone to school together, and then he had gone into insurance and Charlie had gone to blazes. Charlie assumed a patient expression; Constance smiled politely; his wife Alicia ignored him, but on the whole the evening was pleasant. Everyone went to bed early.

Charlie had found out even less than she had, and he had a long list of names of Victoria's friends and acquaintances. They both regarded the list with resignation the next morning at breakfast. They had dawdled in their room until Phil and Alicia were gone; now they had the lovely old apartment to themselves. Phil had kept this rent-controlled apartment for nearly thirty years, and it was as fine as ever, even if the windows were dirty and the woodwork needed a new coat of paint. The rooms were large and bright with oversized windows, the ceilings were high, the walls were thick, and it was very quiet.

"Beckman told jokes," Charlie said. Constance groaned

in commiseration. Beckman told the world's filthiest jokes, it was generally conceded. No one laughed but Beckman.

"There won't be an investigation here?" she had asked in surprise last night, but she understood why not. As far as the city was concerned, Victoria Leeds was Maryland's problem. New York would gather up her belongings and ship them off to her family; case closed. They would hang on to stuff for a time, just in case Maryland sent someone up to look through things; no one had objected to Charlie's going through the stuff they had collected from her office. For all he had gained, he might just as well have stayed in bed, he had added, recounting his day.

"Bergdorf's thinking about retirement. Says they'll raise goats."

"Goats? Does he know anything about goats? Why goats?"

"He likes their eyes. You know, the pupils. He thinks they're really aliens, and they can only see in straight lines, bands, or something like that."

She studied him narrowly. "You're kidding me," she said.

He shook his head. "That's what I said to Bergdorf, but he swore he intends to retire and keep goats. Alien goats!"

She laughed, and after a moment he joined her.

They both went to see Sam Stover, who turned out to be nearly seventy, nearly bald, and dressed in a seersucker suit. Charlie stared at it in awe. He had not seen a seersucker suit for twenty-five years, thirty years. Actually, he couldn't remember if he had ever seen a blue-and-white seersucker suit. It was something you just knew about, learned at your grandfather's knee.

"I'll do anything I can to help you," Sam Stover said. "Victoria was a very special person, very dear to me." He motioned to two chairs that looked as if they belonged in a high school from the turn of the century, heavy, ugly oak, much scarred, and polished from use. He sat behind a desk that was piled high with papers.

Sam Stover was precise in everything he said. He spoke slowly, choosing his words with care, and it appeared that he had never forgotten a thing in his life. He talked at great length about Victoria, how she had been his protégée, his assistant, then his junior colleague, and finally his peer. There had been no enemies, he said firmly; she had not been the type to make enemies. She had been a true professional; any number of careers had been advanced through her efforts with the writers. "It was a good thing for her to move on," he said. "She would have had an illustrious career in book publishing. The magazine, you understand, has been bought out by a Japanese filmmaker, or something of the sort."

He knew exactly what he meant by "of the sort," and it came through as contempt, scorn, derision, beneath civilized consideration. The unspoken words were eloquently expressed in his gesture, the haughty look he assumed.

Charlie finally got around to the last weeks Victoria had been with the magazine, and then the period after she had left. He asked about the manuscript Stover had forwarded to her. "What do you generally do with manuscripts addressed to editors who have left? Is it customary to forward them?"

"Not customary. Not at all. Generally we treat them exactly the same as any other submissions. The publishing world of the magazine is quite different from that of books, naturally. What might be suitable for one would be unsuitable for the other without a great deal of work. But this manuscript, addressed so precisely to the editor of Paul Volte's series, was obviously not meant for anyone else. If there had been even a chance of our taking it, I might have opened it to have a look, but of course, there wasn't."

"Why do you say, 'of course'?"

"Several reasons. One is that we so seldom accept anything that comes in over the transom. That is, freelance, unsolicited, unagented. Life is too short," he added in a brusque tone. "Second, since this person referred to Paul's work, it was to be presumed that the enclosed proposal somehow resembled that, or why draw attention to it, why suggest the same editor should see the new material? We would never have run a second article that in any way resembled such a fine piece as Paul's. Not for many years, anyway, but few on the outside would have known that. And finally, Victoria developed the material with Paul, you understand, and it was possible that the proposal might have been worth her time to develop with this unknown author. That's always a possibility, however remote. It was her option to read it, to send it back unopened, or to pass it on to her first reader, or whatever."

"Lewis Goldstein suggested you might just have wanted to get rid of it, and that was a convenient way, to forward it to Victoria Leeds," Constance murmured.

"Lewis Goldstein is an ass. It would have been easier to put it in the stamped return envelope and send it back to the writer the day it arrived."

"When did the writer call you?" Charlie asked.

"I can't be certain. I think we received the manuscript soon after Victoria left, or she would have handled it herself. Her last day here was the thirtieth of April. I'm certain I had already sent it on to her when this man called me to have me change his address back in May." His voice had gone very dry. Obviously he had never been asked to do anything like that before. "He called and said that he had to have the manuscript back because he had discovered grave errors of fact."

He cleared his throat. "I'm afraid his name meant nothing to me; I had paid no attention to the name on the envelope. I mentioned that the United States Post Office department makes it a rule to forward mail for quite a long time, and he became agitated. I assumed at the time that domestic problems had arisen for him, necessitating the post office box number, and the likelihood was that he would never see the manuscript again if it was delivered to his home address. Therefore, I told him that if it turned up, we would send it to the new address, and that he should write me a letter with that address. He insisted on giving it over the phone, and I jotted it down. It didn't even occur to me to tell him Victoria had moved over to Magnum Publishers. I knew she was out of town, for one thing, but that really was not the reason. I simply didn't think of it. Later, after her return, while we were on the phone I told her about the telephone call and the manuscript. It had already been sent on over to her. I keep a phone log of my outgoing calls; I talked to her on June ninth. I gave her the new address at that time."

It was a miracle that it had ever surfaced again, Charlie thought, regarding the desk. "Had she read it yet?"

"She had. She said it was interesting, might have had something for her, and it was too bad if it had factual errors, but of course that would kill it. She said she would return it. She did not mention the contents, or the subject matter, no more than what I have just said."

"Who sent her the manuscript, Mr. Stover? What was the new address?" Charlie asked. There was no particular reason to pursue this business matter, but there was the remote chance that one of the crew at Tootles's house had lied about having had a contact with Victoria. There was even a chance that it could have had something to do with Paul Volte. Short of plagiarism, Charlie could not think of what that might be, however.

"I thought you might want to know," Sam Stover said and opened a desk drawer. "Naturally I found it for you." He handed a slip of paper to Charlie. The handwriting was elegant and very legible. The name written there was David Musselman.

* * *

140

At two that afternoon they met Sergeant Michael Pressger at the Eighty-ninth Street apartment that Victoria Leeds had leased for the past twelve years. The sergeant was young and very eager. He wanted to rise through the ranks fast, Charlie decided, fending him off as he moved in too close, watching every motion through narrowed eyes, memorizing everything Charlie did, everything he said. No doubt he would re-create it all carefully later. Deliberately Charlie went to a window, studied the view, turned to study the room, even paced it off, and then grunted. The sergeant made a note. Constance glared at Charlie wordlessly; he looked innocent.

The apartment was clean, four rooms, cluttered with too much stuff, but all stowed away as well as the space had permitted. Books, manuscripts, correspondence made up most of the clutter. Two walls had book shelves from ceiling to floor. Her living room appeared to be an extension of her office. The bedroom was almost barren in contrast: a three-quarter-sized bed, chest of drawers, comfortable reading chair and lamp, and a small table laden with books of poetry and plays. In both the living room and the bedroom the tables had marks made by wet glasses, and there was a burn mark on the coffee table in the living room. Constance nodded; just as she had suspected. Victoria had been a wet-glass type. There was an incomplete needlepoint pillow top on the sofa, and a box of colored yarn strands and needles. The kitchen with eating space, and a utility room/second bedroom finished the apartment. It was all comfortable; Victoria had accumulated things she liked over the years, nice prints on the walls, Monet, Chagall, a Turner; there was a good compact disk player—classical music, jazz; thriving geraniums in bloom lined a windowsill. Two needlepoint pillows on a chair in the second bedroom. . . . Charlie came to a complete stop in the living room before a bas-relief of a face, her face he assumed. He looked at Constance, who nodded.

"Good likeness?" he asked.

"Very. Idealized and romanticized, but she caught her. Toni's work, I'm sure. She said she had done a study of Victoria's face." She remembered that Toni had said Paul had bought a second bas-relief identical to this one; she examined it more closely and gradually became aware that the sergeant had moved in as Charlie moved away. The officer was breathing on her neck.

"You know anything about computers?" Charlie asked from across the room, where he was standing at a desk with a computer system.

"A little," the sergeant said.

"I'd like to make a list of the files, not copy them all, just find out what she was . . . oh, oh."

"What?" the sergeant asked, coming to the desk.

"Not sure. Maybe a gold mine. Look, she used a calendar program." He was in a menu program, and keyed in the letter for Calendar. It appeared quickly.

Charlie was able to read through the entries enough to see that she had recorded: *call from M. Check Marion Olsen. Call P.* The date of that entry was June 14. June 15 was the date of her call to Paul Volte to invite herself to Tootles's party.

"I'd like a copy of everything on her calendar from mid-March on," Charlie said to the sergeant then. He scanned the entries following the one that had caught his attention. Everything would need cross-referencing with the addresses in her files, in her little black book.

"Guess I could make a printout right now," the sergeant said, studying the layout of the computer and printer.

Charlie moved out of his way and in a minute the printer blinked awake, cleared its throat, and rattled off several pages. Charlie noticed without comment that the sergeant made two copies.

After they left the apartment, Charlie said he wanted to talk to an old buddy, Curt Mercer, who could very well do most of the legwork involved in finding and talking to the many people listed in Victoria's books. Constance nodded. "And I'm off to the library," she said. "Meet you back at Phil's?"

"Library? What for?"

"They probably have some biographical stuff about Paul Volte," she said vaguely. "Just curious, I guess."

Actually she wanted to find out when his various successes had come about, and how many people close to him had died, or left him, and if the two events seemed linked in time. And this was the kind of thing, she well knew, that would be very hard to explain to Charlie. Not that she believed a word of it, either, she hastened to add to herself. Just curious. Very curious.

Thirteen

Charlie watched her climb the stairs to the library with a feeling of disquiet. Yesterday when they had gone their separate ways a surge of unease had caught him off guard, but now that had changed; unease had become a real fear. The library steps were crowded with people lounging, reading, eating lunch, watching others, doing nothing, hanging out, and he saw menace everywhere. The fact that they had lived in the city for most of their married life made no difference; the populace had not been armed with assault rifles then, he told himself, and ignored the mocking voice that said *then* was only a few years ago, remember; and, he went on in his silent monologue, murder *then* had been newsworthy, not just a filler on page fifty. As soon as she was out of sight, he started to walk.

He was still preoccupied with the danger of the city, not for him because he had grown up here; it held no more real surprises for him, and he knew it was irrational to be this fearful for Constance. He knew very well that if anyone ever tried to roughhouse Constance, she could easily flatten the guy without mussing a hair or breathing hard. She had studied aikido for many years, at his insistence, he added grimly to himself, and she kept in good shape, and worked out with other aikido partners when she had the chance. Their daughter was almost as good as Constance; he had nearly disgraced them and himself by bawling with pride the first time they had put on a public demonstration. He still remembered the hole he had chewed in his cheek to keep the tears back. But that was different. There was no self-defense against a bullet, or a thrown knife. He wondered if Victoria Leeds would have had a chance with years of self-defense training. A rope over the head, a quick upward yank against the carotids to bring almost instant unconsciousness. He doubted that anyone would have been able to fight back, even Constance with all her skills. He wanted them out of the city as fast as they could manage; he wanted her safe in their own house upstate.

He quickened his pace on his way to hire the help that would allow them to leave. Curt Mercer was a good man, reliable, plodding; he believed investigative work was supposed to be boring, and he accepted without question chores of the sort that Charlie intended to load on him: go see all these people and find out if any of them had known Victoria was going to the party, or why. Or if any of them had a suggestion about why she had been killed, or anything else that might be of help.

He was not happy about the vagueness of the assignment; he had learned that it was best to lay it out precisely: go find out if so and so was home Monday from ten to three. Anyone could ask the right questions and find out something like that, while what he was looking for was open, vague, subjective. But he was willing to give it to Curt because he didn't really believe there was anything to learn from her friends. Everyone so far had told the same story: she had not mentioned the party, had not mentioned meeting anyone in particular, had not mentioned anything out of ordinary. He suspected that would continue to be the case. Victoria Leeds had not been a gossip, had not talked much about herself apparently. He was starting to feel that he would have liked her quite a lot; he knew Constance felt that.

When he got back to Phil's apartment, he called Bill Gruenwald, whom he thought of as the tame, friendly sheriff. He gave him the name David Musselman, and the post office number, and they agreed cautiously that maybe they would now learn why Victoria had gone to the party just outside Washington. There was nothing else new, Gruenwald said glumly.

The medical examiner put death at no later than seven-thirty—he had not been able to narrow it more than that. She hadn't eaten anything all day, Gruenwald had said almost apologetically. And the air conditioner had been set to subarctic. Charlie knew enough about autopsies to know that sometimes if you got the year right you were ahead of the game.

He gave the sheriff Phil's number and hung up soon afterward. Then he started to pace.

Constance had been gone for longer than three hours, plenty long to look up Paul Volte. It was nearly five. She would be caught in the gridlock; and it was too far to walk. She wouldn't come by subway, he told himself. She wouldn't do anything that dumb. That's where the guys with the knives and guns were; she knew that. She probably wouldn't get there until after seven, eight. . . . Gruenwald called back.

"Charlie, this Musselman, you know anything about him?"

"Just give it to me," Charlie said in a tight voice. "What?"

"He's dead, Charlie. You know they had two accidents at the condo site? One involved some kids, but the other was a fatal accident. David Musselman fell off a sixth floor structure and was killed instantly. I thought that name sounded familiar. Right there in the file."

Charlie asked very softly, "When was that, Bill?"

"May tenth." There was a brief silence, and then Gruenwald said, "Someone else has that box number now. Your turn, Charlie. Give."

Charlie told him about the manuscript. "And," he finished, "apparently Musselman called the magazine on about May tenth or eleventh to get the manuscript back. Exactly when did he rent that post office box?"

Gruenwald cursed. "I'll get back to you. When are you coming back down here?"

"Tomorrow," Charlie said. "Nine o'clock shuttle."

They made plans for Gruenwald to meet the plane, and then for the three of them to go see Musselman's widow; she lived in Chevy Chase. Charlie hung up, walked to the window, and stared out at the city, seeing little of it.

It was nearly six when Constance arrived; she was carrying a bag of groceries. Charlie met her at the door, took the bag from her arm and set it aside, and then drew her in close in a hard embrace.

"Hey," she said after a moment. "Wow!" She pulled back smiling, but her smile faded at the look on his face. "Charlie? What is it? What's wrong?"

He shook his head. "Nothing now. I kept seeing you getting mugged, getting thrown under the wheels of a bus, thrown down on the tracks in the subway station. Idle hands, idle minds, Satan's playground, or something like that."

"Oh, Charlie," she whispered. "Oh, Charlie."

"What's in the bag?" he asked then in a hearty voice. "And I learned something from Gruenwald that could blow our case sky high again, whole new ball game maybe."

"Ingredients," she said, indicating the bag. "I decided to cook some dinner for Phil and Alicia. Least we can do. You know how much hotels cost here in New York these days, if you can get one on short notice?" She picked up the bag and started for the kitchen. "What did the sheriff say?"

There was a counter with stools in the kitchen; he seated himself out of the way and watched her unload the ingredients: a lovely salmon, lingonberries, sour cream, horseradish. . . . Lingonberries, he realized, meant blintzes. His look was reverential when he turned again to her.

"Well?" she asked.

"Well, it seems that Mr. Musselman died on May tenth, for openers. And he worked at the Buell condo complex. He was the fatality we heard about, the reason for tight security now."

She was frowning at him, her hands motionless over the salmon that she had been anointing with lime juice. "May tenth? But isn't that about when he sent the manuscript to the magazine, and when he called? Are those dates all right?"

"I don't know yet. But it makes for an interesting twist. I think we've found the reason for Victoria's party crashing. And she must not have thought he was dead. She returned the manuscript in June, remember, to the post office box."

"Presumably someone collected it," Constance said in a low voice. "Or else it's still there."

He shook his head. "Box is closed out, new tenants."

Phil and Alicia arrived then, and they joined Charlie at the counter where they had drinks and offered advice to Constance about knives, spices, the location of proper pans and skillets, and she was spared either dodging Charlie's inevitable questions about what she had learned, or else out-and-out lying about it. She knew she was a pretty good dodger, and an incompetent liar.

It had shaken her terribly to see fear on Charlie's face when he caught her up in his arms earlier. He said fear of the dangers of the city, and although that might be what he believed, she did not believe it. They had spent too many years living here for such terror to surface now. But he had been afraid; she had felt his heart thumping, had felt the tremor in his hands when he pulled her to him. At the moment he was laughing at something Phil had just said, the fear pushed out of mind again, so far back that now it would be possible to believe that earlier there had been a simple aberration, a twinge of indigestion, or something equally fleeting and benign. Now it would be impossible to bring it up and talk about it. What fear? he would drawl lazily. Hungry, that's what I was.

It had something to do with Tootles and Ba Ba and that ancient silly Ouija incident, she felt certain. He had buried that, had never breathed a word of it before, but it had soured him for all these years on Tootles and Ba Ba, and had created in him a dread, even a terror that was surfacing now. The fear was inappropriate, out of time, out of place, but that was what made phobias so powerful, their very inappropriateness. Not that this was a phobia, she told herself quickly, well aware that it could turn into one, a phobia that could make an otherwise rational person behave in ways so irrational that treatment could be required. This was an irrational fear that had to be denied, and denial was achieved by transferring the fear away from the self to the other; he feared for her because he could not accept or even examine what had frightened him so badly many years ago.

She thought through this while she prepared the dinner, and chatted with their hosts, and then served and ate the dinner, which everyone agreed was delicious.

As she was drifting off to sleep that night, Constance was jarred wide awake when Charlie grunted and cursed.

"What?" she demanded. "Too many blintzes, too much horseradish in the sauce?"

"What Victoria Leeds said, interpreted by Janet Cuprillo, something about a proposal from a jock. I just got it."

After a second she shivered and groaned. He put his arm around her and drew her close and eventually they fell asleep entwined.

* * *

When Bill Gruenwald met them at the terminal in Washington the next morning, he looked so thoroughly scrubbed, he seemed to shine. Before the handshaking was completed, he said dourly, "He rented the box May eleventh."

"Oh," Charlie said with great interest. "Busy day for Mr. Musselman, what with the funeral and all."

"You got it," Gruenwald said. "I'm parked over this way."

Someone calling himself David Musselman had rented a post office box at the main post office on May eleventh and had kept it until June twelfth. According to Victoria Leeds's assistant, the manuscript had been put in the mail to be returned on June eighth, a Friday. And on June twelfth, someone collected the mail, and turned in the key, Gruenwald said. No one remembered a thing about him. He had put the key in an envelope and left it in the box with a typed note saying he no longer needed it. They hadn't bothered to keep the note, why should anyone? Gruenwald scowled.

"Once he knew who he was dealing with, he didn't need to write letters," Charlie said. "And he did call, apparently, on June fourteenth. Told her to invite herself to the bash, I bet, so they could meet and talk over the proposal that weekend. And that would explain Ms. Leeds's presence, and her ducking out for a date with someone." A date with a ghost, he added silently, and then instantly denied it. Someone who either claimed to be Musselman, or else claimed to represent him, probably.

Gruenwald drove with unconscious ease, and soon they were nearing the Chevy Chase developments. "Mrs. Musselman," he said in a rather flat tone, "has come into a neat little fortune, couple hundred thousand, plus a settlement from the company. Three kids, away with grandparents right now. She was having trouble coping with meals and such." At the next intersection he turned left, and pulled into a driveway. These houses were all expensive, with acres of velvet grass, landscaping done by expensive landscape designers, houses designed by fine architects. Very impressive, and somehow depressing, Charlie was thinking as they followed the curve in the driveway to the front entrance of the house. It looked like a set for a stylish Hollywood movie and real people didn't live in Hollywood sets.

Diane Musselman would have been at home in a movie filmed here. She was blond and pretty, dressed in a silk pantsuit. Her waist was tiny, her breasts and hips generous, a real hourglass figure, Charlie thought, shaking her hand. She carried a wisp of lacy handkerchief that she touched to her eyes now and then although her eyes were as dry as his. An image of the Barbie doll in Tootles's office swam up in his mind, and he struggled to erase it again.

"I know this is a terrible imposition," the sheriff was saying as she led them into the house, through a spacious foyer with many flowers in oversized vases, and on to a comfortable sitting room. It looked as if no one had entered it since the decorators left.

"I must help in any way possible," she said in a tremulous voice. "Please, if there's anything at all I can do, you must let me. I'll try." She was very brave.

"Yes," Gruenwald said. "Something has turned up that puzzles us. Did your husband ever do any writing? I mean articles for publication, books, things of that sort."

She shook her head, her eyes wide and bewildered.

"Did he have an office here in the house, a study, something like that?"

"Oh, yes. He did a lot of work at home."

She took them to the study, a large room with tan leather-covered chairs, a sofa, two desks, a drawing table . . . many books were on shelves here. One of the desks held an elaborate computer system, printer, a complicated-looking drawing machine. In here, as in the other rooms they had seen so far, everything was very neat.

Charlie and Bill Gruenwald exchanged glances, the gloom they had shared seemed to lift.

"Has anyone touched this equipment since your husband's accident?" Gruenwald asked.

"Someone must have," she said defensively. "Not me. I never set foot in here when he was alive, and I certainly didn't after he was gone. Never. But someone from his office came to get some files or something off the computer and he said everything was gone, erased, blanked out. I forget what he said. Gone. All gone."

Charlie let a sigh escape. He looked at Constance, who was watching Diane Musselman with a thoughtful expression. He knew Constance had not reached across the room to touch him between the shoulderblades, or made any other overt motion to get his attention, but she had got his attention. He lifted his eyebrow so slightly that probably no one but Constance would have recognized it as a signal. She had paused at the doorway; now she came the rest of the way into the room, looking around it with great interest.

"This is such a lovely house," she murmured. "So beautifully decorated and maintained."

Diane Musselman drew herself up straighter and nodded. "Thank you," she said.

"Of course, you couldn't be held responsible for rooms you didn't occupy or use in any way. Like this room, so obviously a man's room, isn't it? But for a reader not to have books on tables, on the arm of the chair, that seems strange. I suppose you had to tidy up before other people came around to collect his files."

Diane nodded. "It was a mess," she admitted.

"How about his bedroom? Did he keep books and papers and things in there, too?"

"Yes, he did. It's still a mess. I just can't seem to bring myself to pick it up. One of these days, of course, I will. The housekeeper is after me to let her do it, but someone has to pick up the important things first. You know?"

"I understand entirely," Constance said. "I think if we're through in here, we might have a look at his other private room, and then we'll leave you in peace. It's been terribly good of you to let us impose like this."

Diane led them through a wide hall with nice pictures of irises and roses on both walls, on to another wing of the house. She walked at Constance's side explaining that it wasn't that they hadn't slept together, but she was so tired so much of the time, what with three children to see to, and the house and all, and he had kept such late hours many nights, and had been such a restless sleeper, thrashing about, keeping her awake. . . . Now and then Constance murmured something soothing.

They reached the second private room that David Musselman had used, and this time when Charlie and Bill Gruenwald exchanged quick looks, they both appeared satisfied with this development. There was no computer in here, but many notebooks, magazines, books on a nightstand by a narrow bed, others on two tables flanking a couch that had a worn blanket draped over the back. The bed was unmade; a stack of books was on one side of it.

"I brought some of this stuff in from the other study," Diane said apologetically. "But then I didn't know what to do with it. We don't usually keep books and stuff on the floor."

"You look so tired," Constance said to her at the doorway. "Show me the way to the kitchen and I'll make you a cup of tea, or coffee. Tell me about the children."

She drew Diane out with her, and the two men went to work.

"How did you know?" Bill Gruenwald asked later in the car heading out toward Tootles's house.

"I guessed," Constance said. Charlie snorted. "Well, there weren't any books in sight in the first room she showed us to, remember? Then his study revealed a reader, a man with many interests. The books were art, poetry, biographies, fiction, books on collectibles, coins, stamps, even carpets, but all put away. I doubt that she ever put a book away in the right place in her life; he must have done it, and that left the question of where were the books he was actively interested in at the time of his death. I thought there must be another room."

Charlie chuckled and slouched down in the seat. Bill Gruenwald turned to look at her directly; he had been watching her in the rear view mirror. He made a saluting gesture and turned his attention back to driving.

"Are you going to tell me what you found?" she asked then.

Bill Gruenwald had asked for a large bag or two, and had brought out two filled with magazines, notebooks, books, maps, drawings. . . . He said he didn't know yet what all was in them; it would take hours to sort it out. They had found a heavily annotated copy of Paul Volte's magazine articles, the series on art and architecture. And they had found the hardcover book, not as heavily annotated, but marked up. Someone had to go through everything, he repeated.

No diary, no outline for the proposal he had sent to the magazine, but in all those notebooks maybe there was something to do with it.

There was a how-to book about submitting a proposal, Charlie said lazily. "Poor guy had it right there in black and white, call up and ask the name of the editor if you have to, but he sent it addressed to The Editor anyway. Chickened out about calling. He had underlined that bit of advice."

They had driven out to the countryside by now, away from the heavy city traffic. "What I have on Musselman," Bill Gruenwald said, relaxing even more at the wheel, "is damn little. We were looking at an accident, remember, no reason to start digging too hard into his past or anything. So, here it is. He was the junior partner of a pretty prestigious firm of architects, made a good living with it, and was good at it, apparently. The condo complex was his, with a lot of help from a flock of juniors who did the plumbing, wiring, floors, the detail work. He was the overall honcho above them. Okay. Buell used that firm a lot for primary design work, but not to see the projects through to completion. Apparently, it can go both ways. So it was a surprise when Musselman came around to check on the roof or some damn thing. We had a lot of hard rain all spring, and he said he was concerned about leaks, and he was around a lot. Ditmar said it was peculiar, but acceptable. Others dittoed that. Strange, but not so strange that anyone gave it more than a passing thought. He died on a Thursday after working hours. The roof was awash that day, and lots of mud had been tracked up. If he was worried about leaks, it made sense for him to go have a look. See what I mean? We were looking at an accident. So he went up there, and he got too close to a slippery edge and fell. Nothing indicated anything but that. No one else was with him, no one knew he was going out to look around that day. A watchman, not Pierce, found his body when he made his rounds right after six. Musselman died between five, when the last workman left, and six twenty, when he was found."

Charlie did not stir from his slouched position, and in the back seat Constance gazed out the window at the passing scenery, very pretty here, nice grass, good trees, lush looking farms now and then. No one spoke until Gruenwald said irritably, "All right! We blew it! I can see that now, but at the time? No way. You saw the wife; we got the same story from people he worked with. He didn't have an enemy in the world. No one had a reason to want to harm him. He was in debt, but who isn't? And it wasn't serious. No drinking or gambling problems. Nothing, period."

"Take it easy," Charlie said. "You blew it, but what the hell? It looked good at the time and that's all you can do." He pulled himself up a little bit straighter. "So he dies on

Thursday, and on Friday someone rents the box in his name and calls the magazine to change the return address on the manuscript. You might be able to find out at his office when someone went out there to collect the computer files." Diane had looked helpless when asked for a date. "We've got a busy killer scurrying around tidying up here, straightening up there. Someone who understands his computer enough to clean it out. I sure don't."

"It's a Mac," Constance said from the back seat. "They have powerful drawing capabilities, very good for all sorts of graphic work, I guess. I think most people in art or architecture would understand them, if they use computers at all."

"Well, it's a whole new ball game," Charlie said. "If Musselman found out something funny about the condos and wrote it up in a proposal for publication, it brings in a whole new bunch of suspects starting with Max, Johnny, Ditmar, on down to every foreman, every supplier, God knows who else, backers, bankers. Jesus! And this person might not have attended the damn party at all, just met Victoria Leeds at the condo, talked in any of the rooms, and then after Johnny and group departed, took her up to the sixth floor and killed her. He could have chosen any time to leave when Pierce was busy somewhere else."

"I can just see a mad plumber leaving a letter on her bed, and then taking time out to mess up Marion Olsen's art before going over to kill Victoria Leeds," Bill Gruenwald said with harsh bitterness.

In the back seat Constance stared stonily out the side window at the sparse woods they were passing through.

F o u r t e e n

"About Musselman's death," Charlie said as they approached the condo area, "did you investigate it yourself?"

"Yeah. I'll show you."

"Stop at the gate," Constance said, "and I'll walk on down to Tootles's house. I want to see her, see how she's doing. You can fill me in later, Charlie."

They had left the Volvo in Tootles's driveway and had to go there eventually to pick it up. Constance had already called the motel they had stayed in before and reserved the same two rooms, and she obviously did not want to peer at a spot on the ground where a man had fallen to his death. Gruenwald stopped, as she had requested, and she left them and started to walk on the shoulder of the road.

"That was a nice piece of work she came up with," the sheriff said, shifting gears, pulling on in through the gate.

"Hm," Charlie said, unhappy that Constance had chosen to go alone, unable to say why it bothered him. It was the middle of the day; Tootles, Babar, the students were the only ones likely to be at the house, not at all like New York. Still, the uneasiness settled over him.

"The rain put them behind this spring," Gruenwald was

saying as he drove to the front of the A building—Applegate, Charlie remembered. Max Buell's big, six-year-old Continental was parked there. "A lot of guys weren't working, nothing going on outside, you see, but the painters, plasterers, interior finish people were all busy. Anyway, no one claims to have seen Musselman that afternoon. Could be. He could have driven in, like I just did, parked, and walked in. Elevator up to six, stairs up to the roof." He opened his car door and got out, stood with his hands thrust deep into his pockets outside the building. A sidewalk had been laid, irregular paving stones of a pleasing slate-gray color, bordered on both sides by low-growing plants, nice lawn areas. They walked to the end of the building. "Sidewalk wasn't here then," Gruenwald said. "Junk concrete, bricks, I don't know, just junk littered the ground right here. And this is the place they found him. We've got pictures if you want to see."

Charlie looked from the neatly finished walk up the side of the building; this was on the same side as the deluxe apartments, up there was Six A where Victoria Leeds had died, too. "You'd think someone would have seen him, someone going home or something."

Gruenwald shook his head. "That's what I thought, but they walked me through it. The guys working inside all used the other elevators, the common ones, not the dedicated ones at this end. They stashed their gear in the basement, washed brushes in the basement, stuff like that, and then left by way of the basement doors, the ones closest to where they were. Guys in the other buildings were even less likely to have seen him. Someone driving by at the right moment could have seen him from the road but no one came forward. No one had any reason to be right here until the watchman made his first round, fifteen after six, twenty after, whatever."

"And he didn't let out a peep on the way down?" Charlie

asked sourly. "I guess they all wore headsets, listened to music or something?"

Gruenwald flushed and his lips tightened a bit. "Something like that," he said in a cold tone. "Charlie, ease up. It was raining hard. Windows were closed, tarps over any openings, music was on, guys talking and mostly working in inside rooms. No one heard anything."

"It stinks," Charlie said in a colder voice. "Okay, okay. At the time it looked like an accident. But it stinks today. Let's go talk to Max Buell. Not a word yet about Musselman, you agree?"

Gruenwald shrugged, not appeased.

Since they did not have the key to the dedicated elevator, they had to use the common one at the other end, and then walk the length of the sixth-floor hall to the apartment. The door there was standing open. They entered without ringing or knocking.

Max and Johnny were both in the living room of Six A, standing at a table with an open sample book of paint. All the tarps had been cleared away now; the room looked ready for occupancy.

"I heard what you said, and I still say no," Max was saying, as Charlie and Bill Gruenwald walked into the room. "We stick with the original colors throughout unless tenants or buyers say otherwise."

His voice was low, but there was a sharp edge there; it was very clear who was boss. Johnny looked across the room at Charlie and the sheriff, shrugged, and closed the book.

Gruenwald said, "Mr. Buell, could we talk to you for a moment?" He looked at Max, who nodded and sat down at the table.

"Sure," he said. "Johnny, we'll talk about it again later."

"Right," his son said and left, carrying the large book with him. He looked sullen, and his posture was rigid with repressed anger. He did not glance at Charlie or Gruenwald as he walked out stiffly.

Charlie waited until Johnny had closed the foyer/elevator door behind him, and then sat down opposite Max Buell. "Did you tell Spence to arrange the touring show for Tootles? Are you footing that bill?" he asked bluntly. Max leaned back, his face impassive. A good poker player, Charlie thought; he said, "We can find out, you know. All those gallery owners don't owe you a damn thing, do they?"

"What difference does it make?" Max asked finally, giving nothing yet.

"Damned if I know. She doesn't know, does she?"

Finally Max shook his head. "She doesn't know. There's no reason to tell her."

"I agree," Charlie said, in a more kindly voice. "Absolutely, I agree. Why did you do it?"

Max looked from him to Gruenwald, back to Charlie. "She deserves some recognition," he said. "She's overdue recognition, and it wasn't going to happen unless someone made it happen. She's worked all her life for nothing. Not much money, just a little trust fund, no fame, no glory, nothing. She deserves more." He studied Charlie a moment, then asked, "Who told you? Spence?"

"Nope. He would have had his tongue pulled out before he'd talk. You should know that. A combination of things that didn't quite mesh. Spence could have done this anywhere along the line, but he didn't. Not enough money? Maybe. But the fact is that he didn't arrange it until now. All galleries, not state museums, or college museums. Private. Business deals right down the line. And who's the businessman among us, with money to spare for private art shows?" He shook his head. "It didn't take a giant intellect to come up with you."

"She deserves it," Max said again. "She's a brilliant artist who never quite made it. It's not just charity. Some of the pieces might even sell."

Charlie nodded, as if in agreement again. "How is this complex, all this construction, financed?"

Max looked startled at the abrupt change of subject, then he shrugged. "I put up some, up front, then I went for financing, four different banks involved. They pay in installments, so much with foundation digging, so much with outer walls, and so on."

"That's why it was important to have the showing last weekend? Another installment due?"

"Yes. On completion of a major part, one entire building, for example, a big installment is due. It's like a credit line, enough to keep us paying the bills until we start selling and bringing in money. The showing would have included some prospective buyers, as well as the financiers."

"What now? Another tour planned?"

"No. No," he said quickly. "My God, someone died here! Anyway it will be low-key. Nothing showy, not after a tragedy. Nothing to attract media attention," he added dryly. "Our backers are strong about not attracting attention. We'll have them in individually now, two, three at a time at the most. One of their people will just send a representative, an inspector. It will be discreet." He looked at Charlie shrewdly then and added, "I'm not hurting for money, you know. This arrangement is typical, but I could have done the project without it. And I don't lick boots, or various parts of the anatomy to keep the money flowing."

Charlie laughed. "Gotcha," he said after a moment. "Does your son share your feelings?

"Ask him," Max said.

"I want to see Birmingham," Charlie said when they left Max and the A Building. From all over the site the sounds of hammers, saws, music, voices filled the air; next door the Birmingham building was relatively quiet, all the major construction finished. Painters and plasterers, finishers were at work in it. Charlie led the way down the sloping drive into the basement where two men were painting lines on the floor with a machine. Parking spaces, just like in A.

A worker was spraying stenciled numbers on panels for the dedicated elevators: 1, 2 . . . the number would go on one side of the door that opened in the middle. The other side already had the letter, B. Exactly like the other building, except here it was B, and there it was A.

Charlie stood watching for a few seconds, then turned and nearly bumped into Bill Gruenwald, who was waiting patiently. "Well?" the sheriff said then.

"Nothing. Just nothing. Let's go."

By the time Constance reached Tootles's house she was in an icy rage. She bypassed the house when she saw the two young men and Toni with Tootles and Ba Ba in the side yard. She walked to the small group. One of the boys was painting a grotesque three-foot-high construction full of oddly shaped holes that seemed randomly positioned. The birdhouse, she realized. It had been undercoated and was being painted emerald green.

"We have to talk," she said grimly, taking Tootles by the arm. She didn't know how long Charlie would be, and she wanted this over with before he arrived. There was no time now for niceties.

Tootles looked wary, and pulled against her hand. Constance tightened her grasp. The others looked alarmed and Ba Ba reached for Tootles. "Now," Constance said. "Come on. Down by the creek will do."

She wanted to be away from the others before they started objecting, and not someplace where Ba Ba was likely to follow them. She knew Ba Ba would not venture down the path toward the creek; it was not steep, not difficult, but it was clearly a walk, and Ba Ba avoided walking; a water chute would have been fine for her. Constance began to walk briskly, towing Tootles along.

"All right," she said, when they had put several hundred feet between them and the group at the birdhouse. "I read Paul's biographies, several of them. You gave it to him, didn't you? After Gray Axton died, Paul came to console you. He stayed here a few weeks, and you let him believe that—that gift was transferable, like a bottle opener. Didn't you? He thinks he has your curse, doesn't he?''

"I don't know what you're talking about.''

"Don't let's play games,'' Constance said. "I know what he thinks. I know what you think. Now Toni's trying to talk Paul into giving it to her. And he's just about as unhappy and desperate as you were when you passed it on to him, isn't he? Did you pass it on in some kind of ceremony? Did Ba Ba participate?''

Tootles shook her head, her mouth set, her eyes unfocused as if scanning a very distant horizon.

Constance took her by both shoulders and forced Tootles to look at her. "There was a ceremony, wasn't there?'' Tootles brought her gaze back and nodded slightly. "I won't let it happen again, Tootles! Not to Toni. It stops here.''

Tootles drew in her breath sharply. Her voice was harsh when she spoke again. "You can't stop something like this. Don't even try. You don't know what you're getting into.''

"I can't, but you and Ba Ba can. And you will. My God, you will! I don't intend to stand by and watch another life be deranged by this . . . this superstition.''

"I can't do anything to stop it. Even if I wanted to, I don't know how. I can't make Ba Ba do anything. Forget it, Constance.''

"You can make Ba Ba do whatever you want; you always could, and you will, or I'll tell Max who messed up your artwork and why,'' Constance said.

Tootles's face blanched and she suddenly looked very old and haggard. "I don't know what you mean,'' she whispered.

"You know exactly what I mean. I haven't told anyone yet, but I know. You didn't dare go on tour with that work! And you couldn't just come out and refuse, not after Spence made all the arrangements. What would Max have thought?

What would anyone have thought? But you knew perfectly well that most of the work would be scorned." Constance took a quick breath, surprised to find herself so winded. Fury did it to her, she knew. "You messed up this murder investigation; maybe you've made it impossible to find out who killed Victoria Leeds by mixing your personal problems in with her death. Okay, that's done; I won't tell unless you force me to. But, my God, it's going to stop now! Arrange it with Ba Ba. A séance, whatever you want to call it. Invite Paul, and Toni. Don't forget Toni. And me. I want to be there. You make the arrangements yourself and let me know when." She said grimly then, "And at this . . . this séance, Ba Ba is to dismiss the muse, the spirit, whatever she calls it. Do you understand? She is to send it packing. Tell her that!"

Through this Tootles did not move; she was gazing straight ahead with an agonized expression. Color had come back to her face, but she looked ill and almost wild. "How did you guess?"

"Your note to me, the phone call, your desperation. But by the time I got here, the problem, the cause of your desperation, had vanished. You had solved your problem. Destroy the pieces, no show. Simple. The few you left intact are the ones that are good, aren't they? The others—"

"They're junk!" Tootles said harshly. "I did them after Gray died. Junk, that's all they are!" She studied Constance through narrowed eyes. "You really haven't told anyone?"

"No."

Finally Tootles nodded and without another word started back up the path to the house.

Constance breathed deeply a time or two, willing her anger to subside, before she followed. Blackmail, she thought suddenly, her fury instantly renewed; she had been driven to perpetrate blackmail!

* * *

Charlie was silent on the short drive from the condos to Tootles's road. Something, he kept thinking. Something he was missing and shouldn't be. He was surprised to see Tootles in the shade of a maple tree, leaning against the trunk, looking for all the world as if she was waiting for him. As soon as she saw that he was in the car, she straightened and waved vigorously.

"Well," he murmured to Bill Gruenwald. "Seems I'm being paged. Why don't you just let me out here? Look, if my guy in New York calls with anything about Victoria Leeds I'll pass it on, and I guess it's time to start going over the books at Musselman's company, as well as Buell's. Musselman was onto something. And it's going to take time, maybe lots and lots of time, to find out what. I sure wish we could keep this whole aspect under wraps for a while."

Gruenwald nodded in complete agreement. "We'll do what we can as quietly as we can. What I'd like right now," he said, coming to a full stop, "is to be a fly on your shoulder. Something's on her mind. See you later, Charlie."

He waved to Tootles, made a tight U-turn, and left. Tootles walked toward Charlie with her hands outstretched.

"I'm going out of my mind," she said, her voice low and husky. "Charlie, please, I have to talk to you. Let's go to the barn where no one will disturb us. Charlie, this is more than I can bear. I really feel as if I'm going to crack wide open."

He wanted to put his arms around her and pat her shoulder and stroke her back and tell her not to worry. He was startled by the intensity of his desire to help her, to comfort her. He told himself that she was an aging woman without a bit of charm, or grace, or beauty; she was coarse, and a liar, and her feet were dirty. Also she was up to something that he distrusted completely. It didn't matter, he wanted to hold and comfort her. He took her hands.

"Okay, the barn," he said. "And calm down. What's happened? What's got you so upset?"

"A murder! My life's work destroyed. Maybe my life itself destroyed. Oh, Charlie!"

She ducked her head and withdrew a hand to wipe her eyes. Now he put his arm about her shoulders and steered her across the dirt road toward the barn.

The big doors were closed; inside the barn the light was dim. There were the crates that had been roughly opened, the fronts, tops, sides ripped apart to reveal the messes inside. No one had been back here yet to clean up the mess.

She stopped a few steps inside the barn, and suddenly she bowed her head and buried her face in her hands and sobbed. This time he did hold her close while she wept.

"I didn't realize how hard it would hit me, coming back here," she said in a choking voice a few seconds later. "I just wasn't thinking. I'm sorry. I'm all right now."

She groped in her pockets for a tissue and blew her nose, and then walked away from him, to the far end of the building where there was another narrow door. She opened it and stood in the doorway, taking great long breaths.

With her back to him, she said, "Charlie, will you please take Constance and leave? We made a mistake in hiring you. I'll explain it to Max. I talked a long time with our lawyer today, and he's sure the police don't have enough of a case even to pretend to arrest me."

He had moved closer in order to hear her softly spoken words. "If Max fires us, we'll probably take off," he said. "Why, Tootles? Why do you want that?"

She shook her head, still facing away from him. "You can't understand what my life's been like. You're so orderly, you and Constance, so very much together, so happy with each other. I've never had that, Charlie, not for more than a few months at a time, and then only a few times. Half a dozen months in a whole lifetime! That's what I've had. I have a chance now with Max. Maybe we can make it last. But you have to leave, and Constance has to leave, or it will fall apart again. You're . . . you're a disturbing man, Charlie. I had no idea how disturbing you could still be."

Roughly he took her by the shoulders and pulled her around to face him. "Knock it off, goddamn it! What are you up to?"

She looked straight at him and made no motion to pull free; her hands hung down at her sides. Abruptly he released his grasp of her shoulders and backed away a step, then another.

"I meant what I said, Charlie. I want you out of here as soon as possible. Both of you. She knows how I feel, the attraction I feel, and she . . . she is trying to force me to do something I absolutely must not do, something that will drive Max and me apart, and she understands that very well. Take her away, Charlie. Please. I need this one last chance with Max, one last chance to make some kind of life for myself finally. Charlie, please!"

She did not touch him, did not lean toward him, or make any overt motion, but he felt surrounded by her, within a circle that was Tootles so that no matter which way he looked, which way he turned, how he reached out, he would collide with her.

He shook his head. "Tell me the rest of it," he said, his voice harsh to his own ears. "What does she want you to do?"

"Hold a séance with Ba Ba," she whispered. "And Max won't have it. He really won't tolerate that sort of thing. She has it in her head that Toni is in some kind of danger, and that Ba Ba and I can do something about it by means of a séance. Charlie, I haven't done anything like that since I was a kid. And Ba Ba nearly had a nervous breakdown years ago, fooling around with the occult. It could be dangerous for her. I don't know what's got into Constance's head, why she brought this up. I don't understand, but she says if I don't do it, she'll turn Max against me, and she can. She knows how. She's so clever that way. She knows so much about me.''

Charlie had turned to ice. A moment earlier he had been afraid to move, for fear of coming into contact with her; now he could not move even if he had wanted to. Ba Ba and Tootles in their apartment, he was remembering with a sense of dread and fear, summoning something, striking fear into him with their intensity, their belief. And Constance was using her awareness of that incident from his past in some sort of scheme that she had not even bothered to tell him about. She knew he would not go along with anything like that; she knew, and chose to go around him, bypass him, tackle Tootles head-on by herself. Why?

He felt betrayed, and strangely humiliated. Why? he asked himself again. She didn't believe any more than he did that Tootles had had anything to do with Victoria's death, or Musselman's. Why was she harassing Tootles with such an insane demand, believing her to be innocent? Jealousy? He did not accept that, not for a second. There never had been cause for jealousy between them in either direction. If he had not told her about that stupid incident that had terrified him so, she would not have thought of this, he felt certain, and his sense of betrayal and humiliation arose from that knowledge. In some way she was using his past fear.

If this was all a lie of Tootles's, then what for? She must know he would get to the bottom of it. Like most liars, she built her castles on a grain of truth; the truth was that Constance was holding something over Tootles, something big enough to make Tootles appeal to him for help. He believed that was the germ of truth here. If it had anything to do with Toni, or if it threatened Tootles's marriage to Max, or if Max would not tolerate a séance, or Babar was a basket case, none of that seemed to matter. Details. Constance, apparently, intended to force Tootles to hold a séance with her screwball sister Babar; that was the only important thing Tootles had said.

The very idea of it filled him with a deep fear.

Suddenly Tootles put her hand on his arm. "Charlie," she whispered, "I'm sorry. I didn't know this would hurt you so much. I'm so sorry. Just take her home and forget all this. You will, you know. Let the police deal with the murder, get back to your own lives. I won't forget you, Charlie. I won't forget."

Her touch freed him from the block of ice that had encased him completely. He turned to walk back through the barn. "We'd better get to the house."

"You haven't answered me," she said from the open door, a dark silhouette against the bright light.

He nodded. "I know," he said. At the moment he didn't have an answer. He only had questions. When he left the barn she was still standing at the door at the far end.

Fifteen

Charlie found Constance with a small group of young people who were not officially students on the back porch of Tootles's house, eating sandwiches, drinking iced tea, talking. Constance patted a wicker sofa where she had saved him a seat. He shook his head, helped himself to a sandwich, and sat on the top step trying to be unobtrusive. He decided he had succeeded; the boy who had been talking had not paused.

"I said, I agree. You hear me this time? We're all born creative, I give you that much. I've read some of those tests on newborn babies, on preschool children, and so on. I admit up front that something happens to squelch it real early. What I said was that a *good* study would find out first why it doesn't get burned out in everyone if the pressures are all the same in a family, for instance, and, two, why really creative people so often don't do a thing with it."

The other boy shook his head. "That's where you get off the track. You have to make a value judgment about what is or isn't creative. What you really mean is that a lot of people don't do anything with it that the rest of the world is willing to pay money for. A weaver weaving can be creative, a cook cooking, a gardener producing a beautiful garden . . ."

"Bull shit!" the first boy said. "Let me tell you about my grandmother. She knitted endless booties and scarves and God knows what all, all beautiful, really expert. Creative? Maybe, but she sure would have preferred to be a concert pianist, her ambition at one time, and then marriage, kids, life got in the way. Now and then she played the piano, not very often, and it was terrible to hear her. She would goof up and cry, start over, goof up, and on and on, over and over. I say that's how it is with most of your creative folks, they're hurting to make a real contribution, settling for a pretty cake, or a nice arrangement of roses, or a good paint job on a model car . . . like having your whole body burning with fever and sprinkling a drop of water here or there and making do with it."

He had become very flushed as he talked. Abruptly he lifted his sandwich and took a massive bite.

Toni had not moved during all this. She held a partly eaten sandwich that she seemed to have forgotten. "You have to keep coming back to the capital letters, don't you?" she said softly. "You're talking about creativity with a capital C. Creativity versus creativity; capital A Art versus art."

Charlie found himself thinking déjà vu, the scene he had walked out on thirty years ago, playing itself over again, this time without Tootles, but her input was there, shaping the direction the conversation had taken. Or maybe there really wasn't any other way to talk about what they were talking about.

"It's like the Major Arcana in the Tarot deck," Toni said. "Once they show up, the forces acting on you are outside yourself, uncontrollable. Once you start talking about capital C Creativity or capital A Art you're talking about forces from outside that are uncontrollable, that demand obedience if you want recognition. A pretty garden or a nice scarf can't bring recognition of the sort we're talking about here. A good piece of Art can."

"Even bad Art can," the first boy said. "Most Art is bad,

of course. You know the rule; ninety percent of everything is crap, but it gets the recognition and respect it should have as long as you don't cop out."

Constance knew that Charlie would be ready to leave as soon as he finished his sandwich; this was the kind of talk that sent him off in a dead run usually. It had not surprised her to have him choose the step instead of the seat next to her; to have joined her he would have had to walk through the small clump sitting near the table with the food; it might have broken up the conversation. That had been her first reaction to his sitting over there; now she realized, however, that he was looking at her with exactly the same interest and neutrality that he was showing all the others. He was looking at her no more or less than at the others, and she felt he was trying to figure her out exactly as he would try to figure out any stranger who happened across his path.

Charlie was unaware of her scrutiny. He had been thinking about recognition, the importance some people placed on it. Max saying Tootles deserved recognition, attaching more importance to it than to money. Charlie knew theater people who would never dream of going to Hollywood or working for television; they needed the instant feedback of a live audience, the recognition of their talent, their skill, now, instantly. They said television people played to the sponsor, who didn't give a damn what they did as long as they kept an audience and sold product; movie people played to one person, the director. For some people neither of those options was enough although the money might be very good. Delayed recognition was not enough, either. These young people were giving each other the recognition they all needed, getting it from Tootles, finding it enough for a time, until they were ready to take on the rest of the world. *Which one would succeed out there?* he found himself wondering, looking from one young face to another.

"Your grandmother is a good example of what we were talking about a while ago," one of the boys said. "I mean, for every one who makes it, who doesn't cop out, there are thousands of others with more talent, more skill, more training who don't make it. By itself Creativity is nothing, worthless."

Toni was nodding emphatically. "Luck is what we usually fall back on, but that isn't it, either. Luck is important, but without the other kind of help, no luck or talent or work or determination will put you over the edge."

Her impassioned words were followed by a silence that became prolonged as the young artists all seemed to have turned their attention inward, to contemplate something that had not yet been named.

"What will, then?" Constance asked softly.

Toni turned toward her with a distant look. She opened her mouth and then snapped her lips together hard, and instead of speaking, she shrugged.

It was over, Constance realized with regret, as the boys got up, dusting off their shorts. She had felt compelled to ask, and for a second she had thought there might be an answer. "We'd best be on our way," she said to Charlie. "You'll give Tootles our number, won't you?" she reminded Toni who was standing up, stretching. Constance remembered thinking how Toni was the responsible one; Janet had been the bopper. And how they together reminded her of her own daughter although neither of them had done so singly.

"Oh, sure," Toni said. "No problem. We're off to hang the birdhouse, I guess. When she comes back, I'll tell her."

Toni watched them leave. Constance at the wheel, Charlie slouched down in the passenger seat. As soon as the Volvo was out of sight, she stopped pretending any interest in the silly birdhouse Roger had put together. They all knew he had needed to hammer and pound, and do something with his hands; that had been understood, and they had accepted the monstrosity he had built, but it should now languish in some dark place in the barn.

She wandered back inside the house restlessly. She inspected the dry-erase board, and added Constance's motel number to the other messages, making a heavy black circle around it to attract attention in the hodgepodge of messages already there. She was in the studio a few minutes later when Spence arrived with a dapper little man who looked like the model for the groom on the wedding cake. His cheeks were very pink, his hands delicate and pale. Spence looked like a thug beside him.

"Where's Marion?" Spence asked, at the studio door. The other man was beside him, eyeing everything with great curiosity.

"Taking a walk." Spence had said he would bring out the man from the insurance company, and she knew that Marion had no intention of seeing him. She guessed that Marion had gone all the way to the end of the woods to her little retreat, and that she would stay there until she was certain this man had seen what he needed to see and had gone again. Spence could show him whatever he wanted, she had said before leaving.

In a short while Spence came back alone, and called in to her, "He's gone. If you see Marion tell her the coast is clear."

She grinned. Spence understood Marion better than anyone else on earth, she was certain.

"What's that mean?" Marion's voice floated into the studio then. "Was someone here? Who'd I miss?"

Spence laughed. "I want a drink. You too?"

"Well, maybe, but a small one . . ." Their voices faded to inaudibility.

Toni lay down on the couch in the studio, not to sleep, but only to relax, to rest. The thought of falling asleep out in the open like this made her shudder. She had nailed her window screens in place, and at night she locked her door and wedged a chair under the knob, and still lay awake rigid and fearful hour after hour. But all this would end, she told herself repeatedly, and then what? She tried to think through the next few days, the next months. . . . The house would fill up again, she knew, remembering the mob who had been here when she first arrived. Twelve, fourteen? She didn't even know how many there had been, all talking, all busy. It would be like that again, and this time she wanted to be right here, in the middle of it all, working, critiquing, being critiqued. But first she wanted Paul Volte to come back, because if he didn't return, she would have to go to New York, and she was reluctant to do that, although she would. She had lived in New York for nearly five years, an interlude that she felt now had been snipped out of her life; New York was like a nearly forgotten dream, without value, without interest except for Paul Volte, and if he did not come back, she would go to him. This had to be soon, she knew, without being able to say why or how it could be done, or even if Paul would change his mind and cooperate. All that seemed minor detail-arranging. It would happen, here or in New York.

She had not intended to sleep, but she came awake with a rush of fear that subsided as she recognized Max's voice: "What are you talking about? I don't understand a thing you're saying."

"She will destroy us," Marion said hoarsely. "I can feel it coming. From what she said it seems inevitable. If not me, then you, or even Johnny. It's like a big black cloud hanging there. I want you to fire them both and tell them to leave, no more questions, no more insinuations. Let the sheriff do his job. He's being paid by the government, let him earn it. Or the state police. I thought they had taken charge of the investigation. They have the resources, the manpower to get to the bottom of this without private detectives. Fire them, Max. For my sake. For yours. I wanted to do it, but I can't. You're the one who hired them, they won't pay any attention to me."

There was prolonged silence. Toni realized they were in the small office down the hall from the studio; that door was open, the studio door was open. Even if they had glanced in here, she had been hidden by the back of the couch. Now she did not dare move.

"Honey," Max said finally, "I don't know what in hell's happened between you and Constance, but if you want them out, that's okay with me. Let me talk to Knowlton first, though. It doesn't have to be this minute."

Knowlton was their lawyer, Toni knew, the one who said they needed outside help. He had been very happy with the choice of Constance and Charlie, she understood. She strained to hear what Marion was saying.

"No, of course not this minute. Just very soon. And, Max, promise me something. Promise me you won't talk to her, you won't let her ask you any more questions, or have anything to do with her."

"Damn it, Marion, you've got to tell me what she said! Has she threatened you? Does she think you're involved, after all?"

"No! No, nothing like that. She knows I'm not. It's. . . not me, not you. It's us, the family, everything we've put together, all in danger of crumbling to dust—"

"Jesus Christ!" Spence's gravelly voice interrupted her. "You're talking like a soap-opera queen. It's not good enough, Marion. Even if Max bows out, I'm involved, too, you know. I won't fire them. Goddamn it! You're the only suspect the police have, remember?"

"This is all your fault!" Marion yelled harshly. "You and that stupid show! Why don't you butt out of my life and leave me alone? I don't need you and I haven't needed you for years. Butt out and leave me alone!" Her heavy footsteps pounded down the uncarpeted hallway.

"Shit," Spence muttered. Toni could scarcely hear when

he continued, "Sorry about all this, Max. You were handling her just fine. I should have kept my mouth shut."

"Forget it. Do you know what Constance said to start this?"

"Nope. Something Marion doesn't want told, something Constance has ferreted out that she wants buried again. God knows what. Marion usually couldn't care less who says what about her."

"Well, come on. Let's see where she's got to."

Toni lay without motion for a long time after the voices were gone. Constance, she thought, she would be the one to find out things. She remembered how freely they all had talked to her before Victoria's death. She had, and Paul, Spence, all of them, even Max and Johnny. She was so easy to talk to, so understanding. She bit her lip and finally sat up, got up. What had Constance found out?

Constance drove well, careful but not anxious about it; most of the time she stayed right at the speed limit, only now and then exceeding it a little. Her silence was not because she had to concentrate on the road or the car or traffic; it was because she had not yet decided how to tell Charlie what she had done or why. His silence was just as deep; he was searching for a way to tell her he knew she was trying to coerce Tootles to do something he considered if not obscene, then very close to it, and there simply was no good way to say that.

There were silences and silences between them, and most of the time the silences were as companionable as the conversations, but this was a different kind of quiet that had come between them. Too uncomfortable for him to endure. He cleared his throat and said, "Max had Spence put the touring show together."

"Ah," she said, not surprised.

"He paid for all the galleries. Hired them, rented them, whatever they do."

She nodded.

"Tootles doesn't know a thing about that," he finished. "I told Max I didn't see any reason for her to find out."

Constance glanced at him, then faced the road again. "You remember 'The Gift of the Magi'? You must have read it in school."

He blinked and shook his head. "Give me a hint."

"Oh, it's a lovely little story about a man and wife very much in love but too poor to buy each other Christmas presents."

"Gotcha," he said then. "The long gorgeous hair, the special comb or brush or something."

She nodded. "That's it. Max and Tootles are reenacting it, aren't they?"

"You wouldn't want to give me a little more than that, would you?" His voice was very dry.

She laughed softly. "Tootles messed up that artwork herself, Charlie. She had no intention of taking it on the road because she knew if any critics went to see it, they would pan most of it. She knows very well that she hasn't done work worth showing for many years. But Max doesn't know that, and she can't bear for him to find out she's not the genius he sees. She needs his respect, his adulation even, and this show could have blown it away, or so she thinks. That's what she was so desperate to talk about, it explains the note on the invitation, the phone call, the problem she couldn't see a solution to. Then she did, I'm afraid."

He whistled, thought it over, and finally nodded. "I think you've got it. She could have been working on it ever since they started boxing up the stuff. They boxed it up by day and she messed it up at night. That explains the nutty screws. She loosened them enough to draw attention to them, not because she ran out of time. I bet Palance was supposed to find the mess on Monday when he got back from his camping trip. Wow, thumbscrews wouldn't make her own up to it, would they?"

178

"Are you kidding?"

He looked at her profile, then back to the road. That was what she had on Tootles, and it was strong enough to make Tootles react. The gift of the magi, he thought, nodding at the appropriateness. Max couldn't tell Tootles he had arranged the tour, and she couldn't tell him that her work didn't deserve a tour. Those poor stupid jerks, he added almost savagely.

"You know we can't keep that under the table," he said after another few seconds of thought. "It makes a difference, after all, in how we plot a murder. A whole block of time doesn't need factoring in any more."

"I know," Constance admitted. "But I don't know anything for certain. I didn't actually ask Tootles, and she didn't actually say she had done it."

"How careful were you not to put it into words?" he asked, looking at her profile again. He saw a very small suggestion of a smile twitch her lips and vanish almost instantly.

"I don't think I know what you mean," she said, and turned off the road to the access street for their motel. She looked at him with a bright gaze of absolute innocence.

Her eyes widened then and she grimaced. "Damn," she said. "Just damn. You know what we did? We left our suitcase in the sheriff's car. My new clothes. Your toothbrush. Everything we took to New York, or bought there."

"I imagine he'll be around," Charlie said. "Let's order a pot of coffee up in our room and talk our way through this whole mess. You game for that?"

For the next hour or so, they talked, paced their room, drank coffee, made notes, talked some more.

Finally Charlie tossed down the pencil he had been chewing, and went to the window. The coffee pot was empty; his stomach was rebelling, probably not from the coffee as much as from that sandwich earlier instead of a decent lunch, he thought morosely. It was four in the afternoon.

"It's a bigger mess than ever," he said, watching a yellow station wagon maneuver in the parking lot; the driver had made too wide a turn and was backing up ineptly now. Charlie bet with himself that after another try or two the driver would give up on that spot and find a different one.

"Well, maybe not a bigger mess," Constance said, as frustrated as he was, "but certainly a different mess. It seems to me that Tootles must be completely out of the running as a suspect."

"And Max is in," Charlie said, facing her again. "If Musselman found something on him, or the condo, he sure is in."

Constance was digging around her in her purse; she brought out a notebook and flipped through it, then stopped. He watched silently. "Some questions I asked myself a day or so ago," she said. "Like this one: How long would it have taken to mess up the artwork? Now it doesn't matter if that gets answered or not; it doesn't make any difference since she had all the time in the world. And the mystery of where Tootles went, that's another question I can redline. I suppose directly to the barn where she loosened the screws, and finished up whatever she felt still needed doing. Hm."

Charlie waited but when it seemed she was not going to comment beyond that uninformative *hmm,* he cleared his throat. "Well?"

She glanced at him, then back to her notebook. "Why didn't Paul stay with Victoria? That's so sad, and such a waste!"

"Well?" he asked. "You have an answer, don't you?"

"Not one you'll like," she said. "You know when I was at the library, it was to look up Paul. I told you that, didn't I?"

"So?"

"Let me just read the cold hard dates of various things in

his life," she said, and started to flip through the notebook again. "Here it is. In 1972, the year Tootles's lover died in Vietnam and *Seven Kinds of Death* was a success, Paul had his first success, about ten months after hers. His first articles were very well received, and his wife left him. In 1975, he won a Chicago literary prize for his first book, and got the job he still has. Not the Pulitzer, but prestigious. Two months later, his father had a fatal stroke. In 1980 his second book was a hit, bigger than the first, and his fiancée died. In 1984 he met Victoria and started the new book that's won so many awards now."

Charlie was staring at her in fascination and disbelief. "You don't buy that there's a connection, I hope," he said when she became silent.

"It doesn't matter one way or the other. It's what he believes. What Tootles believes."

"Right," he said, not quite snapping. "I have a question. How are you going to link all that stuff with Victoria's murder?"

"That's a good one," she said and wrote it down. She looked at him with an almost vacant gaze. "Here's another one. Who put that letter in Paul's room for Victoria?"

"Inside job, all right," Charlie said morosely. "Everyone, all the help, deny knowing anything about it." He frowned. "We don't even know if the note the police found was the same one she received that day."

Constance nodded. "The big question is where did Victoria Leeds go that afternoon? With whom?"

Charlie turned back to the window broodingly. The inept driver was gone, the station wagon safely parked in a different slot.

"You haven't said anything about how Musselman died," Constance said after a few seconds.

"There's nothing to say. Just another death, another dollar, another day. He left his Washington office, and drove out to the condo that afternoon without mentioning to anyone where he was going or why. No one gave it a thought. Next, the watchman found his body at the base of Applegate. It was raining hard. Period.''

She was studying his back; something was very wrong, but she could get nothing more than that. Something was wrong. He was too stiff, too distant. Sometimes a case did that to him, but not when there were still so many things that could be learned. This case was still poised at an intersection; it could take off in half a dozen different directions, not a cause for despair just yet.

Usually she could rely on her intuition to guide her in a situation that could become sticky; this time she couldn't because she had not yet told him what she was planning, and there was no way she could tell him that, not yet. He had gone so stiff at her recitation of Paul Volte's career, and his tragedies; that was merely a warm-up, she was afraid, of his reaction when she finally came to tell him everything. First she had to sort it through by herself, find the exactly right way to bring it up, the exactly right nuance of voice, mannerism, attitude. Meanwhile, he was distant, cool, aware that something was missing, something was wrong, and unable any more than she was to do anything about it yet.

Charlie was thinking that if he had met her with a question as soon as possible this afternoon, if he had just said outright, *what the hell are you up to?* then she would have said *what do you mean?* and he would have said he'd had a talk with Tootles, and maybe he could have mentioned her appeal for him to silence Constance, take her away. Then she would have told him what she was planning, and everything would be out, aboveboard, but now, hours later, it was becoming more impossible by the second to discuss any of that. He couldn't explain Tootles to himself, much less to anyone else, even Constance. He could think of no way to bring up that dizzy episode with Tootles in the barn, to try to explain what he had said, what she had said, because now it would sound as if they had met to discuss Constance. Somehow the whole thing had a repellent feel to it that had not been there before. Good old Tootles, he thought sourly.

He swung around then to say, "Let's give the sheriff a call, see if he's free to be wined and dined, and if he'll let us have a go at everything he's gathered to date, starting with Musselman. I keep feeling that we're missing something, and not just our suitcases. Maybe he didn't miss whatever it is even if he isn't aware of it yet."

Sixteen

The sheriff's office was forty-seven miles away, too far, he said, for them to drive and then have to drive back. He met them halfway in the little resort village of Potomac Acres. It was a pleasant drive through gentle woods alternating with lush farmland. They met the sheriff at a restaurant. He had brought a packet that included copies of the various reports he had gathered so far. No point in sitting in his office, which was not all that comfortable, he said almost abashedly; they could read the stuff back in their motel. He would have delivered the same packet to them the next day, he said, if they had asked. No one mentioned the fact that the state investigators had practically told him to go fishing, stay out of the way, get lost, let the big boys handle all this.

At their table, waiting for service, they talked about the weather, which had become hotter and muggier, a storm in the making, he said. Not until after they had placed their orders, and finally were eating, did he mention that he had started the paper hunt for any possible irregularity about the condo financing or building codes, everything he could put together.

"We're being quiet about it," he said over a dinner of

shish kebab. "What with the shaky S and L's, and people scared about their own banks the way they are, we don't want any more uneasiness than necessary." The fact that he was doing this without authorization, and without the knowledge of the state investigators, was not mentioned. "The old man's clean as a whistle from all accounts," he said. "John Buell is an unknown factor, he's not even a full partner, just an employee. We're running a routine credit check on him, but we don't expect much to turn up. Back to the old man, never any company or personal debts that didn't get paid on time, no financial troubles that anyone knows about, no trouble with employees, never a complaint about shoddy construction, nothing. I doubt we'll find anything worth toting home."

Charlie sipped his retsina and rolled the pine-pitch flavor around in his mouth; there seemed to be no liquid, just the biting taste of fumes. Constance had said no very firmly at the wine choice, and had settled for a red wine that probably was okay, he thought, but not really authentic. On the other hand, her moussaka looked better than his lamb grill. He drank more wine. He was half-listening to Bill Gruenwald tell Constance about his ex, who had split when their child was two and was first diagnosed as autistic. The child was in the hospital part of the time, at home with him part time. She was beautiful, he said.

Charlie listened, let his mind drift back to the murders, returned to listen again. No doubt, the sheriff was right about the Buell company. Everywhere they turned, they seemed to run into a wall: wrong times, no one person available for the right period, or if anyone was available, there was no motive conceivable.

"For instance," he muttered, "no one in the house could have killed Victoria, and yet it had to be someone from inside." And, he continued under his breath, aware that it didn't matter what he said since no one was paying attention anyway, no one from that bunch, except Max and

Johnny, could have helped Musselman off the roof. But neither of them could have killed Victoria although anyone could have left the note on Paul's pillow. Not just anyone, he corrected. Anyone from the household, or the hired help. "And you know damn well," he muttered, this time breaking the skin of silence that seemed to separate him from Constance and Bill Gruenwald, "whoever left the note had to have access both to the house and the stationery, and to the typewriter in the condo." Constance and Bill Gruenwald stopped talking and looked at him. "Why roof?" he wondered out loud. "Why not the sixth-floor balcony?" He considered that: the sixth-floor unit again, but why not? Or the fifth?

"Did you check any of the apartments when Musselman took his dive?" he asked Gruenwald.

The sheriff shook his head. "No reason to," he said. "Musselman was on the roof; he left a raincoat up there. Must have been carrying it and put it down, or dropped it."

Charlie asked softly, "Where did he put it down, Bill? Why? Wasn't it raining pretty hard?"

Gruenwald looked unhappy again, the way he did every time Charlie asked about that investigation. He patted his neat mustache, as if afraid it had bristled. "It was raining off and on all day. I don't know why he wasn't wearing it. We found it on part of the housing for the elevator shaft. Look," he pulled a notebook from his pocket and sketched quickly. "This is the layout of the roof. Elevator housing at each end, stairs in the same housing. This end had the door open, not the deluxe apartment side, but this one by the common elevators. We figured he went up the regular elevator maybe to six and took the stairs to the roof. Maybe the rain had let up again. He put his coat down and went to the far side. And maybe he leaned over too far, or his foot slipped; like I said, there was a lot of water up there, and some mud in places. Charlie, that's all we have on it. It seemed like enough at the time." He took a long drink from his stein of beer and set it down heavily. "You tell me why you want the sixth-floor apartment."

"Because you can't tell much about a leaky roof while it's raining if the roof is standing in water. You check the ceilings below, and wait for the water to run off, and then you bring in a licensed roofer. But if he was there to see someone, and if he was pushed, it doesn't make much sense for him and someone else to hold a conference in the rain even if it was intermittent. Better have it indoors on the side where he was found, and that's the sixth-, or fifth-, maybe even the fourth-floor apartment, but then it starts to get chancier to get the right kind of decision about a tumble from the police, the medical examiner. You know, the pros." This was not quite a mocking tone, but too close. He regretted it instantly and lifted his wine again.

Gruenwald shook his head. "That narrows it down to Max Buell, John Buell, the superintendent Ditmar, or maybe one of the foremen. And none of them could have killed Victoria Leeds. Those apartments were all kept locked except when the workmen were in them, and they weren't that afternoon, and the Buells, father and son, had left. That would mean two separate murder cases, one as cold as an icehouse."

"Locked? Why?"

Gruenwald sighed and looked to Constance as if seeking help. She offered none. "Okay," he said. "Locked because there were expensive fixtures in place already. And because the Buells had already started to use Six A as an office, with the table and typewriter up there, blueprints, stuff like that. Things they didn't want anyone messing with."

"Musselman might have had the key," Charlie pointed out, and Sheriff Gruenwald looked chagrined. Charlie shrugged.

"You said the Buells had left. Together?"

"No. Max went to Marion's about four thirty or so. Johnny left right after that, to drive back to the city where he has an apartment. He seldom stays at Marion's. You know, the girlfriend.''

Suddenly Constance remembered the evening that Paul and Victoria had arrived at Tootles's house, virtually ignoring each other. Victoria had been carrying an overnight bag, her purse over her shoulder, and a red-jacketed book with a paper sticking out. She had put down the suitcase in the foyer and had put the book on a long low table with a clutter of things on it. When Constance followed them up the stairs a little later, Victoria had had the suitcase, and her purse, but not the book.

''Do you have an inventory of Victoria's things from Tootles's house?'' she asked, causing both men to looked surprised at the abrupt turn. ''Maybe you can remember,'' she said slowly. ''A book with a red dust jacket. She was carrying it when she got there, and when she went upstairs she wasn't. I just wondered if it turned up again.''

''I'm almost sure not,'' Gruenwald said, after thinking for a second or two, checking off items on a mental list apparently. ''What about the book?''

''I don't know,'' she said. ''I didn't see the title. There was a paper sticking out of it, notebook paper, with writing on it. I wonder if she made notes on the plane, or in the car, and stuck them in the book she was carrying. That's all.''

''Would you recognize it again?'' Charlie asked.

She nodded.

''Well,'' he said. ''Well. Bill, you game for a visit to Tootles's house tonight?''

The sheriff looked resigned. He glanced at his watch. ''I have a few things to do, and then with the drive over, it'll be near ten. That's getting pretty late.'' His unhappiness was increasing moment by moment.

''We can go look for it,'' Constance said. ''We can let you know in the morning if we find anything. I have to talk to Tootles tonight, so we'll be going over anyway.''

The sheriff was shaking his head regretfully. It was one

thing to let them see statements, he said, and quite another for them to gather evidence themselves. He would meet them at the house. He looked at Charlie and added, "And wait, okay? Don't start anything without me."

His tone was pleasant, but it was not a simple request; it most definitely was an order. Charlie grinned and shrugged.

Toni was in the office that had once been a dinette, holding the phone with one hand, tracing a pattern in the wood grain of the window sill with the other, while she listened to the telephone ring in Paul's apartment. Dusk had fallen, bringing with it a stillness in the air that was not peaceful tonight, but more like the low pressure that preceded a storm. All afternoon the humidity had been building, the oppression of the air had increased, and now this breath-holding hush that was not natural had descended. Toni was counting rings. At ten she would hang up, or maybe twelve. But at nine Paul Volte answered.

"It's Toni Townsend," she said in a low voice; she had planned to sound frightened, anxious, and found there was no need to pretend. She was frightened and anxious. "Paul, can you come back, tomorrow if possible?"

"What's happened?" He sounded even more anxious.

She shook her head. "I'm sorry. I didn't mean to scare you. Nothing really, and yet . . . I don't know what's happening. Marion wants to fire Constance and her husband, the detectives. She had a fight with Constance, I think. But I don't really know. Anyway, that will just leave the sheriff and the state police here, and they think she did it, and I guess they'll arrest her, or something."

"Is Max going along with her?"

"I guess so. He can't tell her no and make it stick. If this is what she wants, he'll do it. Spence doesn't want to, but they'll make him, I know. There's no reason for him to hold out. But the two of you could. I know if you were here to back up Spence, he'd keep them working on this. I . . . I'm really afraid for her, Paul. You know, she's so smart about so many things, but she's acting crazy about this. She's being so dumb. I'm sure she doesn't realize that she's in danger. And if Constance has really found out things, this is the worst possible time to fire her. Paul, we need to have all this over, done with. Can you come?"

They talked only another minute or two; he hung up first, and before she could replace her handset, she heard the telltale click of another phone on her line. She drew in a sharp breath and closed her eyes hard; what had she said, what had he said? Her hand that had been holding the phone was wet; her mouth was dry. Finally she turned toward the door to see Spence standing there, leaning against the door frame.

"What the hell do you think you're up to?" he demanded.

"Trying to save Marion," she said fiercely. "If no one else cares, I do."

Spence was studying her openly the way he might study an art object whose authenticity he questioned. He straightened and started to leave, then paused a moment. "Toni, sweetie, if I were you, I'd be awfully careful about not letting on that my ears were bigger than anyone realized. Know what I mean?"

She watched him walk away. His back was very broad and strong-looking; he kept in good shape, like someone who worked out often and regularly. She shivered and at the same moment a gust of wind blew hard against the screened window, entered the room, stirred dust, stirred her hair, made the hairs on her arms stand up; she hugged herself hard. Just the one gust blew now, and when it was gone, everything seemed even quieter than before. Her shivering increased, as if with a deep chill. Who had been listening? Not Spence. There were phones all over the house; anyone could have lifted one in time to overhear her call.

She left the office and went into the bathroom and washed her face with cold water. When she returned to the hall, she

could hear the low mumble of voices from the studio—
Roger, Bob, Jason, maybe one or two more from Claud's
classes. She should have gone to check out everyone instantly, she thought then. By now whoever had listened
would be far from any telephone, probably. Resolutely she
started to walk toward the main part of the house, the living
room, and Marion. She had to tell her before someone else
did, or before Marion brought it up, if she had been the one
on the other phone.

Marion and Ba Ba were both reading; Spence was wandering around the room studying one piece of work after
another. He stopped and put his hands in his pockets when
Toni walked in. She could hear Max and Johnny talking
over some business problem in the adjoining room, the
television room, they called it, although no one ever seemed
to turn on the set. Max and Johnny had been discussing
some problem all evening. Toni drew in a deep breath and
then said cheerfully, "Paul is coming back tomorrow for a
day or two. I was just talking to him."

Spence grinned at her. She lifted her chin with defiance
and sat down close to Marion. *Seven Kinds of Death* was still
in the center of the room, as if it had become a permanent
part of the furnishings. Any day now an ashtray might
appear balanced on it somewhere, or a glass with melting
ice cubes.

"Did he say why?" Marion asked. "What does he want
now?"

Toni shrugged and did not dare look at Spence. "He's
worried," she said. Then swiftly she said, "I told him you
were letting Charlie and Constance go and that alarms him,
I think."

"For God's sake!" Marion exclaimed, jumping to her
feet. "Why is it that everyone is taking it as a sacred duty to
butt into my business? What do you mean, talking about me
with Paul? Who do you think you are? Isn't that a touch
presumptuous, you little ninny?"

Toni leaped up and cried, "I did it for you, Marion! You don't seem to realize that they could arrest you! You're the first one they picked, and nothing's happened to make them change their minds. And, yes, it's presumptuous! I know that. I'll leave in the morning if you tell me to."

Ridiculous, she wanted to scream. She was crying like a baby, tears streaming, nose running, her voice choked and thick. Suddenly Marion put her arms around Toni, stroked her hair, saying, "Shh. Shh. There, there." And she was crying harder than ever.

"Constance won't hurt you," she said in her choking voice. "She likes you too much to hurt you. And she's smart. Let her find out who did it and end all of this. What would we all do if anything happened to you?" It came out in bits and pieces, interrupted by gasps for air, interrupted by shuddering inhalations and exhalations, interrupted by having to blow her nose, and then by hiccups. And all the while Marion held her and stroked her hair, her back.

"I'm sorry, baby," Marion said finally when Toni came to a stop. "I'm so sorry. I didn't realize how upset you were. You've been so good, so calm and collected, holding it all back. Let it out, baby. That's all right. Just let go."

Toni wept harder. She was not at all sure when the act had stopped, when she lost it, but now she could not seem to control herself at all. She leaned into Marion and let herself be held and babied, and she sobbed.

At the door Charlie tightened his grasp on Constance's hand, as they stood silently watching. Across the room in the doorway to the television room Max and Johnny were watching, as was Spence Dwyers at the far wall, and Babar sitting on the edge of a chair, her mouth opened slightly. Toni wept; Marion murmured to her, and no one else moved.

How long this had been going on Charlie didn't know, and how long it might have continued he couldn't guess, but it was interrupted at that moment by the sound of bois-terous voices behind him.

"You chowderhead! Give it back!"

A boy came running from the studio wing; he was carry-ing a sketchpad. Behind him a second boy was tearing after him, yelling. They came to a stop when they saw Charlie and Constance. The one in front grinned and said hi, the other one grabbed for the sketchpad, and they both turned and walked back the way they had come. As soon as they reached the turn in the hall, the chase resumed; pounding footsteps thundered on the uncarpeted floor.

Toni had pulled away from Marion at the noise; when she saw Charlie and Constance in the doorway, she turned scar-let, ducked her head, and raced past them, ran up the stairs. In her shorts and tank top, blushing furiously, she looked like a child fleeing punishment.

"Well," Charlie said then as he and Constance entered the room. "We were passing by, the door was open, and here we are. Hello, all. How's tricks, Tootles?"

She glared at him and didn't even glance at Constance. "Too bad you wasted your time. I'm going to bed."

"What a shame," Charlie said. "You'll miss the sheriff. We'll give him your regards."

She stopped all motion. "The sheriff is coming? Why? Now what?"

Charlie shrugged. "I guess he'll tell you when he gets here." He pretended not to notice that Constance was roam-ing the room glancing at stacks of books, books on shelves, on tables, some on the floor.

"Will you tell your wife that this isn't a public library?" Tootles snapped, and sat down again.

"Well, I don't have to wait up for the sheriff," Ba Ba said and heaved herself up from the chair; it was not easy for her.

Constance had gone nearly all the way around the room. She smiled at Max and Johnny and walked past them. "Ba Ba," she said, "are you going to be around all weekend?"

Ba Ba glanced swiftly at Tootles, then at Max. "I don't know. Why?"

"I might have a party, and I'd really like for you to come."

"A party! My God, are you insane? A party?"

"Well, a very special party, and for very few people. You're all invited, of course, and Paul will be as soon as I can reach him."

"Is that why he's coming?" Ba Ba asked.

Constance was examining a few books that were holding a pottery bowl. She straightened and said, "So he's already planning to come? How nice. When?"

"Toni said tomorrow. But if you asked him . . . did you ask him yet?"

Constance shook her head. "I will when he gets here."

"Tell her, Max," Tootles said harshly then. She was sitting stiffly, her fingers drumming the arm of her chair, one foot tapping furiously. "Just tell her what we decided."

"Well now," Max said in a placating way, "I don't think we decided yet, did we? Spence thinks we should hold off—"

"Goddamn it! *I* decided! Constance, get your ass out of my house. You're fired. And take lover-boy with you! Now!"

Constance scanned the room, paying no attention to Tootles. Then she saw a book with a red dustjacket in the chair Ba Ba had just left. Unhurriedly she moved toward the chair. Charlie was still near the doorway, watching her with a faint grin. He saw the book now, she knew; neither of them mentioned it.

She picked up the book and sat in the chair regarding Tootles. She glanced at the spine of the book, a fantasy romance, and then put it down on the table by the chair. She glanced at Charlie with an expression that told him it was the wrong book; neither of them would have been able to say how she communicated this, but the message was sent and received.

"You know, Tootles," she said calmly then, "I doubt they'll arrest you, after all. Several things have turned up that seem to rule against it. So if you want us to leave, naturally, that's your choice. But my party is really my business. Tomorrow night sounds good. In our motel. It will be a little cramped, but not too bad. I'll have to set a time after I see Paul, find a time that will be possible for everyone. Ba Ba, is nine too early, too late?"

"But I haven't even accepted," Ba Ba said indignantly. "And if Marion thinks it's a bad idea, so do I."

"But Tootles plans to be there," Constance said easily. "Don't you?" She turned her pale eyes on Tootles, who stared back at her with anger and resentment. The silence held for a second, another; neither woman shifted her position. Finally Tootles looked away.

"Not there. Here. After dinner. Nine thirty," she said harshly.

Constance nodded, and then turned her gaze to Charlie to see that his face had become wooden, his eyes flat black, not reflecting any light at all, like two little dull stones. She had seen that expression many times when he confronted a suspect, or a particularly distasteful crime; until now she had never seen it directed at her.

They all looked past Charlie then as gravel was crunched in the driveway in front of the house. Moments later the sheriff and two deputies appeared at the door. One of the things he had done after leaving them, apparently, was to get a proper search warrant.

He was super efficient that night, almost to the point of being rude. "Ms. Leeds was carrying a book with a red jacket when she arrived here," he said, producing the warrant. "She put the book on the table in the foyer. Did any of you see it after that? Did you move it?"

"What book?" Tootles asked. "I don't know what in hell you're talking about now."

"Who might have cleared off that table?" he asked.

"Jesus!" Tootles cried. "I don't know! Ask Alice Weber!"

He nodded. "I will."

Ba Ba lowered herself into a chair, and then turned to look at Constance with horror. "You thought I had it, didn't you? My book there. You thought that was it!"

"Good God," Johnny muttered. "Dad, this is the last straw. I'm going home. We can finish up in the morning."

He went back into the television room, and one of the deputies followed him and began his search there. Johnny put papers together, stuffed them into his briefcase, and started out.

"If you don't mind," the sheriff said. He reached for the briefcase, and after a slight hesitation Johnny handed it over. Gruenwald looked inside, gave it back, and motioned to the second deputy, who walked out with Johnny.

No one else in the room moved or spoke as the sheriff's men continued to search. Gruenwald stayed in the living room until one of the deputies called him to the foyer. He moved the few steps to the foyer, then turned and said, "Ms. Leidl, would you mind?"

Constance got up to join him, acutely aware of the eyes that were watching her every motion. The book the deputy had was orange-red, too thin, too tall. She shook her head.

The fourth time she was called, she hesitated, then slowly nodded. "I think so," she said. The book was a collection of Byron's poems.

Gruenwald opened the book, and began to riffle through the pages. A piece of paper fell out. It was notebook paper folded in half. They watched it fall; he picked it up gingerly with a pair of tweezers as if it might explode, and very carefully he opened it, using the tweezers and his pen, not getting fingerprints on it. On the paper was what appeared to be a map of Tootles's property, and the condominiums across the road from her retreat. Constance felt Charlie near her and glanced at him, but he was gazing fixedly at the paper.

Gruenwald slid the book and paper into an evidence envelope, and said, "It was in the studio mixed in with a bunch of magazines." He nodded to the deputy. "Nice going." Then he went to the doorway to the living room. "Thank you, Mrs. Buell, Mr. Buell. We'll be leaving now. Sorry to have bothered you again." He nodded to Charlie and Constance and left.

"Well," Tootles said. "Son of a bitch, what the hell is going on? Can anyone tell me that?"

Max took her hand and held it, and asked Constance, "You saw her with the book?"

"Yes. I remembered earlier this evening. She had it with her when she came."

"So what the fuck difference does it make?" Tootles cried. "Jesus Christ, I feel like I'm in a Beckett play. Doesn't it matter to you that nothing makes sense any more?" She yanked her hand away from Max and jumped up. "I'm going to bed. This is a madhouse, and you're all loonies. All of you!" She stamped from the room. Ba Ba struggled to her feet and lumbered after her.

Max looked apologetically at Constance and Charlie, and they started for the door. "Our cue," Charlie said. "Good night, Max. She'll calm down pretty soon. Just take it easy."

It wasn't that she needed help in walking out of the house, across the porch, along the walk to the driveway and their car, Constance thought a few seconds later; she was perfectly capable of walking alone. Just as she was perfectly capable of opening the passenger seat door and sliding into the Volvo. And, she thought grimly, she was also perfectly capable of maintaining a silence just as long as he was. She gazed straight ahead and did not say a word.

Seventeen

In their room, still distracted, still silent, Charlie put Sheriff Gruenwald's manila envelope down on the coffee table and regarded it morosely. He picked up the phone to order a large pot of coffee.

Constance watched him adjust pillows, rearrange the light at the end of the sofa, and kick off his shoes before he reached for the envelope. She sat across the table from him. "I don't think you should come to Tootles's house tomorrow night," she said.

He looked up from the papers he had started to sort through. "Why not?"

"You'll hate it. Besides, it really has nothing to do with the murders. With death yes, but not with murder."

Charlie put down the papers and leaned forward, with both hands pressed hard on the tabletop. "Do you know what happened over there tonight?" he asked. His voice was low, but there was a biting intensity in the words, in the way he looked at her. When he became this intense, he sounded like a foreigner who had not quite mastered English, had not yet acquired an ease of pronunciation: he clipped the words, exaggerated the vowel sounds, sounded like a stranger.

"What do you mean?"

"That silly girl has placed you in danger," he said, even more controlled than a moment ago. Anyone from outside would think he was being as casual as the morning weather report, but she knew, and was startled by the subdued vehemence that seemed even more dangerous for being checked so thoroughly.

"And you topped it by telling Tootles she probably won't be arrested," he added. "My God, between the two of you, you're inviting the killer to have just one more go at it."

She started to respond sharply, but choked her words back and instead considered what he was saying. Toni had said she, Constance, had found out things; and she, Constance, had certainly told Tootles she probably wouldn't be charged. She bit her lip in exasperation.

Charlie got up to answer the door when a knock sounded. He paid the waiter as Constance made room for the coffee on the table. When they were alone again, she poured for them both.

"You really think it's someone over there now?"

"I don't know. But I think anything that's said over there might as well be broadcast. What are you planning for your party?" Some of the tightness had eased, but he was still too tense.

She looked at the coffee cup she held and said in a low, hesitant voice, "I think Tootles and Ba Ba and Paul fooled around with séances, or crystal balls, or the Ouija, something like that years ago, and Tootles gave Paul her muse. The dates are right, their attitudes about it, everything. His book is filled with it. Anyway, I think . . . no . . . I *know* that Toni is going to try to get Paul to pass the muse over to her. And it's a jealous muse, maybe even a crazy one. Toni's . . . she's too young and too innocent to have that burden shoved off on her." She watched his expression harden as she spoke, and she heard a sharp edge in her voice as she responded more to his expression than to anything he might say. "I said you would hate it. And I also said I don't think you should be there. Remember?"

"And I don't intend to let you be with that crew without me," he said flatly.

"If you go, will you promise you'll leave it to me? Not interfere in any way? Just observe?"

He looked at her with his hard flat eyes and slowly shook his head. "No promises. I don't think you know what you might be letting yourself in for. Why are you doing this? Do you even know why?"

"I was there when Victoria got killed. It seems that I should have been able to do something, but I didn't. Apparently Victoria was shut out because Paul believes or says he believes that toll has to be paid. I saw Tootles accept the curse and adjust her life to accommodate it. It has to stop. I didn't do anything to help Victoria, but this time I know what I can do. I don't think Toni deserves what she'll be getting."

"You sound as if you believe in it."

She shook her head. "I told you before, it doesn't matter what I believe. It's what they believe. I said it has nothing to do with the murders, but it has a lot to do with death. It has to stop. Even if none of that's true, Toni deserves a chance at a real life, one that includes art and love, maybe a family, whatever she chooses. She deserves that much out of life. What if she were Jessica, Charlie?"

Not fair, he wanted to yell. Not fair. And she knew it. Either of them would do whatever was required for their daughter's sake, but she hadn't seen Tootles and her little sister in action, and he had. God help him, he had. "Okay," he said finally. He stood up and reached across the table, took her cup and saucer from her hands and set them down, and then drew her close enough to kiss. "Whatever it is, we're in it together, remember? I won't promise to keep still, but God, I'll try. I most definitely will try."

"That's all a guy can do," she said softly, and this time she kissed him.

She was relieved that the light had come back to his eyes. Where did he go when they turned hard and flat, nonreflective like that? So far away she was afraid that one day no words would bring him back, no hand would reach him, no warmth would restore him to life. A deep shudder passed through her; she had been thinking of him as dead when his eyes became stonelike. And that was almost right, she knew; the warm, human, loving man vanished and left an iceman in his place. She also knew that she was afraid of the iceman, who used to appear more and more often and stay longer each time. The battles in his sleep had been between the two, the iceman and Charlie; nightmares, the tossing and turning, the insomnia he had preferred to dreaming, all battles for possession—Charlie or the iceman. She knew that victory had never been assured, never from the first foray to the day he turned in his city ID, to the present. The iceman waited, would always be waiting. And if that was believing in possession, she thought, then she was a firm believer, after all.

Charlie poured himself more coffee and took out a notebook, looked over a list he had made. "Let's try the first-things-first on them all," he said. He had a theory that Constance could tell from a brief meeting exactly what was bugging anyone; nothing she said could shake this idea. He called it her first impressions, first-things-first theory. She sighed dramatically, but did not protest; sometimes useful things came out of it.

"Okay," he said. "Tootles."

"Scared to death Max will find out she'd rather teach than do art, and she believes she can't do art any more."

Charlie nodded. Part of the game was that he should not express surprise or disbelief until later. "Max," he said.

"Easy. He thinks she's a genius and is really afraid she'll find out that he arranged the tour and then she'll think it was because he doubts her worth, and thought he had to buy recognition for her. He's terrified that he'll lose her.''

Charlie made a noncommittal noise, then said, ''Spence.''

''He never stopped loving her,'' Constance said, surprising herself. ''He would do anything to keep her well, happy, his friend, whatever, to keep the welcome mat out for him. He wants her to be happy with Max.''

''Anything?'' he asked softly.

She nodded. ''Anything.''

''Paul?''

''Consumed by guilt. And self-doubt. He doesn't know if he is really talented or not, whether he deserves any success, if he was responsible for Victoria's death.'' She considered this, then added, ''He really needs professional help. I don't know how deep his depressions are, but . . .'' An absent expression settled on her face. She raised her hand slightly, and Charlie leaned back waiting.

After a time she looked at him with a puzzled expression. ''You know Victoria really didn't talk nonsense; that comes from the way Janet interprets what she heard. Right?'' She did not wait for his nod. ''Checking out a smoke. Something about where there's smoke, there's fire, and that became going out for a cigarette. Proposal from a muscleman, Musselman, jock. And then there's the curious 'ironic pose' paraphrase. Remember? Where is the note about what she said?''

She found it in her notebook. ''Yes. I wrote her words: 'Paul's ironic pose was wearing him down, and making him tired.' Remember the book she had with her? Byron's poetry. Charlie, try: Byronic pose, and wearing thin, and tiresome.''

He thought about it, then muttered, ''Paul's Byronic pose is wearing thin and getting tiresome. Maybe. But so what?''

''She saw through him,'' Constance said slowly. ''His tragic figure was amusing to her because she didn't believe in it. That's one of the things that baffled me. Her attitude toward him. Amusement." Another thought occurred to her and she sighed deeply, almost theatrically. "Eventually, someone is going to have to talk to Janet, try to get the real words she heard."

They considered this in gloomy silence for another few seconds. "It doesn't change anything, does it?" she murmured finally, and nodded toward his notebook.

He glanced at the open page. "Johnny?"

She hesitated only a moment. "Afraid of his father. He wants to be his father desperately, I think. Tired of being junior. Ambitious and a bit timid, a bit weak. Away from Max probably he's altogether different, though."

He ran his finger down his list, and she said, "There's still Toni." He looked at her, waiting. He had not included Toni because he had seen no reason to do so; she had been accounted for from four thirty on the day Victoria was killed. He had not included Babar because murder was just too damn physical for her. She would more likely talk someone to death.

"Toni would do anything almost to get what she thinks Paul has, the muse, the wild talent. She thinks she's nothing without it," Constance said. She shuddered. "What a terrible desire, to want something you believe will kill people you love. What a terrible price she's willing to pay. Or else, she doesn't really believe it would bring her suffering," she added thoughtfully. She turned her gaze to Charlie and asked, "When do we start to realize the bill will come due, really and truly it will? She doesn't believe it yet. I don't think she believes she'll ever be in love."

This had gone off in altogether the wrong direction, he thought grumpily. He did not want to talk about this "gift" or "curse." He did not want to talk about suffering artists or about art and its price tag. He snapped his notebook shut. "Good stuff, all of it," he said then, forcing a grin. "Now, to work. You want to do Gruenwald's reports in any systematic way, or just dive in for now?''

They just dived in.

By twelve Constance's vision was starting to blur, and for no good purpose, she thought glumly as she got up to walk around the room, to stretch. Everything she was reading she had heard already; absolutely nothing was new, nothing had not been brought up, discussed, dismissed. She stood at the window and watched the western sky flare with distant lightning that was closer now than it had been half an hour ago. She began to hope their silly cats were indoors. Sometimes the cat door jammed. But the Mitchum boys would be watching out for them, she told herself, and still hoped the cats were inside. Poor Candy was terrified of storms, and Ashcan would be a wreck. Anything out of the ordinary threw him into a panic; their absence for so many days would make him feel he had been deserted forever, and now a storm to verify that the gods were indeed after him. And Brutus, she thought with resignation, would become a monster if he was locked out during a storm. He would make life hell for the other two cats if the storm wasn't already doing it.

She didn't even know if there was a storm in New York, she told herself then, and turned away from the window to see Charlie staring off into nothing with a fixed, distant expression. Lightning flashed again, closer, this time followed very quickly by a rumble of thunder. Moving in, she thought. Charlie apparently had not noticed.

She took her seat again, continuing to watch him, saying nothing. She hoped he wouldn't decide to go for a walk. Sometimes he did when he was in this phase, thinking something through from every possible angle, and then over again, and again, finding and answering the questions, the problems, the sticky points.

A new streak of lightning was so bright that it glared in

the room and this time the thunder was simultaneous. Charlie blinked and glanced at the window. "Tell me again about finding Victoria's body," he said. "Start with entering the building."

She began, but now the thunder and lightning, and gusty wind driving rain hard against the windows made talk impossible. She reached for his hand and drew him up. "Watch," she said, pulling him closer to the windows, but not too close. Her mother had always said, *Don't draw attention to yourself during a thunderstorm.*

"It's going to storm," he said.

She laughed and put her arm around his waist; he put his hand on her back, let it slide down to rest on her buttock, and they stood and watched the storm build. It was a tornado-spawning storm, she thought, as the wind blew harder in violent bursts, then died down and blew even harder moments later.

"We could go down to the bar," Charlie said, and she knew he was thinking tornado weather, too. At that moment the lights flickered, flickered again, and went out. "We definitely will go down to the bar," Charlie said then. He had no intention of being on the seventh floor with a blackout, no elevators, and just one nut with a match trying to find the stairs. On the other hand, he knew precisely where the stairs were. He always checked out the stairs, the fire extinguishing system, and usually he was not happy with what he found, but at least he knew how to get out.

He held her hand and they left the room and entered the absolute darkness of the hall where already voices were asking where the stairs were, what happened to the lights, did anyone have a match . . .

Charlie had his little penlight, and down the hallway two flashlights started dueling. He saw that one was being held by a kid, nine, ten years old, and that it was a Teenage Mutant Ninja Turtle flashlight; he grinned and tugged Constance by the hand. Let the kid save the universe, he thought, opening the door to the stairs.

The lounge was dimly lighted by candles, and was much nicer this way than it had been before. The problem would be the air conditioning, Charlie knew, but it was not a problem just yet. He saw Constance to a booth and then went to get them both an Irish coffee. The coffee, he said, because it could be a long night and in a little while the coffee would be cold without electricity to keep it heated, and the Irish because what the hell, it could be a long night.

"You were telling me about finding Victoria's body," he said when he sat down across from her. She told him about it again.

The storm seemed very far away now. No lightning flash penetrated the lounge, and the thunder was muted, the wind vanquished by masonry and steel. In a while someone opened a door out front, and another one in the back, and a breeze flowed through.

"Think back to the elevator ride up," Charlie said, gazing past her with a faraway look. "When Max found the roses, did Tootles admit she had sent them?"

After a moment Constance shook her head. Tootles had looked embarrassed, she remembered.

"Right. And she told you that Johnny ordered them in her name. Everywhere we've turned, we keep running smack dab into Tootles and her lies, don't we? Why would she lie about that?"

Constance felt her throat tighten painfully. "What are you thinking?"

"We both came here believing she wouldn't murder anyone. I think she's counting on that more than she'd admit. But she would, you know, given the right incentive, the right circumstances. Look at her, an aging, nearly penniless woman, a failed artist who is running a school that could be put out of business any day, and along comes a rich man who is crazy about her. She hooks him and she'd do anything to keep him, even destroy her own life's work. Then, suppose one day Max comes home in a state of shock. Musselman's found out something, they argued, Musselman got shoved off the balcony, and Max will go to prison. Protecting Max would be incentive enough, I believe." He paused, as if considering his own words.

"You're making the state's case," Constance said in a low voice.

He nodded, still looking beyond her. "Everywhere, the roadblocks we run into are hers," he said. "She threw everyone off the track by messing up her own work. She ordered the flowers, and then denied it because she has to maintain the attitude that she doesn't give a damn about the condos, or anything to do with them. A lie. Of course, she cares desperately. Max is her financial freedom and first Musselman and then Victoria Leeds threatened to strip it from her. And," he added soberly, "she could have slipped an extra key to the condos to Victoria Leeds, told her to go up there and wait for her so they could talk. When Johnny's group arrived, it would have been a simple thing for Victoria to keep out of sight." He drew in a breath and shook his head sadly. "And it was Tootles, remember, who invited Paul, believing he was still Victoria's lover. Invite one, get both."

"But she claims that Johnny insisted on asking Paul."

"The problem," he said thoughtfully, "is that she says a lot of things, and you have to root around them like a pig after truffles trying to decide which is true, which is a blatant lie."

"You're scaring me, Charlie. You really are."

He pulled his gaze back from that distant horizon and focused on her. "About that party you intend to throw, the séance, let's discuss it."

"I won't let you talk me out of it," she said hotly.

Charlie started to say something, but the lights came back on; they both blinked after the dimness. A group of people entered the lounge, laughing, talking. "Let's go up," he said, reaching for her hand across the table. "There's a lot to discuss. You know, we should use candles more often, travel with them, use them every evening."

His face had turned soft, his eyes seemed to glow. Absurdly she felt a touch of warmth on her cheeks. Then her indignation at his betrayal of Tootles flooded in and she would have withdrawn her hand, but his grasp tightened and they stood and walked from the lounge hand in hand.

When Constance got up the next morning, she found Charlie in their sitting room with a tray that contained a large pot of coffee, sweet rolls, a doughnut, juice, and half a grapefruit. The grapefruit was for her, she knew. He was sprawled on the sofa, the telephone at his ear, another doughnut in his hand, grinning like a kid completing his baseball card collection. She blew him a kiss and went back for her shower, and to dress.

"Well," she asked, rejoining him a few minutes later, toweling her hair.

"Well indeed. This is the way. Push a button and it's breakfast. Why don't we ever have doughnuts at our house? Push another button and the sheriff says, yes sir, I'll get right on it. Push another button and a beautiful blonde strolls through."

She picked up a pillow and threw it at him. He ducked, laughing. She left to comb her hair.

"What did you tell the sheriff?" she asked, when she came back this time and poured herself coffee.

"Not a thing yet. We're to meet him at five, compare notes, here in the lounge. Funny thing is the sheriff can investigate Musselman's death all he wants, but not the Leeds murder. That's state territory. Tough. Anyway, that leaves us a whole day to get our act together. Just so we get back by five. What'd I'd like to do is meet Debra Saltzman and her friends."

She tasted the grapefruit. It was so acidic, so green she felt her whole body cringe; Charlie laughed. "I told you they're bad for you. Have a doughnut."

When they went down to the lobby they found two messages in their box, one for each of them. Charlie read his first: *I can tell you something about the crates that were opened. I'll be in my office at the school from eleven to twelve. Meet me then.* It was signed Claud Palance.

Constance read hers aloud: *You have to come to the retreat at eleven thirty. I have to talk to you. Don't bring Ch. Come alone. T.*

Charlie nodded gravely, thanked the desk clerk, took Constance's arm and they walked out into the day that had been remarkably freshened by the storm. "Divide and conquer," he murmured as they walked to the car. "Get me out of the way and work on you. God only knows what ammunition she planned to use."

"Both of them?" she asked. "You really think so?"

"Don't you?"

After a moment she nodded. Tootles's work; she really was getting desperate.

"Now, let's see," he said behind the wheel a moment later. "Out that way, turn left, five, six miles to the shopping mall. Right?"

She knew he did not need any confirmation. They drove directly to the mall and went into a discount store where he bought some paint thinner, turpentine, a sponge, a large bunch of hideous plastic flowers, and a bottle of cologne. He surveyed his purchases thoughtfully, then nodded, and they paid for them and left. It was ten thirty.

The day was starting to warm up and would become very warm before dark, he felt certain, but now it was nice. Sparkling clean after the rain; a few trees had blown down here and there, but there was no drastic damage. A good cleansing storm.

"It's about an hour in to Washington," she said, thinking about it. "We've never been to the Space Museum, you know. We could do that." They had an appointment to see Debra Saltzman and Sunny Door at three thirty.

"Righto," he said and turned the key.

The day had been designed to make him feel humble and small, he decided late in the afternoon. First the Space Museum had achieved this nicely, putting him out there where he was of less importance than a single raindrop in the ocean. Lunch had been in a restaurant where the head-waiter was pseudo-French, the worst kind, and regarded Charlie as a tourist from Nebraska or worse. And then Debra Saltzman's apartment, penthouse apartment, he corrected himself. It seemed that her father was *the* Saltzman, heir to one of the great fortunes—his daddy had invented one of the dry soup mixes and had gone on to dry salad dressing mixes, dry juice mixes. . . . It was enough to make Charlie's head ache. Debra was dressed in a silk pantsuit with a halter under the jacket; Sunny was in a running outfit with a green stripe down the leg. Both looked exceedingly rich.

"What I'd like," he said to them, "is just a straight account of exactly what you saw and heard when Johnny Buell took you to the condo that night. Okay?"

"You think the killer and Victoria Leeds were already there, don't you? The papers said that's one of the theories," Sunny said, leaning forward in her chair, her eyes gleaming. Two spots of red flared on her cheeks, then faded, leaving a beautiful, controlled apricot tan.

Charlie thought of it that way, a controlled tan, done to a turn, ripe for the picking . . . gravely he nodded. "That's exactly what I think. And I think there's a good chance that something you saw, or didn't see, something you heard, or didn't hear, might provide just what we need to wrap it up."

"See?" Sunny said to Debra with a toss of her head. Her

hair flowed like brushed silk with every movement she made.

"The point is we didn't see or hear anything," Debra said coolly.

"Maybe," Charlie said. "Maybe you know more than you realize. Let's start with approaching the gate."

Watching, Constance thought how very good he was with these young women. He was not deferential in a way they were used to. He had dismissed the apartment, which was breathtaking, with a stunning view of the city, just as he had dismissed the slight inflection with which Sunny had said her last name *Door*. Names, fortunes, none of that interested him, it was clear, but what did interest him was the quality of their perceptions, what they had seen, what they had heard, what they had thought of it all. Constance doubted if anyone ever had treated them with intellectual interest in their young lives.

And what it came out to, she also thought, was a repeat of what they had learned already. No one saw or heard anything. He took them to the gate, through it, down into the basement, up the elevator, and so on until they were back in the Continental and on the way to the city once more. Nothing new. No one else was there. Debra had left her purse in the elevator when they went into the apartment, she had started to go back for it, then didn't because they would leave in just a second anyway. Left it where? he asked. On the shelf under the mirror, she said. She put it down to comb her hair, and forgot it. He nodded. On to the smell of paint in the apartment, the tarps, the curved hallway. . . . What had they talked about with the watchman? Both women filled in the brief conversation; it had lasted only a minute or two and then Johnny had come back.

Both young women had treated his interrogation as an adventure when it began, but they were bored with it quickly, bored with having to back up to fill in details that seemed so minute they couldn't make any difference. Like where everyone stood in the apartment, in the elevator, on the ground waiting for Johnny to come back. Debra said he wanted to know their lines of sight, didn't he? And why didn't he just say so if that was it? He nodded. That's it, he admitted, and they worked with a little sketch, then another. Where were they when Johnny opened the trunk and tossed in his briefcase? Sunny had looked inside; the trunk was big and empty. Debra had watched a contrail point to the city. Where were they when Johnny went back inside? Standing by the car, talking. No one passed them there. Did they actually see Pierce follow them to the gate when they drove out?

"He was walking after us," Debra said. "I saw him, and we didn't see anyone else," she said finally in irritation. "Believe me, I wouldn't lie about it. What for? We didn't see anyone!"

Finally he thanked them, and he and Constance rode the elevator down twenty-two floors and emerged to the street where it was hot and muggy and crowded with tourists. You could tell the tourists because of the cameras, and the women didn't wear hose, and they were sunburned to a degree that looked painful.

"Well," Constance said judiciously, "you told them what they didn't see or hear could be important."

He laughed. "Let's get on the road. This is a sauna."

They were nearly an hour late for their meeting with Bill Gruenwald. He was drinking a beer when they arrived; he looked tired and discouraged.

Charlie was tired, too; he had not counted on the tourists, on the heavy traffic, on the heat that had increased mile by mile as they neared the city. It was not fair, he thought vehemently, for Constance to look the way she did after such a day. She was in beige pants and a beige top with a white belt, white sandals; she looked as if she had stepped out of a cool advertisement only minutes ago. He was dirty, sweaty, crumpled, and the tension he had put aside all day had returned vengefully, much worse, he was certain, than it would have been if he had admitted it throughout the day instead of shunting it off like that.

He liked Bill Gruenwald and didn't want to play games with him, but on the other hand Gruenwald had been ordered off the case, and Charlie needed him. Game time, he told himself unhappily.

E i g h t e e n

"Sorry we're late," Charlie said as they neared the booth.

Gruenwald stood up and glanced at his watch. "Forget it. Technically, I'm off work. I know a little place you might like, few miles down the road. Good food there. Buy you a beer."

"He really doesn't want to be seen with us, does he?" Constance murmured in the car a few minutes later, as Charlie followed the sheriff along a narrow winding country road that was a series of sharp curves.

"Nope. I reckon he's vulnerable politically. Case goes haywire, he gets it in the neck. Way it goes."

The sheriff's turn signal began to flash; Charlie slowed down. They left the blacktop road for a newer one of glaring white concrete, and just ahead there was a sprawling log structure with a sign: Harley's Haven.

"We are there," he said, pulling into the parking lot behind Bill Gruenwald. A few other cars were in the lot, which was quite spacious, and looked well used. Watch out for weekends after nine, Charlie thought. When he glanced at Constance it was to see a look of concentrated absence on her face. That was how he thought of it; she was not home, but off somewhere thinking. She could concentrate herself away during lectures, during Christmas-rush shopping, during movies, during his long discursive discussions with Phil Stern, his lifelong friend, anything.

Once or twice that expression had come during one of their infrequent arguments; he had stormed out of the house wanting to kick a cat or dog, or take a swing at a lion, something. When he returned, she could pick up the argument exactly where they had left off, and he never would learn what had taken her away briefly.

He touched her arm, bringing her back as cool and poised as ever. But he knew that if she had not yet finished whatever it was, it would be up to him to carry on the conversation with Bill Gruenwald, who would never realize she was paying no attention at all.

Inside Harley's Haven there was a nice dance floor, and two dining rooms, one separate from the music area; it was dim and quiet at this hour. They sat in there. A red-haired man came out from the back to greet them. "How's things, Bill? What'll it be?"

"Paddy," Bill Gruenwald said, then nodded to Charlie and Constance and mentioned their first names. "Dos Equis for me."

"Good ribs coming along," Paddy said. "Belinda's cooking, you know, her own sauce?"

Gruenwald groaned. "I'll hang around for them." When they all had ordered their drinks, he said to Constance, "Spare ribs barbecued by Belinda is one of the reasons some folks around here aren't hurrying very fast to get to heaven. When she goes, they'll trail along after her."

Charlie and Constance decided they would hang around and wait for the ribs also. Bill Gruenwald began to talk about some of Charlie's cases he had followed; he asked intelligent questions. Charlie gave him reasoned, intelligent answers, and Constance went back to her "other space" where she could think undisturbed.

They were well into the ribs before she came back fully. The ribs were as good as promised. They came with a sweet/sour cole slaw, biscuits, green beans cooked with ham most of the afternoon, boiled new potatoes, collards with vinegar and green onions and a bowl of fresh black-eyed peas.

It was time to slow down, Charlie knew, or he would have to stop long before he wanted to. Trouble was, he wanted to eat for a week; the motel restaurant, decent as it was, left an empty spot after every meal there. Mediocre food did that, left an emptiness, and you just ate more and more trying to find the one thing that would touch and fill that hole, and never did.

"Charlie," Bill Gruenwald said, "Belmont is getting antsy. I think he'll hold off until early next week and then go calling with a warrant."

"Good heavens!" Constance said indignantly. "With what? He can't have any more than he did yesterday, or the day before that."

Bill Gruenwald nodded. "That's one of the problems. He isn't getting anything else, and he's got Marion Olsen; a motive, the ruined art pieces; time, she's the only one who had the time."

"Have you given him anything about Musselman yet?" Charlie asked.

"Tried. Only way that makes much difference is if the reason is political; someone paid off someone for the variance, or else graft; you know, order it at a buck, write down two, pocket one, pay one. Either way, it gets political and nasty. Belmont doesn't like politics mixed in with his murders, one of the problems. And he wants that to stay the way it was closed, accidental death. Even if we came up with something besides accidental death, he seems to think it's a different case altogether. And it could be, you know. *This* case concerns a bunch of nutty artists, that's how he sees it."

"Well, it really does," Charlie said. "A nuttier bunch you

aren't likely to find. Look, come to the party tonight. You want to see nuts in action, be there."

Gruenwald hesitated. "A party?"

"Party. Séance. Whatever. I don't intend to take part, old buddy. I intend to sit it out in the dining room, or back porch, or somewhere." When the sheriff still hesitated, Charlie dipped his fingers in his water glass and then wiped them carefully. You couldn't get barbecue sauce off without water, he thought, and this was not the sort of place that brought hot lemon-scented towels or water bowls. He paid close attention to the task of cleaning his hands as he said, "If I were you, Bill, I'd be there tonight. I mean, if I didn't have anything better to do, no new movie in town that needs my immediate attention, no hoodlums on big mean bikes roaring around, no shootings in the saloons, why then I'd consider this a sort of special deluxe entertainment opportunity and I sure would be there."

"What time?" Bill Gruenwald asked resignedly.

"We probably shouldn't arrive together. And we plan to get there about nine thirty. Maybe you could have a reason to drop in, you know, a few more questions to ask Max or Spence or someone. You ever find out what time Spence left his shop that Friday?"

"Yeah. Five. Made great time, got to the house at ten to six."

"Uh huh. Anyway, party time, nine thirty or so. Am I remembering right? Was there blueberry pie on that menu?"

All through dinner Toni watched Paul Volte; whenever he glanced in her direction, she quickly looked away, but then found herself watching him again. He ate very little and drank wine and looked sad. It made her want to cry for him to look so sad all the time. A few times when Ba Ba addressed him quite directly, he had looked so blank it was as if he had gone deaf.

217

Johnny was tired, he had announced at the start of the meal; he said nothing more after that.

Spence was going on about two artists who had got in trouble with NEA over what some called obscene art, and they defended as antiwar statements. Spence was hanging their show next week, he said unhappily, and he expected pickets, demonstrations, God knew what all. Fire bombs, he added gloomily.

Only Max seemed normal; he listened to Spence with interest, and he watched Marion with such affection that it was touching to see.

And Marion was angry about something. She scowled and cursed and banged her glass down too hard, and let her silverware clatter too often, but she didn't really say anything.

All in all it was a very strange and awkward dinner; as soon as it was over, Marion said, "Paul, Ba Ba, I need to talk to you. Let's go to the office."

Toni helped Mrs. Weber clear the table and scrape dishes in the kitchen. A few minutes later when she returned to get the tablecloth, she saw the sheriff at the table with Johnny and Max, looking at a crude map.

"Hi," the sheriff said. "Are we in the way here?"

She shook her head. The tablecloth had been folded and pushed across the table to the end. Slowly she picked it up, gathered the napkins, and started to leave.

"Like I said," the sheriff was saying, "we figure they must have already been inside the complex by seven. You had to unlock the gate to drive through, but did you look at the other door, the single door?"

Johnny shook his head. "I never gave it a thought. It was closed, or I would have noticed, but I didn't examine it."

"Of course not. No reason to. Pierce says it was locked at six, but I wonder if he really tried it, or just gave it a glance."

Max said sharply, "If he said it was locked, it was. He's a good watchman."

Toni went on into the kitchen. She felt as if something that had just started to loosen in her throat had tightened all the way again. Why didn't they finish? Be done with it? She wanted to scream at the sheriff with his bland voice, his bland face, his silly little mustache. . . . Without warning, she was seeing his face then, not the way it had looked just now in the dining room, but strangely different, with a deep hurt, a deep secret: a private self she had not seen before.

She dropped the tablecloth on the kitchen worktable and wandered out of the room, down the hall toward the studio, thinking of nothing at all, but examining the face that had presented itself to her, turning it this way and that in her mind, following a line that started at the corner of the eye, down the side of his face where it was smoothed out by his rather high cheekbone . . .

As she passed the closed office door, she could hear raised voices, including Spence's, although Marion had not even invited him to the little talk. Toni continued past the door, on to the studio, to her work space at a long table against the wall.

Not soapstone, too soft, too smooth. Gneiss, or even sandstone. A reddish sandstone, with yellow in it. She reached across the table to a lump of modeling clay, but when she drew it closer, the image vanished. Now she could see only the bland sheriff with his bland mustache, his bland eyes. She stared ahead at the wall; there was a crack in the paint, small bits had chipped off exposing the under-coat that was whiter than the finish paint. She pinched off a bit of clay and pressed it against the crack. She filled in the crack from as high as she could reach to where it disap-peared behind the table. Tears flowed down her cheeks as she plugged the crack with the soft gray clay.

Then she heard a door slam and Marion's harsh voice yelling, "Goddamn it! There's no choice! We do it her way! You hear me? And you behave or I'll get you by the balls and I won't let go! And Ba Ba, you screw up with this and I'll slap you silly from here to Christmas! You got that straight?'' Her voice receded, still at full volume apparently, but she was hurrying away, her bare feet making no noise.

Toni ran to the bathroom that was between the office and studio; she closed the door, locked it, and then pressed her forehead against it hard. After several very deep breaths, she turned and washed her face, and felt she was as ready as she was going to get that night. It was time for Constance and Charlie to show up, party time.

Nineteen

Charlie entered the dining room, his hands deep in his pockets, scowling fiercely, to hear Sheriff Gruenwald say to Johnny, "All we really know is that Victoria Leeds must have got into the condominium before you took your group in. There just wasn't time enough afterward." He looked at Charlie. "Hi, what's up? Oh, I forgot, they're having a party or something?"

"Or something," Charlie snapped. "I was invited to go somewhere else." He cocked his head, listening. "They can't seem to make up their minds where they want the party to happen."

Across a narrow hall from the dining room, with both doors standing wide open, was the television room. The voices became clearly audible:

"This will do just fine," Constance said. "Plenty of chairs, that card table is about right, don't you think?"

"It's okay," Ba Ba said in a lower voice that sounded sullen.

"Good, let's just arrange things in here." Constance was being inhumanly cheerful and brisk.

Charlie sat down at the dining-room table and glanced at

the sketch Bill Gruenwald had made of the condo complex, Tootles's little retreat, the path through the woods. He did not linger over the sketch, but was listening intently to the voices from the dining room.

"How we used to do it," Constance said, "was to have the two Ouija enablers sit at the table, and the others sit around them holding hands. You have to promise not to say anything, or make a sudden movement. You know, respect for the method, the people using the Ouija, the others in the room, and so on. Agreed? Max, I'm not sure you'll like this. Wouldn't you rather join Charlie, wherever he is?"

Max's voice rumbled, nearly inaudible, but he was protesting, that much was clear.

"All right," Constance said, "but you'll have to abide by the rules, just like everyone else." There was a pause; he must have nodded or somehow agreed silently. She went on, "Whoever is at the end, should be prepared to take notes if there is a message. Spence, would you do that? At this end, maybe. Do you have a notebook or something, a pen? Just put it where you can get at it without having to leave the group."

Charlie got up and crossed the hall, to stop in the doorway where he could look into the television room. There was a grand piano, a large television, many cushions on the floor, several overstuffed chairs and a sofa, and additional cane chairs with woven seats. Constance was standing at a card table where Tootles and Ba Ba already were seated with the Ouija board and planchette between them. Tootles looked murderously angry. The others had drawn a line of chairs close to the table. Now Constance sat down next to Toni and took her hand, Max took Constance's hand, and after a second Spence sat down and took Max's other hand. Paul was ashen; he moved like a robot with jerky motions when he crossed to sit by Toni.

Charlie was aware that Bill Gruenwald and Johnny Buell had joined him at the doorway. He took Johnny's arm and pulled him away, his finger to his lips. Back in the dining room he said in a low voice, "They'll close the doors if they catch us snooping. Listen." Babar's voice carried to them clearly.

"Is anyone there? Hello. Is anyone there?" A lengthy silence followed. "Sometimes you have to ask through the Ouija," Babar said, and another silence followed.

"You guys were talking about how anyone got into the complex?" Charlie asked Bill Gruenwald in a very low voice. The sheriff nodded; Charlie lifted his eyebrows in surprise. "That's the easy part," he said, still speaking softly. He listened again, then said, "They, the killer and Leeds, must have seen Buell and his group enter, and simply went through when the gate was open. A step off the access road, behind the trees, and it was done. He left the building open when he took the group upstairs. How long does it take to get inside, duck out of sight?" He cocked his head, and put his finger to his lips again. He took the few steps to the door to the music room and stood there silently. Johnny and the sheriff came after him.

"It's not working," Tootles said flatly. "I can't help it if it doesn't work. There's no way to make anything happen."

Constance was thinking back to her girlhood, a time when she was thirteen or fourteen, one of a group of high school girls who had stayed up all night playing with Tarot cards, the Ouija, palmistry. There had been a lot of giggling, and not a little apprehension and even fear that was always denied as quickly as it became recognized. They had been in the Olsens' basement rec room. Ba Ba had not been allowed to join them; she had been too young at eleven or possibly twelve.

Constance had not played with the Ouija since that night so many years ago. One of the girls had become hysterical, she recalled; how easy it had been then to become hysterical, to have other girls patting, touching, kissing, even envying the one who had succumbed. How they had longed to faint. One good faint would have been worth two cases of hysteria.

Toni's hand in hers had been trembling earlier, but now was still, and had even warmed up. She removed her hand from Toni's, gave Max's hand a little squeeze, and then withdrew from his grasp. His hand had been warm and firm from the start.

"Let me try," she said to Ba Ba, who still looked furious.

"I'd rather not," Ba Ba said. "When it's a bad night, it's best to leave it alone."

"Oh, we don't know that it's really a bad night, do we? Maybe Tootles is just too upset. And she has every right to be upset. It's been one thing after another, hasn't it?"

Glaring, Tootles stood up and went to the chair Constance had just left. She took Max's hand, and then Toni's. "Let her have a go at it," she said in a tight voice. Constance smiled at her, then at Ba Ba.

Toni had been afraid, then she had known nothing was going to happen. The way Marion had been sitting, the stiffness of her shoulders, the set look on her face, her whole attitude had said clearly that there was nothing to be afraid of because nothing was going to happen. Now the fear leaped back, redoubled, quadrupled, overwhelming. Constance would make something happen, she knew. She could not control the trembling in her hands. Marion tightened her grasp on one side, while on the other side Paul's hand was shaking every bit as much as Toni's.

"Is anyone there?" Ba Ba demanded, the same words as before, but with a difference; now it was a challenge.

Constance laughed. "Let's ask with the planchette."

After they moved the planchette around the board to ask, an interval passed that seemed too long to endure; no one moved; the planchette did not move. Babar looked sleek and fierce, Constance relaxed and bright-eyed with interest. Then the little planchette began to slide. Constance glanced at Spence, who was staring at the Ouija with a look of disbelief. When she nodded at him, he released Max's hand to pick up his pen and notebook. Standing in the doorway, fists clenched, Charlie felt a stirring of memory, a stirring of an atavistic reaction to the strange and unnatural that raised the hairs on his arms, down his back. Abruptly he turned and went back to the dining room.

"Jesus," Gruenwald muttered. "I didn't know people still believed in stuff like that. Isn't your wife a Ph.D. psychologist? Does she believe in that?"

Charlie glared at him. "Why don't you do your job and let her do hers," he said in a low mean voice. "You need some more pointers? How about the rope? Trace it. Who around here has rope, and why? Trailer tie-down? Camping rope? Boating? Why nylon? Because it makes a tidy little package that can go into a purse, or a pocket? Were the ends burned to stop raveling? Trace the ash, lighter fluid, barbecue starter, gasoline? What was used? A match? Candle? Gas burner? Cigarette lighter? God, the labs today can tell you the name of the gas company! Have you even thought to look over clothes, see if you come up with fibers, nylon fibers in pockets for example, or fibers from her clothes on the knees of someone's pants? Why don't you just get on with your job and don't worry about what my wife believes?"

Gruenwald tightened his lips into a thin line. He started to gather up the papers he had spread on the table. Johnny Buell looked at him, then very quickly away, as if embarrassed for him.

"Who is there?" Constance asked in the next room. Charlie went to the door again. Constance had a strained, expression; she was pale. She had not counted on this, she was thinking. Ba Ba had gone into a trance that was legitimate; she was in a somnambulistic trance from all appearances, and the planchette was racing around the board.

Charlie's fists tightened. *Something was wrong.* Late into the night they had talked; he had gone over that other time with her, reviving all the terror he had felt that day when Babar had summoned a ghost, a spirit, a something, and it had touched him with fear and loathing. Last night Constance had said, "If this is going to work at all, it has to be as real as it was to you the first time you saw Ba Ba at the board. You have to let it run without interference or nothing will happen. She's probably even better now, more experienced at this, but we're more experienced, too, Charlie." She had said that he no longer was that young kid, groggy with fatigue, stupefied with coming out of a deep sleep into something weird. Last night it had sounded reasonable. Now, watching with his fists balled so hard that his forearms were starting to spasm, all he could think was *something was wrong*. Constance was too pale; he could see a sheen of sweat on her upper lip, the way the tendons in her neck were too tight, the fierce set of her jaw. The thought came to him with the force of a blow to the solar plexus: *she would be the target.*

The planchette moved faster and faster spelling out words: Y—O—U—C—A—L—L—E—D—B—E—F—O—R—E—I—C—A—M—E—I—A—M—S—T—I—L—L—H—E—R—E

"If you are here, you can hear my voice," Constance said clearly. "You have to leave, go back where you came from. No one here needs or wants you any longer."

I—W—I—L—L—N—O—T—L—E—A—V—E—P—A—U—L

"Tell it to go away, Paul," Constance said. "Just say the words. Tell it."

The planchette began to skitter across the board, back and forth jerkily, not pausing anywhere long enough to see if it was on a letter, skidding to the edge, back; then suddenly it flew off the board and landed in Ba Ba's lap. She did not move; her hands remained suspended before her as if her fingers were still resting on the planchette. Slowly her hands were lowered until her fingertips touched the Ouija board.

Her face did not change expression; she looked like a Buddha contemplating nirvana.

"I won't leave," Ba Ba said in a thick unrecognizable voice. "Paul needs me. Paul wants me."

Charlie's stomach spasmed at the sound of that voice.

"Tell it!" Constance demanded, facing Paul, who was shaking violently.

"Get out," he cried then. "Just get the fuck out. Go back to the hell you came from! Leave me alone! Get out!" His voice rose to a near scream. "Get out! Get out!"

"No!" Toni moaned. "I want it. Don't leave!" She tried to wrest her hand free from Tootles's grasp.

"Jesus God," Gruenwald whispered.

His words, so close to Charlie's ear, yanked him back from a wild plummeting fall toward that other room out of the past. For a moment the two scenes appeared superimposed on one another. He shut his eyes hard, and when he opened them again the past was gone.

Max was as rigid as death, as was Tootles. She was holding Toni's hand in a hard grip. And Toni looked ready to pass out; her pale face had taken on a bluish cast. She twisted her hand away from Paul; he jumped up, clutched the table holding the Ouija board, and screeched at it.

"Get out of my life! Get out!"

The Ouija board seemed to jerk convulsively; it twisted and spun around and slid across the card table and sailed off to the floor. The silence and stillness that replaced the frenzy stretched out until, abruptly, Paul slumped, rocking the table that he still clutched with both hands. He didn't fall, and after a second he straightened again. Constance felt as if she had been released from an enveloping restraint. She flexed her fingers.

"It's gone," Paul whispered hoarsely. "It's gone!"

Charlie let out a breath he had not realized he had been holding. Toni moaned again and ducked her head. After a second Constance picked up the board and returned it to the table. Ba Ba stirred and put the planchette on the board. She looked dazed.

In the doorway Charlie felt his muscles start to relax, leaving him feeling exhausted with a dull ache here and there; he turned and went back to the dining room, followed by Johnny and the sheriff.

"Jesus," Gruenwald said again in a low voice.

"It . . . there's more," Ba Ba whispered.

Constance wanted to deny it, to cry out, *No!* This wasn't part of the plan; Ba Ba's part was finished. But Ba Ba was rigid, staring straight ahead as if entranced again. "Let's make sure it's gone," Constance said, and she heard her voice as strained and as unfamiliar as the voice that had come from Ba Ba only moments earlier. "Ba Ba?" They positioned their hands. There was a brief silence and then she said, "Is anyone there?"

Gruenwald and Johnny went back to the door to watch; this time Charlie did not join them. Every instinct was crying out to stop this, stop it now, stop it completely, and never start it again. He felt hot and cold all at once, and he could almost feel the pallor of his face; sweat between his shoulderblades chilled him, and he knew he would not be able to stand in the doorway and watch again.

"Spence," Constance said in her unfamiliar voice.

It took a long time, the letters all ran together as they had done before; the planchette sped up and it was hard to make certain the letters were all noted. Constance said each one when the window paused over it. When the message stopped, Spence read what he had written:

Tell Diane manuscript is in drawer with Buffalo nickels.

"Are you still there?" Constance asked the board. There was a long silence. "It's over." She removed her hands from the planchette. Ba Ba stirred and straightened her fingers; she looked very relaxed and sleepy.

"What the devil does that mean?" Spence asked, studying the message. "Something to do with her work?"

"Whose work?" Tootles asked.

"Victoria Leeds's apparently. Who else works with man-uscripts?" Then he added, "Well, Paul does. You know a Diane?"

Paul shook his head. His face looked waxen.

"She's trying to help find her killer," Ba Ba said in a sepulchral tone. "We have to find out who Diane is and pass the message on to her."

"Anyone here know a Diane?" Spence asked.

"Who has a collection of Buffalo nickels?" Paul said. His voice was so harsh it was nearly unrecognizable. "Come on, enough's enough. Forget it. Marion, I'd rather like a drink. You mind?"

"No, by God, we all deserve something. Come on."

"Well," Gruenwald said in the dining room, "your wife puts on a good party, Meiklejohn. I'll be on my way. See you around."

Charlie nodded. He wiped the sweat from his forehead; he felt gray and very, very old.

Johnny looked as shaken as Charlie felt. He muttered something about a drink, and wandered out of the dining room, headed for the living room where voices sounded faint, very distant.

"Diane Musselman," Gruenwald said in a low voice. "Goddamn it! What the hell are you up to?" He sounded mean and dangerous. "I'll phone Belmont to stake out her place. Damn you, Charlie! Jesus Christ!" He hurried away.

"Drink," Charlie thought clearly then. Drink. He wanted a drink very badly.

"I knew you'd be good," Ba Ba was saying to Constance when he entered the living room. Max was pouring drinks. Toni was on the sofa and no one else was in sight. "I could tell," Ba Ba was going on. "You shouldn't fight it, Con-stance. It's a God-sent gift that can do good things."

Drink, Charlie thought again. He took Constance's hand; it was icy. "Are you okay?"

She nodded. Charlie's gaze happened upon Toni, huddled on the sofa, watching Constance with bitter hatred.

Charlie stiffened, listening, then dropped Constance's hand. "Wait here," he said curtly, and raced to the foyer, out to the porch, in time to see the white Corvette throw gravel as it left the driveway too fast and sped off down the dirt road. He already had his keys in his hand as he ran to the Volvo and snatched the door open, jumped in and tore off after the Corvette before anyone else got off the porch.

The little sports car was faster than the Volvo, and it was being driven by a maniac. Charlie kept it in sight, but did not catch up; he made every turn, every curve, and kept it in sight. At first he had thought they were heading toward Chevy Chase, but very soon he realized he was lost. Although he had a good sense of direction, and would be able to find himself if he had just a glimpse of a map, or if he had driven these roads in daylight, he was driving twisting country roads in the dark, and the roads were narrow, some blacktop, some concrete, some dirt, with mileposts instead of names. Names would not have helped, he had to admit to himself as he made another right turn. He kept most of his attention on the car he was following, but there was enough left over to keep in sight the headlights behind him, pacing him. Bill Gruenwald, he thought, hoped.

All right, he reasoned, Gruenwald had called Belmont or some of his own deputies by now; they would have someone keeping an eye on the Musselman house. Maybe. His lips tightened. They *would* have someone keeping an eye on the house; they'd better.

Up ahead was a lighted area, a gas station, tavern, even, by God, a stop light, he realized, closing the distance between his car and the Corvette.

Constance watched Charlie speed off after the Corvette, followed closely by the sheriff's Ford. She watched until all the lights were gone, and then turned to reenter the house.

"What the devil is going on?" Max stood at the door, also watching.

"I don't know," she said. "It seems everyone decided to go out for a ride."

"Johnny too?" Max sounded disgusted. "Now what?"

"Not me, too," Johnny said, coming from the shadows of shrubs in the yard. "I gave my keys to Paul. He was pretty upset and his rented car was packed in between the Volvo and your car, Dad. It just seemed easier to let him take mine until he cools off." He laughed. "He'll be surprised when he realizes that Charlie and the sheriff both are on his tail."

"Good Christ," Max muttered and went back inside.

Constance and Johnny followed him.

All right, she thought, all right. All she had to do was keep everyone in sight until Charlie and Bill Gruenwald returned. She knew that, but everyone else wanted to wander. Max vanished and returned; Tootles and Spence had been gone, and came back together from the office; Ba Ba wanted to talk to Constance and she kept trying to dodge her. Toni just shivered on the sofa and watched Constance with dull hatred. And Johnny was in and out of the kitchen, also dodging Ba Ba, looking more and more often at his watch as the minutes crawled by.

"Shit," he muttered once. "I thought he'd want to take a spin to the village or something. I didn't think he planned on staying out all night."

"Constance, you really should just try the crystal ball, just once," Ba Ba said. "I just know you'd be sensational with it."

"Who is Diane?" Spence asked, and Ba Ba shrugged.

Constance asked him if he would drive her back to the motel in a little while.

"Whistle when you're ready," he said agreeably.

She went to the office and found a piece of paper, and an envelope and scrawled a note to Charlie, sealed it, and put it in her pocket, just in case. She was not certain she would trust it to anyone here, she realized. Tootles would certainly read it, and Ba Ba and Toni were doubtful. Meanwhile she would keep it in her pocket.

Forty minutes dragged by; no one had relaxed, or sat still more than a few minutes at a time while they waited. Even Ba Ba had become silent and looked fatigued, when suddenly Johnny stood up and said, "Dad, this is too much. Mind if I borrow your car and go home? If and when Paul comes back, feel free to use the Corvette."

Silently Max fished out his keys to the Continental and handed them over. He looked terribly tired. Johnny mock-saluted and left the room. Constance turned to Spence and said, "Me too. Would you mind?"

He looked at her curiously, then shrugged. She said to Max, "If Charlie comes back here tonight, will you give him a note for me, please?" She handed the envelope to him. "Thanks. Goodnight, everyone."

As soon as the Corvette reached the brightly lighted area of the tavern and gas station, Charlie braked, jerked the Volvo to the side of the road. A moment later the dark Ford pulled up behind him. Gruenwald emerged.

"What?" he asked.

"It's Volte," Charlie said in a hard, tightly controlled voice.

"Paul Volte?"

"Yeah. How fast can we get back to the house? You know a better way than the way we just came?"

When Spence got his car headed up the driveway, Max appeared at the passenger side door. "I'm going, too," he said. "Unlock the door."

Spence glanced at Constance. After a second she nodded and he unlocked the door with his control panel. Max got in the back seat.

"I suppose you want me to follow the Continental,"

Spence said, driving out to the road, making his turn. The tail lights were at the intersection; they vanished.

"Yes," Constance said. "I don't think it will be far." She did not look at Max in the back seat; he did not speak again.

The Continental turned in at the condo complex. "You'll have to pass him," Constance said. The other car was stopped at the gate, Johnny was opening it. "Max, do you mind?" she said and ducked down in the seat. In the back seat Max leaned over out of sight. They passed the Continental just as it was pulling inside the complex. "Now stop," Constance said. "Let's back up, right to the gate, and go on foot." She looked at Max. "Why don't you wait for us?"

"No!" He was out of the car before Spence had set the hand brake.

When they got to the driveway to Applegate, the Continental was going down the ramp to the basement. Constance hurried, with Spence at her side, Max trailing a step or two behind. Pierce, the watchman, was standing at the driveway down to the basement. He had looked puzzled a moment earlier, now he looked totally bewildered. Constance held her finger to her lips, and he looked past her to Max, who nodded. Pierce shook his head and moved back a few steps, leaned against the building silently, and watched.

They took the stairs. At the basement level, Constance kept going down until they exited at the sub-basement. There was a dim light, and eerie shadows cast by the rows of storage compartments. It was silent. She glanced at the footwear of the two men; running shoes on Spence, soft-soled sandals for Max, and her own sandals would not make noise, she knew. They left the stairwell and looked down the first row of storage compartments. Empty. Silently they moved to the next row, and this time, Constance dug her fingers into Max's arm and drew him back. Toward the far end Johnny was opening one of the doors.

She had her witnesses, she was thinking, but what could they see from here? Only that he was taking something out. But if they got closer and he ran, then what? She pulled Spence back a bit farther and whispered, "I'm going down the other aisle and get closer."

She could handle him, she was certain. He was big and muscular, but she had the skill, years of training, and she had the edge of surprise.

She had reached the halfway point of the rows when she heard the metal storage door slam, and then his footsteps, heading for the stairs at the other end. She started to run.

"Hold it right there, Mr. Buell. If you don't mind."

The sheriff? Now she fairly flew to the end of the aisle and came to a stop. Charlie was standing there, leaning against a storage compartment, and at his side was Sheriff Gruenwald, holding a gun. Charlie looked past him to Constance; a very wide grin split his face.

"What the fuck are you doing down here?" Johnny demanded. "This is my building! Get the hell out of here!"

"Let's not get too excited," Sheriff Gruenwald said. "What is that you removed from the storage compartment?"

"None of your fucking business. What, you got a warrant or something? You going to shoot me in the back when I leave? This is my property, you pissant sheriff! How do you think you can explain coming here and threatening me? Man, when I get hold of my lawyer—"

"You'll do what, Johnny?" Max's voice was heavy, wooden. "Whose building? What do you have there, Johnny?"

Johnny spun around at the sound of his father's voice. His voice rose to a near falsetto when he cried, "You did this? You called him! Why? I didn't do anything you wouldn't have done in my place! I didn't!"

Max was walking down the aisle toward him. "Give it to

me, Johnny. What is that? A bundle of clothes? Give it to me.''

Johnny moved a few steps toward him, and then he swept out his arm and knocked Max to one side, against one of the metal storage compartments, and he ran. At the end of the aisle, Spence stepped forward and hit him once on the jaw. Johnny dropped and was motionless.

And somehow during this, without awareness of her own actions, or Charlie's, Constance had moved to his side, and he had put his arm around her and was holding her very close.

Twenty

At ten minutes before ten the next morning Charlie and Constance pulled into the condominium grounds. The superintendent Ditmar met them at the curb in front of Building B—Birmingham. Or maybe Baloney, Charlie thought, taking the envelope Ditmar held out to him. It contained the computer card keys to the elevators and various rooms.

"I turned off the electronic door-closer system, just like you said I should," Ditmar said. He hesitated, as if he wanted to ask them if it was true. He shook his head, then turned and walked back toward his little trailer/office.

Charlie opened his trunk and took out the shopping bag with his purchases from the previous day. "This won't take long," he said to Constance. "If they get here before I finish, keep them out here. Okay?"

She nodded and watched him enter the B building with his bag of tricks. Bill Gruenwald and state police investigator, Lieutenant Belmont, arrived together a few minutes later. She greeted them and relayed the message: Charlie would be along in a minute or two.

Howard Belmont was fierce-looking this morning. His forehead was furrowed with deep lines, and his lips were nearly invisible. Bill Gruenwald looked as though he had slept very little, but he was calm and peaceful, almost as if he had taken a week's supply of tranquilizers. She suspected that he had not needed any.

"He began to talk," he said. "Not enough yet, and his lawyer put in an appearance and stifled him, but he started. Once they start, they usually keep on." He ignored the state officer. "And there was a pretty wrinkled note to Victoria Leeds in the pocket of the pants. They had a date for five o'clock. His stuff is in the lab now."

Charlie walked from the building then and nodded pleasantly to Bill Gruenwald and the lieutenant, who eyed him as if he suspected rabies. "Good morning," Charlie said cheerfully. "Let's get the show on the road, gentlemen. What I'll do is give you what I have, and then split."

No one protested. "Okay," he said. "Let's pretend. We are the little group that Johnny Buell brought over here the night he killed Victoria. Right? Honey? You want to drive?" Constance got behind the wheel; the others got inside the car. She made a U-turn and drove slowly down the ramp to the parking basement of the B building.

"Pretend two things," Charlie said. "First, that this is Building A, and next is that we had to use the electronic thingie to open the gate to the basement."

Constance drove to the other end of the basement, headed up the ramp to the street again; she stopped and pulled on the hand brake.

"And here we are," Charlie said. He got out and opened the door for the sheriff and the lieutenant. "We'll take the elevator up to six. I have the key for it."

He opened the door; they got in and the door closed again. Very soon the opposite door opened, and he led them out into the larger foyer. "Keep in mind that all these buildings are exactly the same," he said, leading the way, past the curved hall that would accommodate bookshelves, to the doorway to the living room. "Wait here," he said, "and don't touch anything. Wet paint, you know." The odor of paint was very strong; tarps were heaped on the floor in a table-shape. "I improvised the furniture. The tables have been put away somewhere," he said, walking quickly past the tarps, into the dining room, where he picked up the shopping bag, and then rejoined them. He held it up and said, "Briefcase. And now out."

They retraced their steps silently, back to the elevator, down to the basement, back inside the car. Constance drove up to the street and stopped again.

"Whoops," Charlie said. "Let's check the other apartments. You can come too," he added. He still had the shopping bag. Bill Gruenwald was looking bored; the lieutenant's face was red and his eyes nearly closed. He looked as if he had high blood pressure, and it was rising second by second. When Charlie entered the building on the first-floor level, they all followed him. This time they entered the elevator with the big brass number five.

At the fifth floor Charlie moved swiftly; he went through to the living room where tarps were arranged in such a way they resembled a table. The paint smell was strong. Bill Gruenwald and Lieutenant Belmont exchanged glances. If this wasn't the room they had just left, it was identical to it, down to the tarps on the floor. Charlie very quickly rolled the tarps to make a bundle, and not quite running, but moving fast, he left the apartment by way of the door to the hall. He jerked his head in an invitation for the others to follow as he hurried to the end of the hall and opened the staircase door, and started up. No one spoke.

At the sixth floor Charlie used his borrowed key to open the apartment and led them to the living room where more tarps had been draped over sawhorses, another tablelike shape, and where one tarp had been rolled into a cylinder that could have been a body on the floor.

Gruenwald came to a dead stop. Charlie hurried past the tarps, carrying his bundle, and dumped it in the dining room on the floor. As soon as he unrolled the tarps, the odor of paint rose and spread. He picked up the sponge he had soaked in turpentine and put it in a plastic bag that he closed with a tie, and then shoved into his shopping bag. Still moving silently, he motioned again for them to follow him. They got into the dedicated sixth-floor elevator, where a bunch of fake flowers was on the shelf under the mirror. The odor of the cologne he had sprayed on them was stifling; this time Charlie punched B for basement. When they got down and left the elevator, he went along the row of doors lifting off the panels with floor numbers stenciled on them. They were being held only by finishing nails that fitted very loosely into the holes drilled for screws. Only the number six was relatively tight. It took five seconds to remove that one. He leaned the panels against the wall, and went up the stairs to the first floor and from there out to the street where he stopped at the Volvo, opened the trunk and tossed the shopping bag inside.

Gruenwald had a dazed look on his face. "Voilà!" Charlie said. "Sleight of hand. The case of the disappearing body. Now you see it, now you don't."

"That son of a bitch," Belmont muttered. "That lousy son of a bitch!"

"I should have tumbled sooner," Charlie said. "Everything pointed to him."

Gruenwald snorted. "Come on. Let's have a look at those numbers."

They went back down to the basement and this time examined the numbered panels. "Nothing's very fancy down here," Charlie said. "That threw me, I guess. The brass numbers up on the ground floor are pretty hard to ignore and they're on to stay. But these are stenciled on the panels. Same stencils used for parking spots, and for the storage compartments in the sub-basement."

Gruenwald and Belmont studied one of the panels carefully. They went to the elevator doors and examined one of

239

them just as thoroughly. One side of each door had the panel with the big B already stenciled on it; there was nothing to indicate what floor the elevator served. Until the numbered panels were attached, each door was a blank ride.

"All those identical doors," Charlie said, "no way you can guess which is Six B, which one's Five B, and so on. And this building's identical to the A building. This section looks exactly the same as this section of A building; the painting has progressed to the same place it was over there. The only door that was marked was the door to the stairs. A big six on any of the doors, the other numbers loosely in place, that would have been enough to carry the illusion. One thing missing in their testimony was the arrangement of roses."

Gruenwald thought, then nodded. "No one in that group mentioned flowers," he said.

"I know," Charlie said. "I asked them specifically about the elevator, what they saw, heard, the works. No roses. No flowers. The girls put their purses down on the shelf and primped a little in the mirror. Debra even left her purse on the shelf when they went into the apartment. They couldn't have done that if the flowers had been there.

"And there's nothing upstairs to indicate they were on five instead of six," Charlie said. "The apartments are so much alike no one would have noticed that the elevator was a few feet off to the side. Out the windows they'd see tree-tops, what they expected. Inside both apartments, there were conference tables. So, the mention of wet paint and the turpentine on rags and the tarps on everything was to make sure they would stay put, as well as make sure they truly believed that they had been in Six A and there had not been a body on the floor. The paint smell was another giveaway, but I didn't notice. Everyone said there was a smell of paint, but what people smelled was thinner, turpentine, and all the interiors are latex, water-based. No turpentine anywhere. The painters washed their brushes in the sub-basement, and

I missed that. Anyway, there shouldn't have been any odor immediately identified with paint. No one should have smelled turpentine, and they did; they should have smelled roses, and they didn't.

"So they went up to Five A, where he had set the stage complete with briefcase, and down they came again, ready to swear they had been in Six A. He returned to move the tarps out of Five A, fix the numbers on the elevator doors, and the stage was set to give him a lovely alibi. Planned to the last detail. Then Tootles crossed him up by ordering the flowers, a little surprise for Max. And she crossed us up by lying about them, saying Johnny had ordered them. I called the florist," he added. "She picked them out in person." That was the trouble with Tootles, he thought then; you had to check and double-check every statement she made, and life was too damn short.

They walked out to the street level and stood near the Volvo.

"What about last night?" Belmont demanded. "What the hell were you doing last night?"

"One of the things I hammered at the girls about," Charlie said, "was where everyone was standing, sitting, looking at all times. They saw him open the trunk of the Continental and toss his briefcase inside. There were no clothes in the trunk, no work clothes at all. I never mentioned clothes, or flowers, of course, but there it was, like a puzzle piece that's defined by the hole. Just something else missing from their testimony. That night, if he had to borrow the Continental to pick up his pals at the train station, his work clothes should have been in it, or else in the apartment. He went back to the house to switch cars, remember? Still in his work clothes then. Victoria Leeds came to meet him, thinking she had a date with Musselman probably, and he killed her. He changed into party clothes, but what happened to the work clothes? We figured that if we charged him up with the séance, got him in an emotional state, and then if I baited you," he said to the sheriff, "about following up on lab work and physical evidence, he might do something foolish. I hoped he would take the hint and decide to get rid of the clothes if he hadn't already done that. I thought they might be somewhere around here, but there are a lot of places to hide stuff around a construction site." He shrugged. "Probably he never had a chance to collect them without risking being seen, you sure can't hide much in that little Corvette, so he needed the Continental again. He came down to get the evidence, maybe the only physical evidence there is. Makes me think he believes there's something incriminating there. But it was stupid of him. He should have waited."

They almost always did something stupid, he thought, almost as if they wanted to leave a trail, get caught.

"If we hadn't turned around and come back, he'd have got away with the clothes," Gruenwald said. "Shit, *that* was a dumb thing to do, warn him like that."

Charlie suppressed a grin and nodded meekly. With Constance at one end of the aisle, and Spence at the other, Johnny had had absolutely no chance of getting away. Zilch chance, he added to himself.

"If the manuscript turns up and if it has pretty damning things to say about the job here, or about Johnny, we can nail that to his hide, but if it doesn't . . ." Belmont was gazing thoughtfully into the distance, no doubt hearing a defense attorney mock his case.

"What Johnny could be most afraid of," Constance said, with no warning that she had been noodling with that topic, "is his father. This job is rather like probation for Johnny, isn't it?" She was not inviting comment. Her clear pale eyes were focused on the Volvo, or the trees beyond it, or the horizon, or nowhere.

"Put yourself in his place and you can follow his thought processes pretty accurately," she said after a moment. "If this job goes well, Johnny takes over the company, Max more or less retires, and Johnny's future is rather rosy. He has a girlfriend who is used to a life-style that is elevated, to say the least. He must be desperate to become a full partner, start his plan to expand. If he made a suspicious deal with anyone who could monkeywrench the whole thing, it's understandable that he might panic. He has to keep Max from learning anything that would keep him from becoming a partner, taking charge." She brought her gaze back to the small group, back to Belmont. "So, I think you'll be all right for motive. Musselman died because he knew something that Johnny couldn't afford to have published; Victoria because she knew what it was."

Charlie always thought she went at things backwards. If you get the who and the how, he liked to say, the why pops up at you like a Halloween spook. But she needed the why or she was inclined to distrust the who and how.

"There must be a reason why Max has kept Johnny as an employee, not a partner," she said, just as if he had been arguing with her. "And Johnny knows that Max would dissolve the company rather than turn it over to his son if there's anything crooked in the background; Max is maybe the second most honest man I know."

Charlie grinned and she looked surprised and added crisply, "My father is the first."

Gruenwald glanced at his watch and said, "What about the art that got ruined?" Charlie shrugged. "Maybe he'll explain that," Gruenwald said. "Trying to create a motive for Marion Olsen? Maybe. Well, I have guys over at the Musselman house, making a search. If there's a manuscript, they'll find it. I'm going over there now. You coming, Howie?"

"You kidding?" The lieutenant looked like a kid who had brought a baseball only to learn that the game of the day was basketball.

"And we have to wrap up things at Tootles's house," Charlie said. "Let's get at it, and take off."

Toni met them at the front door. Constance felt very sorry for this young woman who had shadows in her eyes that had not been there a week ago. Toni looked at her coldly, then spoke to Charlie. "They're expecting you," she said. "In the television room. It's the only room in the house that the reporters can't see into."

She had started to walk away when Charlie said, "Hold on a sec, will you? How's Max?"

She shrugged. "Resigned. He doesn't seem surprised, just hurt and resigned." She hesitated a moment, then said, "Now they're saying Johnny got in trouble a few years ago, in college, something about stealing tests. Ba Ba told me, but it seems that everyone else knew all about it."

Toni had finished growing up, Constance thought, watching her when she led them into the house, her shoulders straight, her head high; and Toni would not forgive her.

Charlie took Constance by the arm and they all went to the television room where Ba Ba was pouring coffee. She looked different, too, aloof and distant, so calm she looked doped. Tootles and Max entered the room, and Spence and Paul followed them. It was a subdued group.

"I'll keep this short," Charlie said as soon as they were all seated. Max was pale and remote, much more distant than Babar, and Tootles had been crying hard. Her eyes were swollen and bloodshot. She held Max's hand in a death grip.

"I'll give you everything I gave the police," Charlie said. "Some of this they would prefer to keep under wraps for the time being, but they didn't hire me, you people did. They are always afraid that if their suspect knows what they have against him, he will manage to counter it. That's beside the point right now." No one moved; he could have been addressing a workshop, a class who knew a test would follow. He told them the mechanics of how Johnny had killed Victoria and arranged his own alibi at the same time. "The

244

clothes probably will settle it," he finished. "Or they could find traces of turpentine in his briefcase, or a section of rope. They might go after him for Musselman's death, but maybe not. They will look for the manuscript, naturally, and if it turns up, they may reopen that case and tie the two together. If it doesn't . . ." He shrugged. "We'll wait and see."

There were a few questions, not many. No one looked directly at Max, who stared ahead stonily. Suddenly Max said, "I was too hard on him. His mother was always too soft, and I tried to make up for her, and went too far."

Gently Constance said, "We always think that, don't we? It's my fault. Whatever my child has done, I'm really to blame. It must be in the genes. I imagine killing Musselman was an accident, don't you? But after that . . . he chose, Max. You couldn't go back to day one and reorder his life, make him be someone else. And the man he became chose his actions." She paused, then said, "And, Max, on Monday or Tuesday, they were planning to arrest Tootles for the murder of Victoria Leeds. When you are blaming yourself, casting back for what you said, what he said, what you did, what he did, back through the years, you may find a place where you recognize a turning point, an ultimatum of some sort that you'll feel you should not have pressed. If that happens, just keep it in mind that he knew Tootles was the one they would arrest."

For a time he studied her face without any readable expression on his own, then he nodded, and put his arm around Tootles's shoulders. He nodded again.

"Well," Charlie said, "Gruenwald will be back around, there will be more questions, statements to make and sign, all the routine will be observed. But it's really over." He reached for Constance's hand, but she shook her head.

"One more thing," she said. "The séance was a fake through and through. You should all know that. I arranged it, and I manipulated it from beginning to end." Ba Ba gasped, and Toni jumped to her feet, shaking her head. "Tell them, Tootles," Constance said. "Tell them."

Tootles moistened her lips, but remained mute.

"Ba Ba moved the planchette in the beginning," Constance said grimly. "To give it credence. To make it believable. And I moved it later."

Tootles was staring at her, pale down to her lips. Constance continued to regard her until finally she nodded. "She arranged it," Tootles said.

"Why?" Toni cried. She turned toward Paul Volte. "What you said . . . part of a charade?"

Before Paul could speak, Ba Ba wailed. "I never! It moves by itself! I didn't do it! And you didn't know anything about a coin collection. How could you have known something like that?"

"We saw David Musselman's study," Constance said. "We saw his books on collectibles. Including coins. I don't know if he has such a collection, but he has collections of other things. And he would not have got rid of the manuscript. Architects are trained to be conservative. To conserve, save. He would have saved a copy of the manuscript."

"Good God!" Spence said. "You set a trap for him. Diane is Musselman's widow?"

Constance nodded. "It was a trap. The first part had to look real so he'd accept the rest. Ba Ba is so good with the Ouija; it looks so real when she does it. There isn't any jealous muse, no curse, no gift of the gods. Is there, Paul?"

He had been standing by a chair, holding the back of it with a white-knuckled grasp. Wordlessly he turned and walked out of the room, his shoulders hunched; he looked ancient moving away from them.

"No muse," Constance repeated softly. "Victoria Leeds knew that. Her death had nothing whatever to do with him. She left him months ago because she had come to understand the barrier was his doing, his choice. We think what she said to Janet was that his Byronic pose was tiresome."

She stopped when it became apparent that Toni was no longer listening. Staring at the empty doorway, she was as immobile as a piece of art, her face blank; she seemed oblivious to the lengthening silence in the room. Finally she took a step forward.

Abruptly Tootles pulled Max's hand away from her shoulder and stood up. "Just where are you going?" she demanded harshly.

Toni did not even glance at her. "I'm leaving," she said in a dull voice.

"Right!" Tootles yelled. "Leave! You know where you'll end up? In Hollywood making cute little figures that can chase other cute little figures off cliffs and get a chuckle out of cute little kids high on Saturday morning cartoons."

Color flared in Toni's cheeks; before she could say anything, Tootles drew in a long breath and went on almost savagely. "*I* never told you it would be easy. *I* never promised you a magic wand, or a mysterious muse to sit on your shoulder, or a goddam talisman to make life easier. *I* told you it would take a lot of fucking hard work."

Her gaze swept the room, art on every flat surface, art hanging from the ceiling, crowding the window sills, in every corner. Her gaze hardly even paused at her own work, *Seven Kinds of Death,* but continued to take in all of it.

"You do it yourself," she said in a lower, even harsher voice, "or it doesn't get done. Your hands, your eyes, your sweat. . . . If your fingers bleed you put on Band-Aids; your feet hurt, take off your shoes; your head aches, take an aspirin, but *you* do it. No fucking magic. And you look at it and you say, it wouldn't be here without *me!* Maybe it's good and you say, I did that. Maybe it's a piece of shit, and you say, I did that. Another little hole in the universe is plugged up, and you did it. You look at the world and your hands tell us what you see there, and you say, I'm here! I did that."

Charlie took Constance by the hand. Quietly they walked out of the room. Tootles's voice followed them to the porch, the driveway.

They had got into the Volvo when Spence appeared, ambling toward them in his slouchy way. He put his hand on the door by Constance. "If that was a show last night, you guys sure missed your calling. Some act!"

They both waited. This wasn't what he had followed them to say.

"You didn't clear up the problem of the ruined sculptures," he said.

Very distinctly they heard Tootles scream, "Ba Ba, shut the fuck up!"

Charlie grinned and leaned forward to look past Constance at Spence. "The sheriff thinks Johnny might have done it to supply a motive for Tootles."

Spence's ugly face brightened. "Yeah," he said softly, then again, "Yeah! Johnny must have done it." He reached in to shake Charlie's hand, and then leaned forward to kiss Constance. "You guys are pretty terrific," he said, and shambled away, back toward the house.

Charlie started the car. "Son of a bitch," he murmured. "He knows, doesn't he?"

"I think Spence knows a lot," she agreed.

He started to drive, and smiled when her hand found its way to his thigh. He didn't know which he wanted to do most, go home, or drive to the nearest motel.

"Home," she said lazily. His grin widened and he covered her hand with his.

A few months later a special delivery parcel came addressed to both of them. It was a large and heavy box, marked fragile. Charlie carried it to the kitchen table to open it. It was a bas-relief of Constance, done in a creamy ivory marble. He stared at it for a long time, uncertain if he liked it or not. After a quick drawing in of her breath Constance touched it, moved her fingers over the cheeks, along the chin.

When he looked up from the piece to her, there were tears in her eyes, and he suspected that the work was very good. It was not idealized, not romanticized. The face was strong and rather implacable, and although the bones were very fine, there was an androgynous quality overall. The eyes were cast downward a little. The eyes were knowing, not just looking, but also seeing. It was almost frightening, that feeling of awareness, as if the stone eyes could see through the many layers of defenses that shielded most people from view.

He put his arm around Constance's shoulders, and he was glad that when he looked at her, that piece of stone was not what he saw. He did not voice this because he was almost certain she already knew.